FORBIDDEN WAVE RIDER

A SMALL TOWN SINGLE DAD ROMANCE

EMMA REESE

INTRODUCTION

Never date a pro surfer, especially your ex-boyfriend's best friend.

Avoiding Brody has become my sport.
As I care for the horses in the barn, trying to erase him from my thoughts.
Unspoken emotions weigh heavy as a storm brews above.

Horses panic, fleeing as the storm rages.
The barn comes crashing down.

Trapped.
Bleeding.
Alone.

Craving for Brody saturates my thoughts.
The fear of never seeing him again shatters my heart.
I long for the warmth of his comforting touch.

And as my body grows heavier, a voice calls my name.

Brody.

Finally reaching me but unable to move the scattered
remnants.
His arms wrap protectively around me.
Holding each other in the face of uncertainty.
His tearful eyes meeting mine.

Amidst the ruins, our love becomes the anchor.
Yet our destiny hangs on the precipice of uncertainty.

ROSA

"**W**hat the hell is he doing out there in this storm?"

I turned quickly, my dark hair flying. The rain whipped against the windows, and the wind howled under the doors.

"Mr. Perry?" I asked. My boss was standing by the window and looking out. He leaned on his cane, shaking his gray head. "Did you say something?"

"Look at this guy," he said, pointing at where the ocean was crashing. "I can't quite decide for myself if he's brave or stupid."

I stood beside him, squinting into the storm. In the dark, tossing waves, I could see the shape of someone on a surfboard cresting over the foaming water.

"Definitely stupid. Who would surf in that?" I said, rolling my eyes.

Anastasia Island was full of overly tanned, wannabe pros with their newly minted surfboards and careless attitudes. I couldn't walk two steps out of the surf shop door without running into at least three. This one was no different.

"We should close up shop, Rosa," Mr. Perry said. "You

need to get home before the storm gets any worse. I doubt any customers will be coming in."

I looked around the teal-painted surf shop, taking in the multitude of swimwear amidst the beach toys and other items. Perry's Shell Shop was the last stop on Lighthouse Lane and most of the people who came in were tourists searching for last-minute purchases on their way down to the beach. None of them would be out in the storm.

"I can close up," I told him.

"No, I wouldn't want to leave you here alone with weather like this," he answered, shaking his head.

"Really, it's fine. You can go on home and stall your horses," I said, grabbing the key from the hook. "I'll lock up. It'll be easy enough to leave once I'm done."

He waved a hand. "Oh, I've had those horses on the island for years, doing trail rides and whatnot. One stormy evening isn't going to get to them."

"I can handle it."

He looked out of the window one more time and sighed.

"Alright then, I'll leave you to it. Looks like that surfer kook came to his senses."

As Mr. Perry was leaving, gathering his things, I looked out the window. The man in the water was gone, so I put it out of my mind.

The wind slammed against the side of the shop, and the lights flickered. I glanced down at the cash register as I counted the till. I had the money in my hands and spread it across the counter, ticking it off. Suddenly, something smacked against the window.

"What the hell?" I cried, jumping backward.

A figure was banging his hands against the window.

I stood there for a moment, frozen, contemplating the percentage of waterlogged men in surfing gear that historically turned out to be serial killers.

"I'm coming!" I shouted, running to the entrance that faced the water.

Ignoring all common sense, I throw open the door.

"Do you just leave every customer standing outside?"

I stood there in the doorway with the rain lashing in, staring at the stranger in front of me. He was soaked, and his hair looked as if it were usually a dark, wavy brunette, but it was slicked down to his head, dripping into his bright, blue eyes. The man had his wetsuit unzipped and folded over his waist. His tanned chest and stomach were bare. I tried not to stare at how the rain glittered over the rippling muscles of his torso. Every time he moved, I had to look away from the glow.

"Do you just run headlong into every storm and try to surf?" I snapped, closing the door behind him. "You know, some people might call that stupid."

"Not every storm, no," he said, and I could hear the grin in his voice. "And do I come off as stupid to you?"

I gave him a flat look. "Is that a trick question?"

"Well, you're a real sweetheart, aren't you?" the man said, letting out a barking laugh. He thrust out his hand for me to shake. "I'm Brody Strauss. It's nice to meet you."

"I'm Rosa Rivers, and you're dripping all over my floor," I said, stepping back to stare at the puddle of water that had begun to spread across the hardwood.

"You haven't given me a towel," he said, giving me an infuriatingly charming, crooked grin.

"You haven't explained why you were out in the middle of a storm in the ocean," I told him. I crossed my arms. "You're lucky I even let you in at all."

"You're way too attractive to be this mean," Brody said. "I was surfing out there. I thought that was obvious."

"I don't know anyone who would be on the water in a storm." I glanced over to the rain-soaked windows.

"Well, that explains it, then," he said, grinning. "We don't know each other yet, but we will."

"You're really presumptuous," I rolled my eyes. Looking down, I pointed at his leg, "Your leg is bleeding."

There was a sharp slice across the tanned skin, beading with fresh blood. Confusion gave way to surprise when he finally noticed the cut.

"Oh, damn," he said, whistling. He looked up at me. "You got a rag or something?"

"A rag?" I asked, wrinkling my nose. "Are you living in the Stone Age? I have a first aid kit. But sorry, no rags."

"That'll work," he said with a wink that made my heart flutter. "Could you point me in the right direction?"

"Of what?" I asked him. "Go sit down in that chair."

I pointed to the seat Mr. Perry usually sat in to people-watch on slow days. Brody raised his eyebrows, but he did as I said, sitting down heavily in the chair there.

"Look at that, now we're the same height," he grinned.

"You should show your nurse some respect." I put the first aid kit down hard on his lap.

He looked at me with a smirk. "Your bedside manner could use some work."

I kneeled down, ignoring him. Ripping open one of the antiseptic wipes from the pack and wondered how my day had spiraled into sitting in front of a half-naked stranger and bandaging his injured leg. *Maybe I should have let Mr. Perry stay.*

"So, where's the old guy that's usually here?" he asked, looking down at me with those glittering blue eyes.

"He's the owner, and he's a good guy," I said, shooting him a sharp look. "Were you looking through the window or something?"

The thought of a random, wet man staring through the windows of the place I worked at was daunting. Really, I was fully questioning my own sanity. Maybe it was the fact that the random man was so very handsome that made me second guess. Was I beer-goggling a serial killer?

"I come here a lot to surf. The waves are killer," he said, very casual and not murderer-like at all.

"I wouldn't know," I wrapped up his leg. "Okay, you're done."

He looked down, turning his calf back and forth. "Huh. Not bad for a novice nurse."

"You can't stay here," I said, turning away from him to put the first aid kit back under the checkout counter. "Mr. Perry would kill me if he knew I let someone in after closing hours."

"You want me to go out in that?" he asked, and I turned to look at him as he stared incredulously out of the window.

I crossed my arms. "You can go out the way you came in. Surf home since you're so good at it."

"See, that's the problem," he said, standing up and coming over to lean on the counter next to me. He was so close I could feel his breath against my neck, and I resisted the urge to shiver.

"What's the problem?" I asked him quietly.

"Well, Rosa Rivers, I don't actually have a surfboard," he told me with a shrug.

I glanced at him, my brow wrinkled. "What does that even mean? You said you were out there surfing."

"I did have one, but the ocean decided she wanted it more," he told me, grinning. Outside, the wind howled through the oaks and the palm trees. "Hence, why I'm here. I need a new board."

"That's fine, you can come back when the store is actually open, as opposed to now, when it's very obviously closed," I said. I pointed above me at where all the lights but one were shut off. "We don't sell once the lights go off."

"This is a nice store," he said, nodding. The blue lightning from the dark storm outside flashed across his stupidly attractive features.

"Yeah, it was before you came in and made a mess," I countered, though there was no real heat in it.

Something about Brody Strauss was addicting. He was one of those people it was hard to look away from. I had never seen anyone in real life who looked like he did. He was like something off the cover of a magazine, and I suddenly wondered how he looked on a surfboard in the sunshine, slick with saltwater and tanned golden brown.

"I could make it worth your while," Brody murmured, and when that big hand came up to cradle my cheek, I didn't flinch.

"I already fixed your leg, I think that's enough," I said, meeting the challenge in those blue eyes.

"Thank you for that, by the way," he said, letting out a little chuckle. "I took a nasty fall on the way to the shore. I hit some rocks, narrowly missed my head."

"Well, that's a shame," I whispered, smirking. "Maybe it might have knocked some sense into you."

"You know what, Rosa? Meeting you made almost drowning so worth it."

I couldn't help but laugh.

"Look, you really need to get out of here," I said, but something in me really wanted him to stay. I fought that urge hard. "Mr. Perry might come back, and I need to clean up."

"I'll do that," he said, and his warm body was pressed against mine. "Don't worry about it."

"You're going to clean? Yeah, I'd like to see you with a bucket," I said, my voice shaking.

I'd like to see you with a bucket? Yeah, this was exactly why I went to junior prom with me, myself, and I.

"Your hair looks like chocolate," he said, taking his other

hand and weaving his fingers through the long strands of dark hair.

"Thanks, I guess." I was glad to see I wasn't the only one with questionable pickup lines.

Nothing else mattered as he leaned down and sealed his warm mouth over mine, making my whole body spark to life. I felt the embers deep inside, stoked by the press of his body against me. I felt like I might burst into a million tiny, burning shards as his tongue slipped into my mouth, licking gently. I dug my fingers into his wetsuit, where it was folded over at his waist.

Suddenly, my mind seemed to catch up with my body, and I remembered I had just met this man. Brody Strauss could have been any manner of terrible person, and I would have had no idea at all. I was kissing a complete stranger in my place of work, and he was deepening the kiss, making it so much more difficult to pull away from. I didn't want to pull back, but my mind was screaming at me to stop and think.

He left the kiss with a wet pop as I yanked away.

"You have a lot of nerve, you know that?" I snapped, wiping my mouth. It was all for show, really. His lips tasted like saltwater, and it was pleasant. Still, I had to pretend I had a little common sense, at least. "Where do you get off kissing me like that?"

"Am I crazy, or were you vigorously kissing me back, and now you're pretending like you weren't?" he asked, his mouth edging on a smile.

"You're crazy," I said flatly, stepping back from him. "And you can stop smiling like that too. It's creepy."

"I think I'll be on my way," he said brightly, squinting through the murky glass of the window beside us. "Looks like it's clearing up, and I have a wife to get home to."

My mouth fell open, and a hot tirade began in my throat, ready to bubble out, but Brody just laughed.

"I'm kidding, Rosa. You can laugh, you know. It's not illegal or anything."

"What should be illegal is how annoying you are," I said, but it was a weak response. I was still winded from the kiss. "You should let me take you home."

Brody gasped dramatically. "What do I look like to you? At least take me to dinner first."

"Let's go," I said, bringing my fingers up to touch the phantom feeling of Brody's lips on mine. It was going to be a long night.

2

BRODY

I was almost sure I knew Rosa Rivers from somewhere, and it was itching at the back of my brain.

"This is what you drive?" I asked her, skeptical.

The rain had slowed, and it was just a briny mist now, coating the old, 1960s teal Bronco in rivulets of water.

"Yes, this is what I drive," she said sharply, pulling open the door. "If you don't like it, you're more than welcome to walk."

"Maybe next time," I said as I climbed in, settling my back against the cloth bucket seat. "And I do like it. My great-uncle had one just like it."

"I bought it off a guy down the coast," she said with a shrug. "He wanted two grand and a case of beer for it. It sounded reasonable enough to me."

I almost choked. "That was you?"

"What was me?" she asked, glancing over as she pulled out of the small parking lot.

"You bought my great-uncle Charlie's Bronco. What a

damn small world we live in," I said, feeling completely baffled by it.

Rosa rolled her eyes. "More like a small island."

"I'm surprised we've never met," I told her. "I feel like maybe we've met before. Have we met before?"

She glanced over, her face scrunched. "If I had met you before, I think I would have remembered it."

"Because I'm so unforgettable?" I gave her a grin. "Or because of that kiss?"

"Because you're annoying," she said, and I was pleased to see the red spread across her cheeks.

"Where do you live?"

"Not so fast. Aren't you hungry?"

"Hungry?" Rosa asked like I was speaking a different language. "It's nine o'clock at night."

I took a minute to think it through, looking around the vehicle for any clues about who she was or what she liked. The seats were protected by southwestern-style seat covers, and there was a pink seashell hanging from a leather cord on the rearview mirror. In the back, a single, empty iced coffee cup, along with a pile of clothes, some sneakers, and cowboy boots. Bingo.

"What about coffee?" I said, leaning on the center console as she drove through the moonlit night.

"Coffee? Who's going to still be doing coffee at this hour?" she asked, tossing her dark hair back. I smelled coconut and caramel.

"Dunkin Donuts is still open." I looked at her, waiting for her to look over.

When she did, it was just a quick glance. Something about this girl made me want to spend as much time with her as I could. If that meant going for an iced coffee with the moon climbing high, I would do it. Plus, I was really craving a donut.

"The one at the gas station?" she asked, looking unsure.

"Yeah, come on," I said, letting out a laugh. "I'm not a serial killer. I'm not luring you anywhere."

"That's exactly what a serial killer would say," she told me, giving me a side-eye.

"Yeah, fair enough." I huffed a laugh. "So, what do you say?"

I watched the curves of her delicate profile and the smooth up-tilt of her small nose. Her lips were plump and tantalizing. I kept thinking of that kiss and how she had kissed me back. I wanted to kiss her again, but I would settle for a coffee and a night drive with a pretty girl in cut-off shorts and a tank top.

"Yeah, fine," she told me with a sigh. "I like driving at night anyway."

"Where do you live?" I wondered, watching the island pass by in a blur of yellow streetlights.

"Where do I live?" she repeated, looking at me incredulously. "I'm not telling you that."

"So you can kiss me, but I can't know anything about you?" I asked with a little chuckle.

She hit the brakes, and I grabbed the seat, looking at her like she had gone crazy. We were in the middle of the street, with cars honking as they went around us.

"What are you doing?" I said, glancing back at the cars with their bright headlights. "Drive!"

"I didn't kiss you," Rosa said, squeezing the wheel and staring straight ahead.

"You kissed me back," I told her pointedly. "It's the same thing in a different font."

"I didn't kiss you, and I'm not moving this vehicle until you agree," she said, looking over at me with her eyebrows raised. "What we do is up to you."

I couldn't help but laugh. "You're crazy. I like crazy."

"I'm not driving until you agree," she said again, resolute.

"Okay, I agree. You didn't kiss me. It was a figment of my imagination," I said, grinning. "Can we go now?"

"We can go now," she said, nodding. "I'm glad you decided to see things my way."

"Have you ever dated a surfer before?" I asked, and she looked at me, making a disgusted face.

"Is this you asking me out?"

"No, that's me asking if you've dated a surfer before," I said. "You're exactly our type."

"I think I should be offended," she wrinkled her nose.

"Is that a yes?"

"Yeah, I actually have dated a surfer before, and I never will again," she said, keeping her eyes firmly on the windshield.

"That bad, huh?" I said with a small laugh.

"Let's just say I'll pass on surfers from now on." She turned the Bronco into the parking lot. "We're not parking."

"Why not? Do you only go inside with men who aren't in borrowed tourist t-shirts?" I looked down at my neon orange attire.

"What do you want, Brody?" she said, ignoring me as we pulled into the drive-thru.

The sound of my name on Rosa's lips made me grin, and I leaned over her to see the menu, fully aware of how close we were. She huffed a sigh in my ear, and I turned to look at her, glancing down at her mouth. She licked her lips, and her face went red.

"I'll take whatever you're having," I leaned back into my seat.

She sputtered for a moment and then seemed to recover, looking annoyed. After ordering they asked us to pull around. The girl at the window was smiling at us both.

"Aw, you guys are so cute. How long have you been together?"

"I don't even know this guy," Rosa told her, and the girl laughed.

"Oh yeah, I'm the same way with my boyfriend," she said, and Rosa stared at her. She continued, "I'm like, I don't even know him."

"Right," Rosa said.

I snorted.

"Well, anyway, here's your drinks," the girl said brightly. "You two enjoy your date!"

"Don't say a word," Rosa told me as we drove away.

We kept going, and I put her straw in her drink. "My lips are sealed. Pull over. I like this spot."

"This spot?" she pointed at the big structure climbing into the sky. "This is the lighthouse, you know. I'm sure a lot of people like this spot."

"The ocean is behind it, just through the trees," I said. "If you let the window down, you can hear the gulls and the waves. I love that sound."

Rosa sat back, sipping her drink. "Have we seriously met before?"

"You know, I was wondering the same thing," I tasted my drink, then winced. "This barely has any sugar. How do you drink this?"

"You should have ordered something then," she said with a shrug. I looked over, and she seemed contemplative. "Maybe it's just that all surfers are the same. If you've met one, you've met them all."

"I don't think so," I yawned as she cut off the engine. I leaned my seat back a little, rolling my head over to look at her. "Did you bring me here to kill me because I wet the floors?"

"What?" She asked, offended. "This was your idea to come here!"

I grinned. "Just making sure you're paying attention."

"If you have a girlfriend, I feel bad for her."

"That wasn't very subtle, you know. If you wanted to know if I have a girlfriend, you could have just asked."

"I don't care if you have a girlfriend," she said, scoffing. "You probably have five kids and a wife, too. I don't care about that either."

"If I had a wife, I don't think she would be happy I'm with a pretty girl in the dark."

"You didn't say you don't have kids," she said, though she didn't actually sound like she cared very much. She was just making conversation.

"You don't like kids?" I asked her, grinning. "But you seem so maternal."

"Oh, ha-ha," she replied, letting out a sigh. "I need to be getting home. I have to be up early in the morning to help clean up after the storm."

"Why doesn't the old guy just hire a cleaning crew?" I asked. "There are plenty around the island."

"It's not usually a big enough mess to hire a crew. Plus, Mr. Perry is a one-man show. He would have to pay for everything."

"He's your grandfather, right?" I asked her. "Why don't your parents help?"

"What?" Rosa asked, looking confused. "Mr. Perry isn't my grandfather, and my parents live in Daytona."

"Oh, I was wondering why you didn't call him 'grandpa'," I said with a small laugh, but something she said caught my attention. "You said your parents are in Daytona? Is that where you're from too?"

"Yeah, I moved here after a bad breakup a year and a half

ago," she said with a shrug, getting a far-off look in her eyes. "Mr. Perry gave me a job. Why are you asking?"

"Did you happen to know a guy named Sam back in Daytona?" I looked over.

She flinched, swallowing hard. "There are lots of Sam's in the world, Brody."

"Sam Wesson," I said quietly. I waited for her to respond, and she didn't. "You're her, aren't you? You're my best friend's ex."

"Your best friend?" she asked, turning angry green eyes on me. "The one who cheated on me with one of his surfing groupies?"

"Cheated on you?" I asked her, shaking my head. "No, he said you guys just drifted apart, and one day you left him high and dry in Daytona, taking all your stuff with you."

"Wow, of course, he did," she said, slamming her coffee down hard enough in the cup holder that it spilled over her hand. "If you're best friends with him, you're a lousy person."

"Now, hang on a minute—" I began, raising a hand to stop her voice from getting louder.

"Do you want me to tell you what really happened?" she snapped. Her tone wavered a little. "I came to one of his stupid little competitions one day, and he told me over and over again it was bad luck to have me there. It turned out it wasn't bad luck; he just didn't want the bleached blondes knowing he wasn't single."

"You saw him?" The information was slowly sinking in. "Did you see him with another girl?"

"No, I just imagined it," she said, rolling her eyes. "Yes, I caught him. He won, and some little blonde in a tiny bikini threw herself into his arms. I didn't even let him know I showed up. I just packed my shit and left. I never looked back."

"He didn't say anything about that."

"So, you think I'm lying?" she asked, sounding hurt. "You don't even know me, Brody. Apparently, you don't know your best friend that well either."

"Alright, that's enough," I shook my head. I wanted her to tell me more. I wanted to know if my best friend was the kind of guy who would do something to a woman like her. "Why don't we—"

"No," she snapped, cutting me off completely. "I'm taking you home."

"Rosa—" I began, feeling a little guilty for some reason.

"Where do you live?" she said, whipping the Bronco into reverse. My night had taken a sharp turn, literally. "Tell me now, or you can walk."

3

ROSA

I took a deep breath. The sweet scent of hay and the minty-medicine aroma of liniment wafted around in the stable's cool breeze. I pushed my manure fork into the pine shavings and plopped the soiled wood bits into the wheelbarrow in the stall's opening.

Night still hung heavy in the air, and the near-morning was peaceful as the stable woke up around me. I had always been fond of the smell of stables, especially when the dew was still heavy in the grass outside and the smell was pure and fresh. This close to the ocean, the brine was heavy in the breeze, and waves washed over the shore nearby. Mr. Perry's stables were some of the nicest I had ever been to, though they were a little run-down just from use over the years. The salt had eaten away at some of the wood panels.

The grazing horses blew their breath into the air of the small paddocks, enjoying being let out for a while. The grass beneath them was sparse but bright green, and they tore at the pieces, chewing them happily. The two stablehands whom Mr. Perry employed began their day with barely-hidden yawns and sleep-heavy eyes, holding their shovels and rakes. The teenagers waved at me, and I waved back. If the three trail mares were in foal, the stablehands would have been up hours earlier on a long, hourly rotation, but this far into the year, the last of the colts were old enough to be left alone.

I stepped out of the stall, wiping my arm over my forehead. Even without the sun, Florida was humid, and sweat beaded on my skin. The horse in front of me was just passing ten years old, and she was easily my favorite. The white stripe down her copper-brown face looked almost too bright in the light from the lamps. The carved plank outside her stall, hanging on the door, read *Cinder*. She was easily the meanest horse out of Mr. Perry's small herd, but that was why I liked her. She only really liked me.

"Hey there, gorgeous girl," I murmured, smiling as she nuzzled my hand for snacks. "Sorry, I didn't bring any cookies today. Maybe tomorrow."

"She's going to hold you to that, you know," a familiar, gruff voice informed me.

I looked around to see Mr. Perry coming into the barn, backlit by the slow orange of the rising sun behind him. He was leaning heavily on his cane, shuffling over the concrete.

"What are you doing up so early?" I asked, closing the stall door.

"Oh, don't worry about me, dear," he waved a hand. "I just wanted to check for damage to the fences after that storm."

"I can do that for you. I already dropped by the shop to clean up the broken branches and swept the parking lot."

"Rosa, you need to be more careful. I don't like you being there all by yourself in the dark."

I gave him a fond look. "Thank you, but I like doing it. I needed to keep my mind busy."

I refused to think about how Brody Strauss had completely ruined my night and made me so damn mad in the process. It had been a strange night to begin with, being with him at all. It didn't feel real to me. My car still smelled like saltwater. One thing that did feel real was the kiss. It felt horribly, terribly real, and very, very perfect. Brody was a good kisser. It was too bad the talent was wasted on the man.

"What happened?" my boss asked, concern deepening the wrinkles in his face. "Did you lock up okay last night? Perhaps I should have stayed and helped."

"Oh no, everything was fine," I assured him, giving him a weak smile.

"You look sad," he told me, patting my arm. "Even Cinder can see it."

The horse came to the stall door and put her head over, nuzzling my shirt sleeve. I couldn't help but laugh. Mr. Perry glanced out to where Cinder's yellow mother was grazing happily out in the field. She was just as beautiful as the little horse before me. Cinder's father, Mr. Perry's stallion, stomped his hooves in the back pasture, the one with the palm trees, his red copper coat glimmering in the low light. Cinder seemed to have his spirit. I knew Mr. Perry favored the stallion, always giving him treats.

"Do you think a lot of kids will sign up for the lessons and the trail rides this year?" I asked him, pretending I didn't hear him say that I looked sad.

"I think this year will be as good as any other, and maybe even a little better," he said jovially. "It's always better to look on the bright side of things. The kids will come."

"Cinder, are you ready for the hordes of sticky children?" I murmured, running a hand along the muscles of her thick, deep red neck.

I could still remember that first week a year ago, when my only job had been to muck out the stalls, and Cinder took a liking to me. A week later, Mr. Perry offered to let me work with him at the sea shop, telling me that if his horses liked me, he was taking that as a good sign. Horses were always a good judge of character. I wondered if Cinder would like Brody, but the thought made me want to huff. I kept my frustration inside myself.

Cinder just blew out a breath in response, pushing her nose into the fresh hay inside the net.

I stood back for a moment and let out a long exhale. The lights in the barn's alleyway glimmered over her shimmering coat. At that moment, I wished she was my horse. When I was little, I always wanted one. When the chance came to work at a horse barn, I took it. Working alongside Mr. Perry and his kindness was just an added bonus.

"If you don't tell me what it is, you'll just keep it to yourself, and it'll fester like a sore hoof," Mr. Perry said sternly, leaning heavily on his cane. I was going to deny it again, but he waved a hand. "Come on with me into the office here, and we'll dish out the feed together. That way, our young stablehands will have less on their plates."

Instead of going to the bins in the back of the small room, though, Mr. Perry sat down heavily at the desk. It was covered in horse-related items and he didn't even try to disguise the fact that this was a thinly veiled attempt to get me to talk to him. It would have been funny if I hadn't been so scatterbrained. Mr. Perry was like a father to me.

"This doesn't seem like dishing out the feed," I told him pointedly. "I know what you're doing, but I'm really okay."

"I didn't say anything. Nothing at all," he told me, raising his hands in surrender. "Can't an old man just rest for a moment?"

I stared at him for a minute and finally sighed. "Okay, fine. Do you know a man named Brody Strauss?"

"Strauss?" he repeated, rubbing his chin. "Hmm, well, I've heard the name before. I believe the family lived around here at one time."

"Where did you hear it, and what did you hear?" I asked, leaning forward a small amount, trying not to seem too eager. "I mean, if you can tell me, it's fine. If not, that's totally fine, too. It's not a big deal."

"Well, a few years back, there was a surfer who got caught on the rocks just off the pier," he said, shaking his head. "It was a damn tragedy, is what it was. He was there at night during a storm. He had a young son, I believe."

"I think his son was that guy in the water last night," I said, knowing the words were true as I said them. "Like father, like son."

"Last night?" Mr. Perry asked, looking down his glasses at me. "You didn't stay too late, did you? Did that surfer give you any trouble? You say he's the Strauss boy?"

I took a deep breath, taking in the familiar, comforting smell of horse feed and pine shavings. The last thing I needed was another man on my mind. My last boyfriend had been enough to traumatize me into never dating again. Did Brody give me any trouble? Yeah, I guess so. He didn't seem to believe me about Sam, but most people didn't, so that wasn't new. Mr. Perry did, though. He was kind in that way.

"No, I just went home after," I told him easily. I hated lying to Mr. Perry, but I didn't want to put unnecessary stress on him either.

"Well, that's good," he said, nodding.

"Now, what's wrong with you?" I asked my elderly boss, staring at him. "You think I can't also tell?"

He chuckled. "You're a sharp one. Exactly the kind of person I need around here."

"Did something happen?" I asked him, concerned.

A month ago, one of the horses escaped and caused havoc in a neighbor's yard, and Mr. Perry was nearly sued. He would have been if I hadn't gone over with cookies and a bottle of wine to smooth things over.

"Something of sorts," he said, looking wistful. He looked around the room, his eyes landing on the horse posters and the ribbons on the walls. "Well, my girl, I'm thinking that it's time to retire."

"From what?" I asked, feeling completely blindsided.

"From everything, but most of all the shell shop," he told me, giving me a sad smile. "These old bones need a rest."

"You're not selling the shop?" I asked him, my voice cracking. "Mr. Perry, the shop has been open for longer than I've been alive. You can't just abandon it like this."

"You're right about that. I'm not abandoning it. I'm hoping the shop will go into capable new ownership," he said, staring at me. "Rosa, I'd like you to take Perry's Shell Shop off my hands."

My mouth fell open. "You want me to buy the shop? You want me to own it?"

He looked proud, nodding. "What better way to keep it alive? I know you'll do the place the justice it deserves."

"Can I think about it?"

My mouth felt dry, and my whole body must have been made of concrete at that point. I was floored by Mr. Perry's confession. How could he just drop the store on me like that? It wasn't that I didn't want it, but it was a lot to think about at the time.

"Of course you can. Now, I'm going to have some tea and toast at the house," he said, letting out a breath as he stood and balanced on his cane.

"I'm going to ride Cinder," I said hollowly, and for someone so observant, the man didn't seem to notice how upset I was. Maybe he didn't want to see it.

"Have a good ride, my girl," he patted my shoulder as he left the room. "Let her run."

That was exactly what I needed.

. . .

"Alex?" I called out to the stablehand, who was shoveling manure nearby. "Can you saddle Cinder for me?"

Usually, I would have done it myself, but I was afraid I might forget a step with how much I was thinking. My mind was going a mile a minute. Alex didn't seem to mind.

"She's antsy," he said, giving me the reins and a leg up into the saddle. "She tried to bite me when I put the saddle on."

"She just needs a good run," I said, letting out a long breath. "We both do."

Alex nodded, looking warily at Cinder's blowing nostrils. We trotted out past him and worked around the yard for a minute before I let her run. With Cinder kicking up dirt and putting long, fast strides between us and the barn, the thought I was avoiding surfaced.

I would never be able to afford to buy Perry's Shell Shop.

4

BRODY

he seagulls burst into flight above me, soaring on smooth, white wings across the blue sky. I dug my toes into the hot sand as I stood at the sign-up table on the beach, the salty breeze pulling at my hair as I eagerly waited for my turn to go up. I couldn't believe it, but my heart was pounding with excitement. The next surfing competition was just around the corner, and I couldn't contain the amount of anticipation that seemed to bubble out of me. I could have spent all my time on a beach or in the waves, and I wouldn't have complained. I tried to tell myself it wasn't about proving anything. I knew it was, though. It was about proving something to myself.

I watched the people in front of me move up, and I knew I could beat all of them. I was one with the waves, and I belonged to the ocean. As I moved forward in the line, a small smile pulled at the edges of my mouth. All of this was so familiar. The organizers, who were also the judges, greeted me with smiling and bright faces, their features filled with respect for me. It took a while to earn my spot at the top, but I did it. I went ahead and signed my name on the registration sheet, feeling a rush of hot confidence moving through my body. I knew I would do it, and I was excited about it. This place was my domain, my kingdom, and I was ready to conquer the waves and whatever else I could in the process.

Just as I was about to make my way from the sign-up table, a vaguely familiar voice reached in and interrupted my thoughts.

"Hey there, Strauss, fancy meeting you here, huh?"

I rolled my eyes before I whipped around to see the younger man, Logan Reynolds, watching me with an annoying glint in his gaze. This was going to be an aggressively passive-aggressive conversation, I just knew it.

I gave him a quick smile, and I raised one of my eyebrows, sizing the man up where he stood with his board. It reminded me that I still needed to buy one. I couldn't believe I lost mine on the waves the other night, but at least I knew how to take a risk. Unlike some surfers, I wasn't just there for the recognition. Logan Reynolds was skinny and tall, and he had a mop of truly wild, sunburned blonde hair that seemed to defy gravity the way it stood on end. I could tell his board was brand new and expensive. His parents seemed to think that if something took more money, it meant that it worked better, which usually wasn't true. To me, it was clear that Logan had a ton of confidence, but I couldn't help but muse about whether or not he actually had the skills to back up that inflated ego. I had watched him at a few small events, and he seemed okay. It seemed to be mostly his bravado that kept him going. That was a flame easily put out with time.

"What's up there, Logan?" I answered evenly, my voice laced with a small hint of amusement. "Nice to see you here, little man. Are you sure you're ready to take on this kind of competition?"

I could see him floundering for a moment, and it was exactly what I wanted. He had come up to me hoping to psyche me out somehow or show off, and I had gone off-script.

He recovered and chuckled, his narrowed eyes betraying his anger. "Oh, you really have no idea, Strauss. I own these waters. My parents might have cut me off, but I'm going to show everyone what I'm made of, and I don't care what anyone thinks about it."

"Your parents cut you off?" I asked him, surprised. "Now, why would they do that?"

Maybe I was wrong about the surfboard. Maybe he bought it himself somehow.

"They don't approve of my lifestyle," he said with a grin and a shrug. "Who cares?"

"You don't care if you don't have money?" I wondered, snorting a laugh. "How does that work?"

"I make do."

I watched him, and I really couldn't help but be fascinated by the man's ego. Did I sound like that? I hoped not. Talking to him reminded me of how I was when I was younger, and the hunger to prove myself was burning bright like a star within me. It was still burning now, but there was a confidence deep within my heart that I knew what I was doing. This kid was just pretending to know. He was barely eighteen, and he thought he had it all figured out. Surfing wasn't as easygoing as people liked to pretend. If I were being honest, experience had taught me that just having a world of arrogance alone would never get you very far in the fierce competition of professional surfing. Little did Logan know, being a professional took skill, artistry, and a deep connection with the ocean's waves and rhythms. You needed to know the waters.

"Well, kid," I told him, knowing it would piss him off, "I

do hope you're prepared to be traumatically humbled by the competition. Whatever you think you know, learn it again. The ocean can be really uncaring, especially to surfers who underestimate it. And little men with a lot to prove."

He scoffed, his confidence seemingly unwavering, but his face went red. "Yeah, I guess we'll see about that, old man. You have no idea what it takes. I've been committed, and training my body every day and night for this. I won't let some washed-up, has-been surfer steal my thunder while I'm on the rise."

"Man, I'm twenty-four. And I don't have anything to prove to you," I told him, snorting a laugh. "You'll learn one day."

"I don't care how old you are, Strauss, I'm going to wipe the floor with your ass," he said, pointing at me. All of the easy bravado had been burned away by childish anger.

I chuckled, shaking my head. "Bud, you can't even pay for your own stuff. You need to humble yourself. You don't even realize that it's about respecting the waves and understanding their power. You have to find your own harmony in that chaos."

The younger man's eyes narrowed. There was a small show of doubt that seemed to momentarily cross his red face. But just as quickly, the look was replaced by a cocky glare.

"You know what?" he asked me, chuckling and sounding a little forced, "I don't need your useless advice at all. I don't need any advice at all. I'll prove myself to the world on my own terms, and you'll look stupid."

It was so funny to me to see someone so stuck on their own ego. I tried not to laugh at him, but it was really difficult when I could see him squeezing his board so tight that his fingers went white. He was obviously bothered, but he was pretending he wasn't.

I nodded sagely, deciding to have mercy on him. "Alright, yeah. Fair enough, then, Logan. Have a damn good day. May the best surfer win and the younger one lose."

I spun on my heel, and I could hear him sputtering behind me. I did laugh then, throwing my head back in mirth. I sobered after a moment and found my way to my pickup truck. I blew a kiss to the remains of my old surfboard in the back bed and hopped in the front seat, pulling away from the beach parking lot and making my way down the road.

"Aw, there you are," I said with a grin as I drove up to the spot with the best waves.

The section of the beach was cut off from the rest, and it was also conveniently in perfect view of Perry's Shell Shop, not that it mattered. I couldn't imagine Rosa wanted anything to do with me. I called Sam after that night and told him he needed to be honest with me. I wanted to know what really happened between him and Rosa Rivers. He told me to mind my own damn business at first, and then he caved. Basically, he was an ass, and so was I. I wasn't even sure how to make it up to her. She had saved me and I had essentially called her a liar. What a dick.

"I guess it's just you and me," I told the beat-up surfboard in my hands.

It was one I found at a flea market a few years back for dirt cheap. It would do for now, but I really needed a new one for the competition at the end of the coming week. I would need to brave the surf shop sooner or later. Sure, there were other places, but they were further down, and they also didn't have Rosa Rivers running the register. That was definitely an added bonus.

I took my board into the water and waded out. I got on and paddled right out into the vast swell and sway of the ocean before me, the briny breeze pushing against my face as

I got myself right on the surface of my chipped board. The waves around me cascaded in with a gentle sort of rhythm, giving me the chance to balance on their cresting foam. To me, it looked like a spectacular day to be out on the water, with the sun casting a golden halo on the ocean. It was also that the beach itself was relatively empty and kept private from the world, save for a couple of scattered beachgoers and curious tourists. The swells here were way too much for people who only wanted the gentle lap of the ocean, so they usually didn't stay long on the beach.

I slid effortlessly across the cut of the water. Without my consent, my traitorous mind wandered back to Rosa. I had only met her the one time, but she was stuck in my mind so solidly that it was alarming. Something about her was making me want to be around her. It was strange. I had never felt this way before. From the moment she gave me her sarcastic grin, I knew I was hooked. Too bad I messed it all up. I knew she worked at Perry's Shell Shop, just a little stone's throw away from where I was now in the water, lost in the pull of the salty waves. It felt like torture not to go see her, though it didn't technically make sense.

All of a sudden, a quick little flicker of movement caught my gaze, and I looked over. I squinted, trying to make out the form of the figures that seemed to be making their way towards the sea shop, looking very suspicious to me. It was two men or small women, their faces covered by dark masks. They moved up the beach and then the hill with a very obvious air of aggression and purpose. I watched them, frozen for a moment. I could feel my heart skip a few beats as a heavy feeling of foreboding and horror washed over my being. I just knew that something was not right with what was going down. Maybe it was all that time I spent searching for a reason for what happened to my dad that made me so ready for situations like this one.

My instincts seemed to kick in, and I paddled my way quickly to the shore, my mind turning and racing with terror-filled thoughts of Rosa's safety. The waves seemed to work to turn themselves against me, growing harder and more lashing with each passing minute that went by. I refused to be pulled away from the destination I was set on. I knew I had to reach that beach and the sand to warn Rosa and maybe even Mr. Perry of the coming danger. It was only the Bronco in the parking lot, though, and I knew deep down that it was only Rosa inside the store, all alone.

With one more press of energy, I finally reached the low edge of the crashing water, my legs shaking from the push to the shore. I tumbled my way onto the sand, pushing my soaked hair out of my eyes. I scanned the world around me for any sign of the men with the masks. I looked up, squinting through the sand in my eyes. The shop stood right there before me, its big windows mirroring the glittering sun beams, but there didn't seem to be any sign of Rosa. I could feel the panic that threatened to choke me. It pulled at my chest as I realized she might already be there inside the shop for her shift, completely unaware and clueless of the danger coming toward her. I didn't dare say her name. I didn't know what they were after.

My brain was screaming at me to go save her. Without a second thought and with apparently absolutely no self-preservation instincts, I ran quickly towards the shop on the hill, my heart thumping loudly in my ears. It sounded like the ocean, pounding and crashing so that I couldn't hear anything but the horrifying thoughts in my mind. I crept on bare feet, barely feeling the hot asphalt of the small parking lot. I reached out, and the wooden door swung open with a sharp creak, letting me in on a scene of mess and chaos. There was glittering, shattered glass covering the floor under the door where the window over the lock had been busted, and the air was thick with the scent of the ocean. It should have been comforting, but terror gripped me. I looked around quickly, my eyes searching for Rosa's pretty form amidst the mess inside the shop.

Then, I saw Rosa. She was crouched in a corner of the shop with a bat in her trembling hands, her eyes wide with terror and what seemed to be anger. Her gaze caught mine, and I saw the pissed-off glint there in those green eyes. She put a finger to her lips, telling me I should be quiet because they were obviously still inside. I felt relief wash over my whole body as I rushed to where she was crouching, wrapping myself around her body in a protective curl of an embrace. I thought she might pull away, but she surprised me. She let out a tiny little cry and then buried her face in my chest, her body shaking where it met the length of mine.

"Everything is going to be okay," I murmured in her ear, my voice filled with confidence that I wasn't sure I really and truly felt. "I'm not going to let anything happen to you, okay?"

"They're in the back," she whispered, nodding. "They haven't seen me yet, but I was cleaning the window, and I saw them coming. How did you see?"

"I was down at the beach," I admitted, giving her a small smile. "I saw them walk up the hill, and they were wearing masks. I put two and two together and got four."

"Wow, what a genius," she snapped, but I could tell she was just scared.

"We need to call the cops," I said, keeping my voice low.

In the back room, there was a sharp sound like a drawer being opened. Then muffled cursing, then footsteps. Rosa raised the wooden bat.

"When the cops get here, those guys won't have kneecaps," she said, her lip curling.

"Whoa, what?" I said, grabbing her arm. "Hold on there,

mob boss. They might have guns."

"Okay, then, what do you suggest we do?" she asked, looking annoyed. "I didn't even need your help, you know."

"No, I know. You were gonna make a necklace of kneecaps to take home," I told her, leaning to look around the corner. "I'm going to go make sure they're still in there."

"Of course they're still in there. That's where Mr. Perry keeps the expensive jewelry his mom gave him when she died," Rosa whispered. "It has to be someone from around here, Brody."

"Well, we're about to find out," I said, putting my hand on her thigh to keep her down.

"This is his livelihood, and we can't just let them take it away," she said, her voice low and dangerous. I had no doubt she would bounce up and knock them around before they ever laid a hand on her, but I wasn't about to let any of it happen.

"We aren't going to let them," I said. I shot up and ran loudly into the main room. "Hey, assholes! Get out here and say you're sorry!"

"What the hell are you doing?!" Rosa hissed.

Loud, heavy footsteps sounded, and the door to the back room opened with an ominous creak. Two tall, gangly figures stepped into the light, covered in black.

"I just know you guys are ugly under those masks," I said, giving them a big grin. "Take them off and let's see."

Something glittered in one man's hand, and he brought it forward, wiping it on his dark jeans. It was a big-ass knife.

"That's a big-ass knife," Rosa said casually out of nowhere, and then she whipped forward, knocking one of the men in the ribs.

He grunted in pain, falling back, and the knife clattered to the floor.

"Go hide!" I told her, and then the other man slammed

into me, knocking the wind out of me. "God, you're bony. Are you twelve?" I groaned, my body hitting the shelves that held the novelty t-shirts.

"Get away from him!" Rosa cried, sounding frantic, as I heard the bat smack against the guy's back.

"Ow, what the hell?" said a familiar voice, and I froze.

"Logan, is that you, you little asshole?" I asked, shoving the man back against the checkout counter.

He froze, and the other guy tried to go for the knife on the floor, but Rosa was faster.

"Don't even think about it unless you're not a fan of having ten fingers," she snapped, and I found her so damn sexy at that moment.

"You want to be bad cop or good cop?" I asked her lightly, and she rolled her eyes. "Okay, bad cop it is."

I reached forward, ripping off the thick mask. Of course, Logan's stupid hair fluffed out of it, looking ridiculous.

"Who is that?" Rosa asked. "Justin Bieber?"

I nearly choked on my laugh. "This is Logan. He's just a kid. He was going to compete in the surf competition this weekend, but I think being in jail might put a crink in those plans somewhat."

"Who's your friend, Logan?" Rosa asked, pointing her bat at the kid crouched on the floor.

"You're crazy as hell!" the boy said, ripping off the mask. "Don't touch me with that bat, or I swear I'll sue."

"What are two rich kids doing here, stealing from an old man?" Rosa asked, her brow wrinkled as she stared at the red-haired boy who was covered in about a million freckles.

"Oh, I get it," I said, letting out a disbelieving laugh. "This is how you got that fancy board, huh?"

"I don't know what you're talking about," Logan grumbled, looking away.

"So you've been breaking into surf shops and stealing

money along with boards and gear, right? That's how you're getting by even after your parents kicked you out?" I asked.

"Wow, that's embarrassing for you," Rosa told him, wrinkling her nose. "What about you, carrot top? What's your excuse?"

"Logan is my friend," he said, but he looked wide-eyed and very, very young.

"Yeah, bad friends will get you in a shit ton of trouble, kid," I told him. "Get out of here."

"He had a knife," Rosa said, staring him down. "We shouldn't just let him go."

"Pick it up," I told her, nodding. "It's just one of those prop knives. He's probably a theater kid."

"I am not! I'm a serious actor!" the kid cried.

"Go home," I told him. "Go back to the gated community before I call the cops."

The kid left in a hurry, nearly tripping over his own feet in his quick movements.

"Really?" Logan said. "You just let him go like that?"

"Are you just going to throw your friend under the bus?" I asked, laughing.

"He's probably the bus driver," Rosa said.

"Who is she?" Logan asked, giving her a dirty look.

"Hey, don't look at her like that," I told him quickly. "What are your parents' numbers?"

He went white as a sheet. "You can't call them."

"I'll call them or the cops, it's up to you," I said with a shrug.

"The cops," he said quickly, nodding.

"You got it, boss," I said, pulling out the phone. Rosa walked away, and I watched her. "Where are you going?"

She turned, wincing. "I have to call Mr. Perry. It's been a long morning."

That was the damn understatement of the year.

5

ROSA

*B*rody's jeep smelled of the ocean and the brown leather seat covers.

"I didn't need your help, you know," I said, staring out of the window.

"Oh, you're welcome," Brody answered, scoffing.

Truthfully, my hands were still shaking. It had been hours of talking to the cops and telling my side of the story. Mr. Perry was probably still there at the shop too.

"You didn't have to take me home," I told Brody. "I have a car."

"Did you not hear the cops? They were checking your car for evidence," Brody told me, glancing over. "Did you want to stay there all night or something?"

"I don't see why they needed evidence," I said with a shrug. "I mean, Logan pretty much confessed to what he was doing."

"The other kid. They need to know who he is to charge him," Brody said. He drove in silence for a moment, thinking. "I'll bet Logan is pissed about not being able to surf."

"What do you mean?" I wondered. I tucked my hair

behind my ears, annoyed that Brody didn't put the top up on the jeep before we set off.

He grinned. "That little punk was talking himself up about the surf competition coming up, making sure that I knew he was going to beat me. Look at him now."

"The surf competition this weekend?" I asked. "Is that why you were out in the water?"

"I was out in the water because I like the water," he answered. "No matter the weather."

I rolled my eyes. "Yeah, I know how low your IQ is. You don't need to explain."

"You think you would be a little more grateful to the man who saved you," he said, grinning.

"Can you just take me home?" I asked him, sighing.

Brody Strauss was the forbidden fruit. He was the man who was the closest to the one who had broken my heart completely. I loved Sam Wesson, and I was dumb enough to trust him with our relationship. Of course, he found the bouncy, glittering, tanned girls on the beach to be more entertaining. Honestly, maybe I was better off. The last thing I really needed was to get myself involved with another surfer. Daytona was bad enough.

"Oh, I'm not taking you home," he said, smirking.

I glanced sideways at him. "Okay, Ted Bundy. Let me out here. I'll walk."

"I'm not taking you somewhere to make you my next victim," he said, laughing. "I'm making you dinner."

"Who says I want dinner?" I said, crossing my arms.

He laughed again, and the sound of it was warm and inviting. He smelled so damn good. The urge to kiss him again was overwhelming. I had to dig my fingers into my sides to keep from launching myself at him. The worst part of it was that he had no idea. He was just living his life, driving the jeep, and blissfully unaware of how much I wanted him.

"Hey," he said suddenly, his voice going warm and gentle. He stopped at a four-way. "Look at me, Rosa."

I closed my eyes for a moment, weighing my options, before I finally looked at him, keeping my arms crossed. I kept my face carefully flat and impassive.

"What?" I asked, turning a little.

I shouldn't have looked at him. I should have ignored him fully. His handsome face was open and genuine, and it made my chest ache. He might have been a surfer like Sam was, but Sam had never once looked at me like that. There was none of the raw emotion that was openly showing on Brody's features.

"It's okay to show fear," he told me gently. I tried to push down the feeling of butterflies in my belly. "Everyone gets scared sometimes."

"Oh, you were scared then?" I asked him sardonically. I expected him to say no, that he would never be scared. Maybe I thought he would laugh at me or make a joke.

"Yeah, I was," he admitted with a shrug. "I thought something might have happened to you. I thought I wouldn't get to you quickly enough."

That made my breath catch. I swallowed hard, looking away. I wasn't even sure what to say. Brody was very open about what he wanted and what he thought. I wasn't used to that. I wasn't someone who shared things with other people. It wasn't easy for me to just open up. Sharing a part of myself was terrifying to me. I wasn't always like that, but getting my heart broken changed a big part of me. Before that, I was soft.

"Well, I had it pretty much handled," I said finally, trying to keep my tone easy and light.

"Oh yeah, completely handled," he said, shifting back into his seat with a laugh.

I let out a sigh of relief, but I also felt the absence of that warm gaze.

"Are we there yet?" I asked him, clearing my throat. "Do you live in another state or something?"

He laughed. "Once you taste my baked spaghetti, you won't care where we are."

"I don't like spaghetti," I said, glancing at him. I fully intended to keep it going until I saw the look on his face.

"Oh yeah?" he answered, a frown cutting across his features. "I probably should have asked first, huh?"

"I was kidding, Brody."

"Oh, right," he said, his smile returning. It made me feel warm.

"Is it true that surfers are less intelligent than the average person?" I asked, staring out of the window as I tried not to smile.

To my surprise, he let out a real, surprised bark of laughter.

"You tell me," he said, putting the jeep in park. He glanced over at me. "We're here."

He parked us in front of a small bungalow that was nestled in a copse of wind-bent, ancient oak trees. The house was warm and inviting, just like Brody. There were signs of him everywhere. Battered surfboards were leaned against the faded blue siding, and there was even a ripped wetsuit hanging from the rails of the small porch. There was a tire swing in one of the trees, and I assumed the person who had the house before him must have had kids. When I was supposed to take him home before, it was at a friend's house because he said he had to pick something up, and it was apparently close to where he parked his jeep. This was miles away from that. I realized he trusted me enough to let me know where he lived, the place he called home.

He had also saved me, no matter what I tried to tell myself. Fake knife or no fake knife.

"I can come and pick you up tomorrow to get you to work," he said, shrugging.

"You don't have to do that," I told him. "Though a ride home after this would be nice."

"Yeah, I can do that," he said, smiling at me.

"Look, about what I said before…" I started, shaking my head, "I really appreciate this."

"My spaghetti or my driving skills?" he asked, and I could hear the grin in his voice without looking. "Or was it my scintillating company?"

I cleared my throat. "All of it."

"Rosa." His voice was soft and entreating, urging me to look at him.

I glanced over, and the ache in my chest for him only seemed to grow. He was watching me, his gaze moving to my mouth. Oh, this man was going to do me in for sure. I wanted to press my mouth to his again and find out if he always tasted like the ocean.

He let out a breath. "Alright," he said finally, shaking his head and leaning in.

Warm hands came up to cradle my face, and then his lips were on mine.

My hands were on his shoulders, squeezing hard enough to bruise. My head was swimming, and my heart was beating out of my chest. His thumb caressed my cheek, his touch pulling a shiver through my body. One of my hands went into his soft, dark hair, and his tongue licked into my mouth. I wasn't thinking about the circumstances that brought us to this moment. I was only thinking about Brody Strauss, and I wished he was reaching under my top to press those warm hands to my skin. He kissed me hard and frantic, his breathing ragged. He kissed like he had been waiting for it. Maybe we both had. This kiss was a twist of emotions—a hard landing from a soft fall. A panic settled over me. Maybe we would both regret this when it was said and done.

"Brody," I said gently, breathing into his mouth as I pushed back a little.

He laughed, soft and happy. "Yeah, that was a lot," he murmured, his thumb soothing my skin. He kissed my cheek, pulling back. "Sorry, but I couldn't take it anymore."

I could feel my old heart coming back, bursting to life with the touch of his warm hands. That first kiss had been the catalyst, and this one was the result. Before Sam, before old wounds tore me open and I came back scarred, I was someone who always saw the bright side. I would look up at the glittering stars and see the potential and the hope in the world. After him, I knew that the stars were just dead things, sparkling at me with their last, dying light. Around Brody, I felt warm and bright. It was terrifying.

"Yeah, I get it," I told him quietly, though I knew it wasn't a real answer.

I was taking the coward's way out. If I didn't acknowledge what he said, I could pretend he never said it at all. Whatever was happening between us, it felt so very different from anything else I had ever experienced. Something was pulling us together, tying a knot in our hearts like a tether.

"Right," Brody said, and he didn't sound unsure or disappointed, but it was there in the set of his dark brows.

There was some sort of allure surrounding Brody Strauss that seemed to pull me to him effortlessly. It was as if he possessed an intangible quality that made it impossible to resist his magnetic presence. Every encounter with him left an indelible mark on my consciousness, a lingering sensation I couldn't quite shake off. His presence seemed to awaken the buried emotions in me that had been dormant for a long time. He had an intense hold on me, and the more I tried to resist it, the stronger it grew, like an unseen force pulling at the very core of who I was. It was a risky sort of business that called for a delicate balancing act between desire and willpower. Brody was surrounded by an atmosphere of warmth and intrigue. He was bright and sunny, but there was something else underneath all of it. The way he kept trying to help me and his sarcastic nature made me constantly wonder about his genuine motives. What did he want from me? But maybe it was this uncertainty that caught my interest and drew me further into his orbit.

I found myself aching for him, craving his presence in ways that didn't really even make sense. With everything else on my plate, I didn't need to have to worry about him, but it seemed inevitable. As much as I tried to pretend he hadn't already charmed me without even really trying, it just wasn't happening. It was as if he held the key to unlocking a hidden part of myself, a part that I had long forgotten, or perhaps never even knew existed.

The intensity of my desire both exhilarated and terrified me, for I knew that indulging in it could lead to unforeseen consequences. But I couldn't help but wonder if he felt the same way. Did he notice the jolt of electricity that seemed to happen every time our eyes met? Did he see an unspoken connection that seemed to bind us together and go beyond the realm of rational thought? Or was I just a piece in his complicated plan, a little distraction in his intriguing existence? I wondered if he thought of Sam when he thought of me.

As I pushed down the nagging urge to surrender to him, I couldn't help but question the nature of whatever was burning between us. Was it a short fling destined to soon fade into the depths of my memories? Or was it something deeper—a cosmic clash of souls that I couldn't begin to understand—that was more profound?

As I continued to navigate the emotional warfare of my own emotions, only time would be able to provide the answers to the questions in my head. Something about him really drew me in, and it was hard to ignore. Suddenly, I found myself wondering if we could be something. I also wondered if my thoughts were even appropriate. That was a part of it and most of the reason I was fighting it so hard. Brody was Sam's best friend, and maybe they were more alike than I thought. There was no way to tell.

"Are we getting out?" I asked him, watching him closely. I waited for a moment, trying not to think of the kiss. "Brody?"

Yeah, it probably wasn't the most mentally sane move to ignore it and pretend we didn't just kiss passionately, but oh well. I didn't want to confront feelings right then.

"Rosa," he said seriously, turning to me. "I really had no idea about Sam, you know."

I looked at him, surprised. "What do you mean?"

I really, truly didn't want to talk about my ex-boyfriend with him, but I was curious. He was the man who probably knew him better than anyone else. Maybe he would tell me what I did to deserve being treated the way Sam had treated me. Actually, no, there was no excuse for that. Sam was just a shitty human being. Despite that, I was still curious to know what he thought about the whole situation and what he had to say about it.

"I know that Sam likes women. He's always been that way," he said, wincing.

"Yeah, he likes blonde women. I told you that," I said, making a face.

"No, I mean, he's always been the kind of guy who could go up to a woman in a bar and she would just go home with him," he said with a shrug. "It comes naturally to him."

"Does it come naturally to you?" I asked, though I wasn't really sure why exactly.

"I don't need to approach women," he said with a snort. "He's just—"

"He's just what?" I snapped, annoyed with him. If he took up for Sam, I knew that would feel like another betrayal for me. "Are you going to make some stupid excuse for him?"

"I'm not making excuses for him," Brody argued. "I'm just saying that's how he is."

"Oh, so that's how you explain him treating me like garbage?" I said, my voice rising.

"I told you, I'm not making excuses. I think you deserved and deserve better." He squeezed his long fingers around the steering wheel, looking ahead of us at the house with thoughtful eyes.

The cool night wind brought the scent of the briny ocean into the open jeep. I took a deep breath, making sure I stayed calm.

"I know I deserve better," I told him easily. "But Sam is the reason I haven't tried with anyone else."

Brody nodded. "He's an idiot. He didn't know what he had."

"I'm sure he would love to hear you talk about him like that," I said, letting out a dull little laugh. "It's crazy we never met."

"Yeah, I know, but I would have remembered meeting you," he said, chuckling.

It was little stuff like that. He had my heart racing, and he didn't even know it. Maybe that was what he meant about not needing to approach women at bars. He was so easy with it, so not afraid to say whatever he wanted. I was sure women probably just flocked to him, hanging on his every

43

word. Suddenly, I imagined him in a bar, plaid shirt unbuttoned to expose his tanned chest and the trail of dark hair that disappeared into his khaki shorts. He would probably have women all over him.

"It's odd he never introduced us," I said, nodding distractedly. I was busy trying to get the thoughts of Brody out of my head.

"I think you were his first real girlfriend," he told me. "Maybe that's why we never met. He wanted you all to himself. Can't blame the guy."

"I can and will blame him," I said, rolling my eyes.

"Yeah, that's not what I meant," he replied with a wince. "Anyway, are you ready to go in?"

"Yeah, I'm starving," I said, glad to be back on easy conversation terrain. "I can't wait to see how that famous Strauss spaghetti holds up to the hype."

"We'll see," he said, grinning.

Surprisingly, he came around to my side to open the door for me. I thanked him, but all of a sudden, he looked shifty. He rubbed the back of his neck, and I followed him to his front door, curious. The windows were lit up warm and yellow with light, and I wondered if he left the lights on by accident and why he didn't seem to care.

The door swung open before he could touch it though, and there was a small figure standing at the door.

"Dad!"

6

BRODY

*R*osa was staring at my son like he had two heads and seven arms.

"You have a son?" she asked, her eyes wide.

"He has a son, it's me," he said, coming up to her quickly and thrusting out his hand. "I'm Corey, and my last name is Strauss."

Rosa shook his hand slowly. "Hi, Corey Strauss."

"You're supposed to tell me your name now," Corey told her, beaming at her.

I decided to quickly cut in and give Rosa a break. I scooped my son up and moved him off to the side, shooing him in the direction of the living room and the movie playing.

"Corey, why don't we give Rosa here a minute to think," I said, nodding at him. "Go watch some TV. Is Greta still here?"

My son shook his head. "She left a few minutes ago. She was half asleep."

"Of course she was," I said with a grin. I looked at Rosa.

"Greta is the elderly woman who babysits for me. She lives a house down from us."

"Right," she said, looking between the two of us as Corey left for the living room.

"Why don't you have a seat, and I'll get dinner started," I told her, gesturing to the small kitchen island.

Yes, I was avoiding the real elephant in the room. It was never a good time to bring up that I had a son waiting for me at home. There was a reason I had asked her to drop me off at Greta's house. I didn't know how to casually mention I had a son to the woman who had dated my best friend until that best friend cheated on her. Truthfully, I thought he was ridiculously stupid. I looked at Rosa, and I wondered how anyone could hurt her. I saw her ready to tear those guys apart when they broke into the surf shop, and I was hooked. She was like a mother lion protecting her cubs or something. It was hot.

"So…" she said, sliding into one of the seats, and I already knew what she was going to say. "You have a son."

"Yeah, we pretty much already established that," I said, flicking on the lights. Warm golden light flooded the kitchen, where it had just been the TV glowing through before. "Do you like cheese toast?"

"Who doesn't like cheese toast?" she answered, rolling her eyes. "Except when it's used as an excuse to not talk about certain topics. Then no, I'm not really a fan."

I stopped, putting the pot down into the sink on the island and filling it with water. The island had been an add-on. I wanted to feel like one of those chefs on the cooking channel. Two of my burners were also situated there, leaving enough space to eat on the other side of them. It made me feel more secure to have a place where I could cook for Corey and watch him play. We had made this house a home in the time we had spent here. Despite the trouble with his mom, Corey seemed to be pretty happy.

"Which do you want to talk about?" I asked her lightly, putting the noodles on.

"Which what? What do you mean?" she asked, her eyes going wide again. "Do you have another one I don't know about?"

"No," I laughed. "Which do you want to talk about? The kiss or the kid?"

She sucked in a breath of surprise and coughed, hand on her chest.

"Why did you say that so casually?" she asked, wheezing. "Those are two very different subjects."

"Well, which one pulled that reaction out of you?" I asked, trying not to laugh. "We don't need to talk about that one. I don't know the Heimlich maneuver."

"Why didn't you say that you had a kid?" she asked me, settling after a moment.

"And when was I supposed to say that exactly?" I pulled out all the ingredients I would need and started cutting up tomatoes. "Oh right, I should have mentioned it in between almost drowning and nearly being stabbed by a fake knife."

"I mean, that just seems like something you would tell me," she said, but then shook her head. "I guess that sounds stupid. We don't even know each other."

"It feels like we do," I said, shrugging.

"Because of Sam?" she asked, wrinkling her nose.

Really, it had nothing to do with him. There was just something about her that made me feel bright and alive. I liked the way she was dry and sarcastic, but there was also sweetness underneath. Things like that were even sweeter when you had to work to keep them there. She had obviously been hurt and it made her want to keep a wall up.

"I haven't even talked to him in a few months, honestly," I

told her as I mixed various vegetables into a soft, maroon spaghetti sauce.

"Uncle Sam?" my six-year-old shouted suddenly, appearing behind Rosa, who jumped in surprise. I was used to Corey's habit of popping up at random intervals.

"Oh, Uncle Sam, huh?" Rosa said, looking at my son and then at me accusingly.

"Hey, don't look at me," I said as I dropped the spoon and raised my hand in surrender. "Sam hasn't seen the inside of my house in a long time. We really don't talk much."

"Uncle Sam is really cool," Corey said, pushing his dark waves out of his eyes. "He's teaching me how to whittle."

"Whittle?" I asked my son, looking at him. "What are you talking about, Corey?"

He looked back and forth between us, seemingly trying to think of what he was going to say. He finally just grinned, shrugged, and made his way out of the room again.

"What was that about?" Rosa asked, raising her eyebrows. "You tell me you haven't seen him in a while, but apparently he's been teaching your kid to play with a knife?"

I couldn't help but laugh. "Have you ever whittled?"

"You're good at that, aren't you?" she said, smiling a little. "Changing the subject, I mean."

"I haven't talked to him," I told her honestly, looking her straight in those bright, pretty, almond-shaped eyes. "Kids say stuff that doesn't really make sense. They just do."

"Not me," Rosa said, and I could hear the teasing in her voice.

"You were probably a math kid, huh?" I asked, staring at her across the counter and watching the way her hair glittered in the soft, golden light.

"English, actually," she said, her voice going a little wistful. "I always wanted to write a book. If it was up to me, I would spend my days writing and riding horses."

"Mr. Perry's horses, you mean," I said, looking up to catch her answer as I poured the noodles into the now-boiling water. When she nodded, I said, "So, why didn't you?"

"Why didn't I become a best-selling author and live my life on a horse farm in bliss?" she asked with a snort of disbelief, raising her eyebrows.

"What, like it's hard?" I replied, and she laughed, the sound warming me from the inside out.

"I can help with that, you know. I'm not completely useless in the kitchen," she said.

"Oh yeah?" I asked her, grinning. "Do you cook?"

"For sure. If you count cut-up fruit and microwave meals," she said with a small laugh, a hint of pink coloring her cheeks. "It's never been a big deal to me."

"A good meal is worth more than you think," I told her. "My mom wasn't really able to cook for me every night, and I had to sort of fend for myself, you know?"

She shifted, nodding. "So, your mom wasn't around then? If you don't want to tell me, you don't have to. I guess it's really none of my business."

It was strange, but something about the way she said it felt like she already knew what she was asking about. But there was no way she could know about my dad, right? If she had known, I assumed she would have mentioned it. Then again, I never told her about my son, so that was something to consider.

"No, it's okay, I'm not ashamed of it," I told her, though my chest twinged painfully with that old emotional hurt. I pushed it down. "My mom just had really low lows, you know? She needed a little help, and I was the only one there to take care of us."

The entire truth of it was that her husband was swept away by the ocean, and she just couldn't function the way she could before. She needed me and I was more than happy to help. She was my mom, and I always wondered if it was my fault in the first place.

"Brody," Rosa said softly, and when I looked at her, her eyes were glittering.

"Don't look at me like that," I told her, shaking my head. I cleared my throat. "Come and help me with the meatballs, will you?"

She seemed to relax. "You like scorched meatballs? They're my specialty."

"Oh, I think I can handle it," I said with a chuckle. I moved behind her as she came around the counter, grabbing the ingredients. "You have to really get into it," I said. You have to be serious about rolling the meatballs."

She looked back at me, her eyes sparkling with a hint of mischief, and she nodded. "Sure, Brody," she said, her voice soft and melodic. "I'm pretty good with meat."

I coughed a laugh. "Well, thanks for sharing that with me."

Her cheeks went red. "Just shut up. You know what I mean."

The whole kitchen was filled with the rich, savory aroma of simmering tomato sauce and the faint, pretty scent of Rosa's soft perfume. It was a heady mix that made my heart thump fast in my chest. I showed her how to roll the meatballs, our hands brushing against each other. I was behind her, my front pressed to her back, and she tipped her head back a little, resting on my shoulder. Each touch of her skin against mine sent a little jolt of electricity through me, making me very aware of her presence.

"Am I doing this right?" she asked, her voice soft and thrilling.

"You're doing fine," I told her easily.

"What about your son?" she wondered, pausing for a moment.

"He likes to nap before dinner," I told her. "He's done it

since he was a toddler. Something about the smell of cooking food makes him sleep."

I knew what she meant, though. If Corey found us in the kitchen, tucked together like we were, what would he think? He was young, but not that young. I wasn't even sure what was happening between Rosa and myself, and there was no way I would be able to explain it to my son.

"I'll grab the baking pan," she said, and shimmied out of my loose embrace.

"I sprayed it already," I told her. "Grab the cheese?"

It felt so domestic being in the kitchen with her. It was like having a real family, and not just Corey and myself. Yeah, we were a family, but it wouldn't hurt to have someone else in his life.

"Can I ask you something?" Rosa murmured, putting the cheese on the counter beside me.

"You can ask me anything," I said, shooting her a sideways grin as I popped the meatballs into a little pan to sear for a moment before putting them in the sauce. "Are you going to ask for my number?"

"I think it's a little late for that," she said with a snort. "We jumped straight to dinner."

"What is it that you want to ask?" I wondered.

"Do you still see your mom? Does she see Corey?" Rosa asked, sounding hesitant.

"Oh yeah," I answered her easily. "She lives close to the Lion's Bridge, over by the bay. She likes to see Corey on the weekends when I have time to take him over there."

"My parents are back in Daytona," she said, sounding a little sad. "I just can't go back there, you know?"

"You should go see them," I told her, bumping my shoulder gently into hers. "I'm sure they miss you."

"I miss them too," she said, her voice breaking. "It's been months now."

"Who do you miss?" asked a new voice.

"Corey," Rosa said, clearing her throat. She went around the island to my son with his tousled, nap-wild hair. She put out her hand for him to shake. "Hi, we weren't properly introduced before. I'm Rosa, your dad's friend."

"He has friends?" Corey asked, and I rolled my eyes.

"No one is more ruthless than your own kids," I said with a snort. "Thanks, son."

"Can we be friends?" Corey asked Rosa, ignoring me completely.

She grinned and it glittered like the sun. "Of course we can. We can't tell your dad, though. He'll get jealous."

"Very funny," I said, looking at them both. "Corey, why don't you go set the dining room table? We'll finish this. That is if you and your new bestie can be parted."

Corey's little laugh was adorable, and I tried very hard to keep the stern look on my face.

"I'll go set the table, Dad," he said finally, reaching on his tiptoes to grab the plates and forks.

"Thank you," I told him, giving him a smile when he looked back at me.

"He's a good kid," Rosa said as she sprinkled cheese over the spaghetti in the baking pan. "I haven't had much experience with them, but he seems to have a good head on his shoulders."

"You helped out at the winter trail rides, didn't you?" I asked her, and then I realized my mistake.

"How did you know that?" she wondered, turning to look at me and stopping what she was doing.

I chuckled awkwardly. "Corey wanted to go last year, but when we got there, it was all full. I saw you."

"You're a stalker," she said, but I could tell she was just teasing me. "But yeah, the trail rides were a big hit."

"Were?" I asked her, putting the pan in the oven when she opened it for me.

"It's a long story," she said, shaking her head.

I couldn't help but steal glances at her, admiring the way her hair fell over her face as she concentrated on her task. At one point, she even looked up with those pretty eyes and caught me staring at her. Instead of looking away, I held her gaze, and the sparks seemed to fly between us. I wanted her to know that she was something to look at. I didn't want to hide it. There was a warmth in her features that made my heart flutter with anticipation. This felt like something to be guarded and kept safe. This felt like it would be the one to hold me down. It sounded crazy, but I could feel that pull to her already. She gave me a small smile, her cheeks turning a soft shade of pink. I wanted to hold her in my arms, and I wanted to know what all that soft skin under her clothes tasted like.

"Is this how you get all your dates to cook for you, Brody?" she teased, her eyes twinkling with amusement. "I mean, I'll admit it's a pretty effective tactic."

I chuckled, feeling a warmth spread through me. "Only the ones I really like," I replied, hoping she'd catch my meaning without me having to actually say it.

"I think I singed the cheese bread," she said, wincing as she bent down to pull it out. "So maybe you have bad taste in chefs."

"But not in women," I said with a shrug.

She blushed deeper, her pretty face going bright red, but she didn't look away from me, and I counted it as a win.

"Food!" Corey called from the small dining room, and we both laughed.

"Well, you heard the man," Rosa said, grinning.

"Here, put those oven mitts on, and don't burn your

fingers, okay?" I nodded to the half-open drawer with the watermelon-themed mitts.

"That's sweet," she said, grabbing them. "But watermelons? You picked these out?"

She was wondering if I had a girlfriend or a wife I was hiding from her. It was pretty obvious to me where her mind was going.

"I stole those from my mom's house to carry out an especially hot tray of oatmeal raisin cookies a week ago," I said, reaching down to brush my hand over hers and nudge the mitts against her fingers.

"That makes sense," she said, looking relieved.

"Dinner's served," I said as we came into the dining room with the food all put onto plates.

My son was reading a book from his summer reading list, and I was proud of that fact. He put it politely down as we came in, and Rosa made a sound of surprise.

"You're reading that new dragon series?" she put down the pan and asked, pointing. "Me too!"

"Really?" Corey asked her, and his entire face lit up. "None of my friends like it."

"I have the entire set if you want the next one too," she told him kindly. "They're really good. You have good taste."

"Thank you," Corey said politely, beaming at her.

"Here you go," I said as I fixed his plate. "Cheese bread pushed to the side away from the noodles, just like you like it."

"Where should I sit?" Rosa asked. She looked unsure, and I didn't like it.

"Beside me!" Corey said, nearly bouncing with excitement. "Sit right here, Rosa."

"Perfect," she said, looking pleased.

"Alright—" I began, sitting in my seat, but I was interrupted.

The doorbell was ringing, shrill and annoying throughout the house. Corey and Rosa looked at me expectantly, and I sighed with a small grin, making my way to the door.

"Hello—" I began once again and then stopped short at the face in the doorway. "Sam?"

7

ROSA

"It's okay," I told Corey. "Your dad will be back in just a second."

Corey jumped as it sounded like the front door burst open and hit the wall behind it. There was the clatter of silverware against porcelain. The bright noise filled the room as we sat at the dinner table. What was going on? My heart was thumping hard. The sudden intrusion startled us both, causing Corey to drop his hand down and shake his plate, nearly toppling his spaghetti over the sides.

"Rosa," a familiar voice echoed through the room, and my body went cold.

I felt my heart drop into my stomach at that sound. I knew immediately it was Sam's voice. His hazel eyes were wild, his blonde hair disheveled, and his breath reeked of cheap beer.

"Sam," I said, swallowing hard as I stood up quickly, my chair scraping the floor.

My mind flashed back to a year and a half ago, and all I could see was the empty road in front of me, and the empty feeling in my chest. There was freedom there too, buried under the heart. Somehow, I felt better after I left him, and, even without his mistakes, I didn't want to be with him. The thought made me feel better, and I felt stronger for it.

"You're at his table, huh?" Sam slurred, pointing at me. "Yeah, that figures. Everybody always liked him better."

"I don't know what you're talking about," I said, watching him cautiously. I stood beside Corey, who was looking wide-eyed between all of us.

"Take your dinner to your room, son," Brody said sternly, and that strong voice sent shivers dancing down my spine. "Now."

Corey looked at all of us one more time, and then he was up and taking his plate with him. He disappeared into the dim hallway. Brody was at my side in an instant, a warm presence. We were a united front against this man we both knew. Right then, he was just something standing in the way of the happy dinner we were trying to have.

"Sam, what are you doing here?" Brody asked him. His voice was calm, but I could see the tension that tightened in his strong jaw.

"I need to talk to Rosa," Sam said, ignoring Brody and staring at me. His gaze was intense, and I felt a shiver run down my spine.

"How did you know I was here?" I asked. "How did you know what city I was in?"

He laughed, loud and jarring. "Oh, Corey sent his Uncle Sam a message on his tablet. He said his dad had a special friend over. He called her by your name, *Rosa*."

Brody cursed. "He wasn't even supposed to have that this late at night."

"Sam, this isn't the time or the place," I said, trying to keep my voice steady as I spoke with this man who was once supposed to be my future. I was glad that he wasn't.

"No, I think it is," he retorted, his voice rising. "I think it's exactly the right time. It's time we talked about you and Brody. Or maybe I should talk, and you should just listen."

I felt my cheeks begin to burn. "What are you even talking about? You're not making any sense. You came here just for this?"

"He's here for the competition, right?" Brody commented, his voice tight and tense. "That's why he's on Anastasia Island."

"There's nothing going on," I told my ex-boyfriend, keeping my voice calm.

"Don't play dumb, Rosa," he spat, only slurring his words a little this time. "You've been seeing Brody behind my back. I bet you were seeing him for years."

I was taken aback by his accusation. "No, that's not true. I didn't even know Brody when we were together. We just met a few days ago. Are you really trying to blame everything on me? After what you did?"

He scoffed, crossing his arms over his chest. "Oh, yeah, right. And I'm supposed to believe that?"

"Yes, Sam, because it's the truth," I told him, my voice firm.

"You don't need to bring up old shit to try and prove a point," he said, throwing his hand out, moving toward me a little. "You could have just forgiven me, but you hold grudges."

"You need to leave." My voice was firm and I was proud of how serious it sounded. "This isn't your house, and you need to go now."

"This is my best friend's house, right, buddy?" he said sarcastically, giving Brody a nasty grin. "I'm welcome here at any time."

"My son is here, and you're not in the right state of mind, Sammy," Brody said, his tone going gentle. "I need you to go home. I can call you an Uber or something to get you back."

"No way, I'm not going anywhere until we sort this whole thing out," Sam said, his voice stubborn. He did seem to be slowly sobering up, though, maybe at the mention of Corey.

"I'm going to tell you one last time," I said, gritting my teeth, "there is nothing to sort out."

"I'll be damned," Sam said with a scoff.

"I don't understand why you're doing this," I said, feeling deflated and very, very tired. "You didn't give a damn when I left, and you didn't care about me enough not to stick your tongue down another woman's throat right in front of everyone."

"Hey, come here," Sam said, stumbling towards me with his arms out and his face crumpled with regret. Brody pulled me back, and Sam stared at me with bleary eyes. "You left me for him. I know you did. I can see it all over your face."

"Sam, you cheated on Rosa," Brody interjected, to my enormous relief. His voice was stern and serious. "She left you without a note in another city. You're my best friend, but you really have no right to come here and accuse her of anything. Do you understand?"

Sam's face turned red. "You got a lot of damn nerve, Brody. You were supposed to be my friend."

"I'm your friend, but what you did was wrong, and I think you know that," Brody said easily. "Rosa deserves better than that."

"You don't know anything about what happened between the two of us. Whatever she told you is probably a lie. That's why we broke up, you know, because she's a liar," Sam said, looking very proud of himself.

My stomach churned. "I'm a liar? Oh, you have got to be kidding me."

"That girl kissed me, and you said it was my fault," Sam slurred again, looking weepy.

"You smell like a bar," I told him with a sigh. "Go home

and stop pretending you give a damn about anything but yourself."

"You're better than this," Brody said sadly. "Or at least I used to think you were."

Sam opened his mouth, and he looked like he was about to explode. But instead, he turned on his heel and stormed out of the little house, smacking the door behind him.

The room was silent for a moment, and the only sound was the constant ticking of the clock on the wall. I jumped when I felt a hand drop gently on my shoulder. I turned to see Brody looking at me with concern. I could feel my whole body shaking.

"Are you okay?" he asked me, his voice gentle.

I nodded, swallowing the lump in my throat. "Yeah, I'm okay. I can't believe that just happened." A laugh bubbled up out of my throat, but it felt more like a sob. "I don't even— I mean, what just happened?"

"Okay, I think you need to sit down, Ro," Brody said, and the nickname made butterflies flutter around in my belly, making me feel giddy.

"Maybe."

I let him wrap his arm around my waist and tug me into the kitchen area. He pushed me gently down to sit in one of the bar chairs.

"I'll be right back," he said, and then disappeared into the back rooms. "I'm going to start some coffee, too."

"Yeah, that sounds good," I said, nodding.

I sat in Brody's kitchen, nervously fidgeting with the hem of my shirt. The scent of freshly brewed coffee filled the air, mingling with the aroma of warm pancakes from the candle Brody lit when he came back in, telling me that Corey had gone to sleep. Brody, with his messy hair and kind eyes, stood across from me, leaning his body against the counter lazily, like a big cat. I took a deep breath as I watched him, gathering the courage to say what had been weighing on my heart for what seemed far too long a time.

"Listen, there's something I need to tell you," I began after a moment of silence, my voice barely rising above more than a whisper. His gaze met mine, encouraging me to continue. "I was just thinking. I don't think I ever really loved Sam, at least not the way I should have."

His eyebrows furrowed in confusion, and I could see the concern etched on his face as he stepped closer. "What do you mean? You were together for years, weren't you? He always seemed pretty happy to me. I figured you were too."

I sighed at that, trying to find the right words to explain the tangled mess of emotions that had taken me over for so long. Of course, I couldn't completely explain something like that to him. Unless he was in my head, he wouldn't have understood. I did wonder if Brody had been around when I was with Sam, would I have wanted him then too? At the moment, it felt as if my feelings for him had sprung on me, and I didn't even really know how to make sense of them myself. In all other aspects, Brody would have been just like Sam. The only difference was that he wasn't a god-awful person, at least as far as I knew. I was so afraid he was going to turn out to be just like his friend.

"I know. I get that it's hard to understand for you, but I think I was really just comfortable with him. If you know what I mean. We had been together for so long, and it felt safe. But looking back, I don't think I ever truly loved him." I took a deep breath and then let it out again.

Brody stood before me, and his eyes softened, his expression filling with understanding. "Hey, no, it's okay. Sometimes, it's normal to confuse comfort with love. Honestly, it happens to the best of us. It's nothing to hide."

I nodded, grateful for his patience. "I think maybe I was just so scared to be alone, scared to face the unknown on my own. Sam was just so familiar to me, and I clung to that familiarity to keep me sane. Deep down, I always felt like something was missing."

"You're different now, though. I couldn't imagine anyone using you or walking all over your feelings," he told me thoughtfully.

"Yeah, well, I guess I learned my lesson," I said, blowing out a breath.

Brody reached out with warm fingers and gently took my hand in his. His touch was giving me a sense of comfort and peace. "Rosa, you know you deserve to be with someone who makes you feel complete and happy too. You have to find someone who ignites a fire within you, not just someone who keeps you warm at night."

My eyes burned as tears welled up. I hadn't even realized how true those words were. "I think that's exactly it, yeah. When I was with Sam, I was just going through the motions and going along with what was expected of me from him and everyone else. But around you, Brody, it's completely different. I feel alive with you, like I'm finally living my life in line with who I am. I'm riding horses more and doing things for myself."

I watched as a small smile tugged at the corners of his lips, his thumb gently pressing over the back of my hand. "That's how it should be, I think. I've been in a few bad relationships myself. It's never easy to let that part of yourself go. You have to, though, if you want to be a better version of yourself."

His words filled my body with warmth, and I couldn't help but lean into him, seeking solace in the protection of his embrace. I couldn't believe Brody was like this. When I first met him, I never would have thought he was anything other than a brainless surfer. It turned out, he was so much more than I ever cared to admit to myself.

"You're right," I nodded, pulling back to look at him. "I don't want to be who I was back then. I don't want to be stuck in that mindset."

"Rosa, if I had known what he was doing to you, I would have put a stop to it," he whispered, his fingers brushing under my chin to make me look up at him.

"I believe you," I said, my eyes meeting his earnest gaze.

When he leaned down to kiss me, it wasn't as frantic as it had been in the jeep earlier. It was the soft move and press of those lips against mine, the warmth almost overwhelming. He sucked my bottom lip into his mouth, and I couldn't help but sigh. His big, warm hand came up to cover my cheek. and I felt safe.

"I'm sorry he came here," he murmured, kissing me again and again. "I thought I knew him, but I guess I was wrong."

"I don't blame you, but I'm glad he's gone," I said truthfully, pressing my body as close against his as I possibly could. I was craving more of him. I was aching for him.

His talented tongue licked into my mouth, and I felt my whole body *sigh* into the kiss. His grip moved down to clutch at my hips and I dug my fingers into his shirt, pulling at him. The kiss deepened, and we backed up, thumping my lower back into the counter until he slipped his hand there to cushion me. I moaned as his other hand slid up my body to squeeze my breast gently, and he swallowed the sound with his mouth.

"Brody," I breathed, and the sound of his name was full of lust.

I could feel how much he wanted me too, and I moved my hand down to palm the front of his jeans. He tipped his forehead into mine, sucking in a breath. The hand on my breast slipped down my side to grasp my thigh and hook my leg around his hip. In one quick move, he hoisted me up onto the counter and situated the weight of his long, lean body between my legs, right where I needed him.

He looked up at me, and I nodded, leaning down to kiss him once again, this time letting out a full, shaky breath, knowing his hand was between my legs. I gasped as his long fingers pulled my shorts to the side and slipped into the wet warmth. My fingers pressed into his back, and I was panting, kissing him desperately. I wanted him so bad it hurt.

Suddenly, one of the back rooms banged open.

"Dad?" a high voice shouted. "Are you here?"

There were footsteps down the hallway, and we broke apart as if we'd been burned.

8

BRODY

"Can we go see Rosa?"

The words were the first ones I heard when I woke up, bleary-eyed and half-asleep. And he repeated them all morning.

The sun was shining through the windshield, and the sky was a brilliant blue all around us. We drove down Lighthouse Lane to the hill overlooking the ocean.

"Breakfast?" I asked Corey, glancing over at him in the seat.

He was the spitting image of me at his age, all dark hair and big eyes, watching the world with wonder. I remembered riding in this same jeep with my dad as a kid, my heart full of hope. Of course, that hope had been dashed, but that was the past. I was going to do better for my own son. I wanted to make money for him and win for him. I wanted my life to matter because of him.

"Do you think Rosa likes breakfast?" he asked me, sounding very curious.

I couldn't help but laugh. "I'm sure she's a fan."

Rosa had been all my son would talk about. The day

before, when we went to the beach together, he was constantly wondering if she might like to go too. I knew she probably needed space, at least for a day or so. I didn't want to push it. Corey had taken a liking to her, though, and he was a persistent kid.

"Look at that cool shop!" he said around a yawn. "Are they open?"

"They just opened," I told him. "Do you want to go in?"

He nodded enthusiastically, and I helped him out of his buckled seat. The sun was climbing higher in the sky, and something caught my eye out on the water. It was a surfer, which was surprising. No one ever really surfed in this area but me, which was why I liked it.

"Let's go, Dad!" Corey screeched like a banshee at me.

"Okay," I said with a laugh. "Lead the way."

The surf shop on the hill was alive with warm light. The Bronco was parked next to a small, older, maroon car, and I wondered if they already had customers this early in the morning, besides us.

I went to open the door, my hand on the curved knob, and an elderly man stepped out. He had a kind face but looked at me with narrowed eyes.

"Are you the one who's gotten my Rosa into so much trouble lately?" he asked.

"Trouble?" I answered him, holding Corey's hand. "I think I helped her get out of it, actually."

"Is that right?" he said, eyes still narrowed. "Well, I'm Marcus Perry. I'm the owner of this little shop. I suppose you already knew that."

I did suspect that this was the famed Mr. Perry, and I had seen glimpses of him at times, so I did know what he generally looked like.

"It's nice to meet you," I said. Older gentleman always prided themselves on having manners, and I was sure Mr.

Perry would appreciate it on my end. "I'm Brody Strauss. This is my son, Corey."

Mr. Perry glanced down at Corey, who grinned up at him.

"Strauss, huh? I've heard the name," he said, nodding sagely. "You keep my girl safe, you hear me?"

"I hear you loud and clear," I told him seriously.

He looked down at Corey. "Young man, I have a frosted coke in the drink cooler with your name on it. What do you say?" he said, his mouth tilting up in a grin.

"Can I, Dad?" Corey asked me, looking hopeful.

"I don't see why not," I told him. "A growing boy needs a cold coke or two."

"Wise words," Mr. Perry nodded. He looked back at me as Corey went in with him, his voice low. "I'm not joshing you, son. You take care of her, or I'll take care of you."

"Got it," I answered, my eyes going wide. That was a lot of murder in those old eyes.

After that, Mr. Perry was the sweet old man again, hobbling after my son into the shop. I couldn't help but laugh a little.

"What's so funny over there?" a familiar voice asked me.

I looked over and found Rosa at the check-out counter, haloed in light from the window behind her.

"Oh, Mr. Perry was just making sure I knew to take care of you," I told her, and she gave the old man a warm smile. He winked back. "We were wondering if you might want to have breakfast with us."

"I'm working," she told me, looking back down at where she had been going over something. "I'm sorry, I can't."

I had expected as much. She was pushing me away. I had brought drama into her life, and she didn't want it anymore.

Mr. Perry came over, leaning on his cane. "Oh, you work

and worry too much, my girl. We don't have any customers right now. Why not step out for breakfast?"

"You want me to leave?" she asked him, looking as if she wanted him to bail her out of the situation.

"Only if you bring me back a sausage roll," he said. "I love those things."

"Gross," Corey commented, and Mr. Perry laughed.

"Well, I suppose you like pancakes with extra strawberry sauce and extra whip cream, huh?" he asked my son, who nodded enthusiastically.

"He's a fan of the sugar," I said, patting Corey's head.

"Oh, please, Rosa!" Corey said, hopping a little in his flip-flops. "Come with us!"

"He won't leave until you do," I told her, shrugging.

She seemed unsure for a moment, and then she sighed, smiling a little. She grabbed her bag and gave Mr. Perry a little hug.

"Call me if you need me, okay? I won't be more than an hour at most."

"Take as long as you like," the old man told her, waving a hand as he went behind the checkout counter. "I have a feeling it's going to be a slow day, and I can handle it just fine."

"If you say so," she said, sounding unconvinced.

She followed us out into the parking lot and went to her Bronco.

"What are you doing?" I asked her, holding Corey's hand.

"Does he have a car seat?" she nodded at Corey.

"He has a booster seat, why?"

"Well, let's move it over then," she told me. "We're taking my vehicle. It's the least I can do."

"What do you mean?" I stared at her. Maybe I had read her all wrong. "I think you just don't want your hair to get messed up."

She laughed, shaking her head. "Well, you've saved me a couple of times now," she said, her cheeks going pink. She stopped, looking over my shoulder. "Is that who I think it is?"

I looked too, squinting in the bright morning sun. The surfer on the water had become more clear. The way he moved and cut through the waves was unmistakable.

"Sam," I said, staring at his form. "What the hell is he doing?"

"No cussing," Corey commented, shaking his head at me.

"Sorry, buddy," I told him. I looked at Rosa. "Did you tell him where you work?"

"Why in the world would I tell him that?" she snapped, looking annoyed. There was also fear underneath it. She reached down, and Corey took her hand. "Let's just go have some breakfast."

9

ROSA

*A*pparently, a lot of people had the same idea.

Flocks of tourists had come to the white, sandy beaches in droves, presumably to watch the surfing competition over the weekend. I was just glad this stretch of beach was Sam-free. I kept glancing over my shoulder to try and make sure we were in good company. My neck was aching from the stress of looking around so much.

"We're okay, you know," Brody's voice said from my right. "He was over by the shop. We're miles away now."

Corey had decided we were getting breakfast from the oceanside diner by the volleyball courts. We had bags with cartons of crepes and bacon, along with scrambled eggs, and Brody had flattened a thick blanket on the sand for all of us to sit down on.

"I was just bird-watching," I answered with a shrug.

I was really trying hard not to look at him too much. Looking at Brody meant remembering his hands on my body and the way my heart felt like it would beat right out of my chest. Being with Brody was intoxicating, and it was difficult to ignore his presence. Corey waited patiently while his father opened the food.

"If you look closely enough, you might see a dolphin out there," I told him, pointing out at the horizon where the water met the bright blue sky. "They like to jump into the air."

"My mom says dolphins are really mean," Corey replied, and I felt Brody stiffen beside me. "She says they'll eat me if I go in the water. She never lets me in the water."

"You've never been in the ocean?" I asked him, surprised. I looked at Brody.

I really expected a kid with a dad like Brody to spend most of his time in the water. It was strange he would be kept from the spot his father spent most of his time.

Brody sighed. "His mom found out about my dad, and she banned him from being in the water. She was terrified of what might happen."

I hadn't touched the plate Brody made me. I was too busy listening to what he was saying. Corey dug into his crepes, making quite a mess on his small hands.

"What do you mean?" I asked, though I already knew about his dad's surfing accident from Mr. Perry. I couldn't believe he was actually going to tell me.

"My dad was a champion surfer," Brody told me, looking sad and wistful. He patted Corey's head. "Hey buddy, why don't you go make a sandcastle for us to look at?"

Corey nodded, giving me a grin before he left. Brody looked back at me, and I got it.

"You don't want him to know," I said. It wasn't a question, and I couldn't say I blamed him.

"Yeah, I don't think he would understand anyway. He never met my dad," Brody said, smiling sadly. "When he gets older, I'll tell him about how awesome he really was."

"So, what happened?" I asked him, moving a little so that our knees brushed.

In the face of his sadness, I could only feel compassion. There was none of the anxiety from earlier, when all I could think about was his touch. Something in my heart was reaching out to him. A big part of me wanted to help him, but I could only listen to him.

"When I was a kid, my dad would drag me to the beach every morning," he told me. "We would get up at the crack of dawn, and the whole stretch would be empty."

"I bet you just loved that," I said teasingly. "Little kids love getting up."

"Well, I definitely developed my coffee addiction around that time," he said with a grin. "There was this little gas station by our house, and the coffee was awful."

"But you drank it anyway," I said, nodding.

"I drank it anyway," he confirmed, and when his fingers wrapped around mine, I squeezed his hand. "My dad made it, so of course I did. I thought I was so damn cool."

I looked at Brody and remembered patching him up. It felt like eons ago that I had cared for his wound, and now we were having breakfast with his son, talking about his tragic, dead father. We had been through so much. It had been a crazy few days. Now I knew why Brody was the way he was, and I just wanted him to say it aloud.

"He seems like he was great," I said, giving him a soft little smile.

He nodded, looking sideways at me. "We slept in that day, so my dad was in a hurry. He rushed us into the jeep and I remember missing our normal cup of coffee."

"There was a storm?" I asked. He was watching his son dig around in the sand.

"There were dark clouds on the horizon," he said, rubbing a hand over his face. "My dad misjudged the distance, and the storm hit just as he was paddling out. He didn't stop."

"Why not?" I wondered, hoping I wasn't overstepping my bounds. "If he knew, why wouldn't he go back to the beach? Back to you, I mean?"

He just shrugged. "I guess he wanted to surf. A big wave came up behind him, and I never saw him again."

I felt confused. "So he knew it was dangerous, and he still stayed?"

"He was really passionate about surfing," Brody told me, his voice sounding a little strained. "You wouldn't get it, and I wouldn't expect you to."

"Yeah, I don't get it," I told him honestly. "I'm sorry you lost your dad like that, though."

To my surprise, he pulled his hand out of mine. He was staring at me when I looked at him.

"What are you trying to say?" he asked, his tone accusatory.

"I'm not trying to say anything," I said with a shrug. "I said I was sorry your dad passed in such a tragic way. It shouldn't have happened."

"It wasn't his fault, Rosa," he said shortly.

"I didn't say it was his fault," I replied. I was getting annoyed. It was like I couldn't say anything right. "You didn't have to tell me about your dad if it's a sore spot for you. I'm not trying to poke at it."

He shook his head. "It's not a sore spot for me," he said hotly.

"Okay, whatever," I answered without looking at him. I didn't really feel like going back and forth with him. "Can you pass me that syrup packet?"

"You're changing the subject," he said, and when I looked at him, his gaze was searching. "Tell me what you really think."

"Why don't we just enjoy breakfast?" I asked, looking away again. I was hoping he would drop it. My opinion was on the tip of my tongue.

"No, Rosa. Tell me," he said, and I could feel him staring at me.

"You really want to hear what I think?" I said, finally, dropping all of the pretense. "I don't think you do."

"No, if you've got something to say, I want to hear it." He was obviously trying hard to keep his voice even.

"Alright then," I turned to him. "If you really want to hear it, then fine. Here it is. It was irresponsible of your dad to surf in a storm when he knew you were waiting on him. What he did was dangerous, and I can't understand why you did the same thing when you have a son waiting, too. I don't get it. Why repeat his mistakes?"

Maybe I should have kept my opinions to myself, but he did keep pressing me. I wondered if anyone had ever told him the truth, or if they tried to comfort him with platitudes and vaguely sincere condolences. I wanted to do that for him too, at first, but I couldn't keep this to myself. I couldn't believe a man would push himself to his limits while he had someone depending on him.

But Brody was fuming. "His mistakes? That's my father you're talking about. You didn't know him. He was amazing."

"Having flaws doesn't make a person any less of who they are," I told him. "They just make them more real."

"You don't know anything," he shook his head.

"Yeah, you can think whatever you want," I snapped, standing. "My dad is an accountant, and my mom is a teacher. Neither one of them would ever intentionally put themselves in harm's way to prove a point."

He laughed, though it was humorless. "Oh yeah? Are we still talking about my dad here? Or are you talking about me?"

I debated opening that can of worms. I had been bothered by the knowledge of Brody's storm surfing session ever since learning he had a son. Before that, really, when Mr. Perry told me about his father.

"You know, I guess I just don't get it. You have a young son waiting for you at home, someone who looks to you for happiness, and you just throw yourself into danger," I said with a scoff.

I was standing with my arms crossed, staring down at him, and he stood too, kicking sand over the blanket.

"I'm not trying to prove a point," he said sternly. "I go out every day and try to make my dad proud. He rode every wave, and I won't back down. I want my son to know I never gave up. Not once."

I was fuming. "Well, that's stupid."

"Stupid?" Brody asked, his eyes going wide. His shoulders were wide too, wide and strong, but I tried not to notice. "Alright, I'm packing this stuff up, and we're leaving."

"Oh, but you don't give up, right?" I asked him, scoffing.

Instead of snapping at me or telling me off, like I thought he would, he froze. He looked at me, and then he looked back at the water. His next words were chilling.

"I don't see Corey."

I moved forward, looking. "He has to be around here somewhere, right?"

"Corey!" Brody shouted, frantic. "Corey? Oh my God, where is he?"

"Hey, calm down," I soothed, reaching out to him and touching his arm. "We'll find him. He probably got bored and wandered down the beach or something like that."

"C'mon," he told me quickly, grabbing my hand. "I need to find my son."

"Wait, I'm sorry, Brody," I said quickly. "I never should have said anything about your dad."

"It's fine, let's just go," he said, and I followed behind him. He stopped as we went by the sandcastle, only half-finished. "Oh, please no."

"What?" I asked him, frantically looking around. Had he spotted something in the distance? "What is it? Do you see him?"

"His footprints, Rosa," he said faintly, pointing. "They don't lead down the beach. They lead into the water."

At that moment, I heard a faint yell. I whipped my head around, and I saw a shape in the distance, bobbing in the water. It was him.

Without a thought and without even telling Brody, I took off running into the water. He wasn't too far out, but he was struggling. It was a miracle to see his parents must have at least gotten him swimming lessons, but he was still no match for the ocean.

"Corey!" I cried, gurgling on water. "Don't give up! Keep paddling!"

I heard Brody faintly calling my name from the shore, but I didn't care about anything but the little boy struggling in the water. I was glad that I had taken those lifeguard classes when I first got to the island and wanted to dip my fingers into every pot.

"Rosa!" I heard him call out.

"Grab my hand!" I screamed at him, reaching my hand through the water to get to him.

Little fingers reached out to me, but they slipped away, and my heart dropped. I was panicking in the water, flailing around, trying to find him as the salt made my eyes burn. I saw his dark head bobbing out of the water and lunged, grabbing him and pulling him to me. My legs were aching from treading water and searching, though, and I felt my body growing heavy. We slipped under the water, and I could only see darkness for a moment. I was terrified that he was right there and I wouldn't be able to get to him.

Suddenly, something grabbed my hoodie from behind, yanking us out of the water and into the bright, blessed air again. I sucked in a breath, and Corey was sputtering and spitting water. I held him tight to me, as if he might slip away into the dark depths.

"Grab onto the board!" Brody cried, and I realized he had grabbed his surfboard from the jeep and paddled out to us.

My fingers slipped on the slick surface, but I finally managed to wrap my arm around the very end. With my other arm, I tried to push Corey up to his dad. Brody grabbed for the coughing little boy and kissed the top of his head, looking at me gratefully.

"I think he's okay," I said with a voice that was raspy and painful. Saltwater burned my throat.

Slowly but surely, we made it back to the shore. My body felt like it was made of lead. I flopped down, drenched and exhausted.

"Are you okay, buddy?" Brody asked, his voice shaking. "You aren't supposed to go in the water."

Corey coughed again. "I wanted to be like you."

Brody sucked in a breath and looked at me. His expression was haunted, and I just nodded.

"I think he needs to see a doctor. Maybe you too." He reached out and cupped my cheek with his free hand. "You look pale."

I kissed his palm. "Drop me off at the shop. I'll be okay. Just make sure they see about Corey."

"Saved me," Corey said through his coughing.

I reached over, patting his cheek. "You would have done it for me, little man. Don't worry about it."

"If I was a grown up," he said, nodding sagely.

I huffed a laugh and stood up in the sand, following

Brody up the powdery white dunes. When he dropped me off at the shop, he kissed my cheek quickly and left again. I didn't even tell Mr. Perry when I got there. I didn't want him to ask me what was wrong, and I didn't want to talk. I sent him a text asking for the rest of the day off, and he said that was fine. He told me I could just work with the horses the next day if I wanted to. He was a good man.

I wanted to be on the back of a horse, running my troubles away. I felt like I could sleep for a century. I went to the cottage and crawled into my bed like it was a cave for hibernation.

I only woke up when the morning sun gleamed through my window.

"I could have just stayed in bed all day," I grumbled to myself as I slowly got ready for the day.

The horse barn was alive with the sounds of stomping hooves and snorting. I went straight to the tack room and found what I needed for Cinder. The little red horse was waiting in her stall, and I brushed her down, feeling my anxiety begin to calm. My hands were still shaking, remnants of the scare from the day before. I finished grooming Cinder and put the brushes away. The little mare nudged me for a molasses treat when I came back in, and I laughed, petting her nose.

"Alright, pushy, I'm going," I told her, unable to stop my smile.

Despite everything that had happened and the worries on my shoulders, I felt happy knowing that Cinder and the other horses were waiting for me whenever I needed them.

These four-legged creatures are usually the answer to every-thing, Mr. Perry's voice echoed in my head, comforting me.

I left the stall and stopped short, catching sight of Mr. Perry's office. I felt a cold wave of sadness at the thought that he wanted to retire from everything. I wondered if that meant he wouldn't be here as often. I had always loved the horse barn office. This place felt more like home than anywhere else. The place was worn and well-loved, touched by kind hands, and well-maintained. I thought that I wanted something like this for myself. I didn't want to lose this place.

I sighed, sitting down in the office chair. It was old, and there were pieces dangling off the armrests. The floor had scuff marks from years of boots scraping and walking across it. There was a new, thin computer pushed a little to the side on the desk in front of me. I had finally convinced my boss to buy something to keep his documents on other than actual paper. He was reluctant, and he never used it, but I was glad he finally caved. I imagined Mr. Perry doing the very same thing for years and years. This place was as much his baby as the shop was. He was a man who put his heart into everything. He helped whoever he could. I hoped I could be like him one day.

"What the hell am I going to do?" I said aloud.

Suddenly, footsteps sounded over the concrete. I looked up in surprise.

"I went to the shop. Mr. Perry said I could probably find you here. I guess he was right."

I cleared my throat. "Brody."

10

BRODY

*R*osa was looking at me like she wanted to throw me out of the barn.

"Hey," I said cautiously, standing in the doorway.

I had never been inside of this horse barn, or any other for that matter. When Corey wanted to go on those trail rides in the cold months, we had only gone far enough into the sheltering oaks to catch a glimpse of the riders and the horses. That was the first time I had ever caught sight of Rosa. She was holding a big, black and white horse, helping a small child onto it's back with a joyful smile on her face. I remembered thinking I must have looked like that when I was in the water, surfing the foaming crests.

"What are you doing here?" she asked me, sitting up straight.

"I was looking for you," I told her simply. "I guess I found you, huh?"

Well, that sounded really creepy. I mentally kicked myself. I really liked this woman, and I was making a fool of myself over and over again. I came here to make amends with her.

"I mean, how did you know I was here?" she asked me,

but then seemed to realize something. She sighed. "Mr. Perry, right? He must have told you I was here."

"Yeah, he said you might be in a mood," I told her, and then regretted it.

Telling a woman that multiple people thought she was in a mood wasn't really a great conversation starter. I really needed to work on my people skills in my spare time.

"You know the best way to put someone in a mood is to tell them that you think they're in a mood," she said, rolling her eyes. "Mr. Perry means well, but I'm really fine here."

"Are you saying you want me to go?" I asked her, raising an eyebrow.

"I'm saying that I'm fine," she told me flatly.

"I'm not here to fight with you, Rosa," I said gently. I stepped further into the room and took a seat on the worn leather chair in front of the desk. Sunlight shone brightly through the windows, illuminating dancing dust particles in the warm, damp air. "I wanted to say that I'm sorry for yesterday."

Rosa was watching the small fan spin around on the table under the window. There was a coffee maker there and a little mini fridge as well. I wasn't even sure if she heard me.

"You want coffee?" she asked instead of actually addressing what I said. "I think I'm going to make a pot."

"It's like melt-your-shoes hot outside," I answered her, confused. "You're going to make a hot pot of coffee in this weather?"

"It's never a bad time for coffee," she told me, turning her back to me to start the machine.

"It's nearly lunch time," I reminded her, pushing my hands into my hair and then brushing it down after. "Didn't you drink coffee at breakfast? Or do you wait until lunch?"

She shrugged. "I've been pretty busy brushing my horse—

well, she's Mr. Perry's horse, but still. I'm going to go for a ride. Why are you judging me right now?"

"Not judging," I said, cracking a small smile, though her back was to me. "Just curious."

I got up from the chair and moved behind her, close but not quite touching. She stopped what she was doing and glanced back. Then she started putting the grounds in the filter.

"I don't want to fight with you," I murmured, smoothing a light hand over her hip. "I was terrified yesterday. I thought I might lose both of you."

The coffee began to bubble into the pot, and Rosa turned, looking up at me.

"I'm sorry, Brody," she said, shaking her head. "I shouldn't have said anything about your dad. It wasn't my place."

"No, I shouldn't have snapped at you like I did," I answered. "That was wrong."

She put a hand on my chest. "How's Corey doing?"

"He'll be alright because of you," I told her honestly. "You saved his life."

I couldn't remember the last time I had been so afraid. For Corey, I always pretended like nothing bothered me, and I was never scared. In the face of real danger, though, it was hard to be brave. I didn't care how I looked. Rosa had been so brave, it was almost unbelievable. Not that I expected anything less from her. I remembered how she was ready to take out a couple of thieves with a baseball bat a few days before.

"I should have called," she told me, looking up at me with big, limpid eyes.

"It's only been a day," I said gently, reaching up to sweep her hair back. "I knew you needed time to yourself. Anyone would be shaken after what you've been through."

"What we've been through, you mean," she corrected me, smiling gently. "I am sorry, though. Where is Corey?"

"He's with his mom."

"Oh no, what did she say?" she asked, her eyes going wide.

A wave of guilt washed over me. I knew how my ex-girlfriend would have acted if I had told her what happened. I had seen her freak out over the smallest things to the biggest situations. My head was so full of chaotic thoughts, and I didn't need to be yelled at. Corey didn't need to see her going off on me either. It was just counterproductive.

"She didn't say anything," I told her, letting out a sigh.

Rosa's brows dipped. "What do you mean by that?"

"Well, I didn't actually tell her," I said, wincing. "I know it sounds bad, but I just didn't feel like she would take it very well."

"Do you mean the fact that he was in the water, or the fact that I was the one to go in after him?" Rosa asked. "I'm sure she wasn't thrilled to learn about me."

Once again, I felt guilty. "Uh, yeah, she doesn't really know that either."

"Oh," she muttered, dropping the hands she had on my chest and belt loop.

I could practically see the wheels beginning to turn in her head. Since I hadn't told anyone about her, she assumed I wasn't serious about whatever this was between us.

"No, Rosa, you don't get it," I said, cupping her face in my hands. "You don't get it. Heather isn't exactly the best in crisis situations. She would just make it all worse."

"Heather," she repeated, testing the name out on her tongue. "Is that her name, then?"

"Yeah, that's her. Heather Akins," I told her.

She nodded, seemingly unthawing. She let me pull her into a hug, and when she pulled back, her mouth met mine in a swift kiss. The touch of her lips ignited a fire in me, and I had to push that desire down for the moment. I needed to make sure we were okay.

"What do you think? Can we make up now?" I asked, giving her a small smile.

Rosa grinned. "Sure, we can, but only if you let me give you a riding lesson."

The thought of being on the back of a thousand-pound animal was daunting, but I would do it for her. It would be fun. Besides, I had always liked a little danger with my women.

"Maybe I will, but only if you agree to learn how to surf," I said, grinning.

"Well, that sounds like a fair deal to me," she said, nodding as she stepped closer. She looked up at me. "So, should we shake on it or what?"

"Oh, I've got a better idea," I said, leaning down to press my mouth to hers once again.

Kissing Rosa was becoming an addiction for me. The feeling of her lips on mine always seemed to make me feel warm. The want that seemed to consume me when she was around was unlike anything I had ever experienced before, with any woman. The feeling that fell over me was an intense and all-encompassing emotion I wasn't even able to explain. Every inch of my body yearned for hers, as if she held some sort of mysterious power over me. It blew my mind that my best friend had all but thrown away what he had with her. I couldn't imagine leaving her for uncertainties. Just having her around started a burning, raging fire within me—a hot desire that consumed my thoughts and emotions without any way to really control them.

Whatever this really was, it wasn't like anything I had ever been involved with before. Every moment with Rosa, even the fight, was like that moment when you finally catch the perfect wave. She was the wave, and I was at her mercy.

When we were together, there was just an undeniable pull between us, like an invisible force that drew me closer. Now that we had made up, everything felt right again in the world. It was like our souls were together, tangled by an unspoken connection that seemed to come on so very suddenly.

I couldn't believe we had never met. I was almost sure that if we had while Sam was living in Daytona, I would have wanted her then too. Her pull was irresistible, and I found myself constantly craving her smile, her touch, and those soft, wide eyes.

This feeling was not just a fleeting want for me. Somehow, it ran deeper than that. My mom used to say that some souls just recognized each other, and it really felt like that. It wasn't going to be easy to let go of Rosa, though I hoped I wouldn't have to. Something about her was just so tempting. What I felt for her was a deep longing that resided within the depths of my being.

It wasn't just her physical beauty; she had that too. It took nearly losing Rosa and Corey all at once for me to realize how I was really feeling about her. Maybe it was wrong because of the connection between the both of us and Sam, but it was a risk I was willing to take. She was a hell of a woman, and she was worth it.

I didn't even want to think about how pissed I was when Sam scared her like he did the other night. I had never wanted to fight my best friend before, but I felt the intense need that night, for Rosa's sake. It was as if Rosa was the only key to unlocking a hidden part of myself, a part that had been dormant until she came into my life and shook it all up. She brought out a primal, hidden nature that I felt keenly.

It felt so odd to me. Despite how much I could feel the intensity of the connection between us, it was still so different. When I loved a woman, I loved her hard and passionately. I hadn't had someone like that in a very long time, and I wasn't looking for anything either.

It sounded ridiculous, even in my own head, but I couldn't fully understand its strength or why the connection had chosen her as the one I wanted. I was fascinated by the way I felt for her, and it made me want her even more. The more I tried to understand it, the more fleeting it seemed to become, leaving me in an endless state of longing for her.

The craving for her was a double-edged sword, and it was simultaneously exciting and awful. Rosa and her gleaming hair completely took over my thoughts, but it also brought me a sense of peace. There was a constant battle between the absolute bliss of being near her and the agony of not being able to fully have her, though I wanted her so badly. I liked how she made me feel like I was on the edge of a cliff, and I wanted to fall right off. I wondered if there was soft water below or if jagged, high rocks would destroy me.

"What do you say we go for a picnic?" she suggested, her breath a ghost across my cheek. We can pack the saddle bags and count it as your very first riding lesson."

"As long as you're with me, I don't care what we're doing," I murmured with a grin.

She smiled for a moment before she stepped back, suddenly serious and professional. I missed her touch, even though it was just seconds after I holding her close.

"Alright, so we need to get the saddles and the food in the mini fridge," she said, turning and pointing behind us. "I packed chicken salad sandwiches for me and Mr. Perry, but he's not coming by today. There's apple slices for the horses, but they won't miss them. Can you grab two water bottles?"

"I can do that. Do you need me to help with the horses?"

I wasn't sure how much help I would actually be, but I still thought I should offer.

"I can do the horses. We'll just save the saddling lesson

for another day," she told me, waving her hand carelessly. "I'm going to ride Cinder. She's that big horse to the right."

"She's beautiful," I said, nodding. The animal stomped and snorted in her stall, clearly ready to get up and go wherever. "Now, what horse am I going to be riding?"

"You can ride Slim," she said, grinning over her shoulder as she left for the stalls outside of the barn's office. "Don't worry, he's the laziest horse in the entire place. You're good to go. Or not go, really."

She laughed at her own joke, and I couldn't help but smile. She was so damn adorable. With everything she did, I was just falling deeper and deeper for her.

"I'll grab the sandwiches," I told her. "Where are the, uh, the saddle things? The bags?"

"The saddle bags," she called back, supplementing the blank spot that had entered my mind.

"Yeah, those."

"In here with the tack," she called back to me once again. "I can get it all in a minute."

"No way, I'm helping," I said, leaving the office to follow her. I would have followed her anywhere at that moment. "Wow, this is a lot of horse shit."

She rolled her eyes. "No, the horse shit is in the wheelbarrow."

I let out a burst of laughter. "Thanks for the heads up."

"Grab that saddle to your right, and be careful," she said, smirking. "It's pretty heavy."

"I think I've got it," I said, making a face at the way she was underestimating me. "Oh damn," I said as I lifted it and the thing nearly dragged me down.

"Told you," she said, and I saw her staring at me.

"What?"

"Oh, nothing," she said lightly, and then she laughed. It

was a happy, carefree sound. "It's just, you know, a girl could get used to this."

She had a look on her face that I thought I could understand perfectly. I put the saddle down, and smiled as she came over. She wrapped her arms around my middle, squeezing those tanned, thin arms tight. She looked up at me, and her eyes were full of something dark. I wondered if it was want that I was seeing there.

"Is that right?" I asked, grinning. She nodded, looking up at me with eager, lust-filled eyes.

When I leaned down to kiss her, she made a sharp sound of desire into my mouth. She looped her fingers into my belt and pulled me to her, as I pushed my tongue into her mouth. She gripped at my shirt, shoving her hands under to scrabble at my skin. She wanted more, and I did too. My hands grazed her hips and then her ribs until my fingers squeezed at her breasts gently, making her moan into my mouth. I felt myself growing hard in my jeans, wanting her more than I ever had. She pushed at me until we tumbled into the stacks of dry, yellow hay bales waiting behind us.

She laughed, laying on top of me. "Smooth moves, Strauss."

"Hey, that was your fault," I told her, laughing too. I brushed her hair back, whispering. "This hay is itchy as hell."

"C'mon, cowboy," she murmured, smiling against my lips. "Don't you like to have fun?"

She pulled back to look at me, her gaze soft. It was very alluring. I tangled my fingers in the soft, long hair at the nape of her neck, pulling her into me. Our lips were about to meet, when the scuff of boots across the floor made us both jump apart in the hay.

"Oh, Ms. Rosa," said a startled, young-sounding voice. "I'm sorry, I didn't know you were here."

We stood up, and I smoothed down my shirt, knocking hay off of me

"Alex," she answered him, and her cheeks were pink even as she tried to sound casual. "We're going for a ride. Could you saddle Dragon for me?"

"Dragon?" I asked, my eyes going wide.

Rosa looked back, grinning at me. "Like I said, laziest horse in the barn."

Alex looked a little confused, but he nodded anyway.

"You know," Rosa said, a coy look on her face, "no one can interrupt us out there."

11

ROSA

*B*rody's big hands explored the planes of my body.

We were settled on a blanket under the swaying oak trees, hidden from civilization by the thick oceanside forest. I could hear the water rushing over the sand just through the trees and bushes to my left, and it made my whole body feel relaxed and ready. This felt so right between us. I was hot all over, like fire burning through me.

"Rosa," Brody said, pressing open-mouth kisses to my neck.

The sound of my name on his lips was like a prayer, whispered into the yellow sunshine and the shaking leaves above us. The horses pawed and stomped where they stood tied to one of the sloping branches. This felt like some sort of hazy, lust-filled dream we had fallen into. I felt the passion between us as if it were a tangible thing, swirling over us like a growing flame.

Our eyes locked and he hovered over me, his gaze dark. I could feel an intense energy as it seemed to surge through the air around us, enveloping us both in the heat of our want. It was as if an invisible pull had coaxed a storm to brew within our souls, causing our hearts to beat in sync with every touch. It was insane to me, but the intensity of our connection was not something I could deny anymore. It was as if we were two candles dancing in the darkness, drawn together as the wind pulled and tossed around us.

Yes, this man was the best friend of my ex, but that didn't matter anymore. I wasn't going to deny what I wanted. I wasn't going to let Sam ruin anything else for me. Every word exchanged between us seemed to have an electric charge attached to it, sparking a deep longing in me that went beyond mere mindless chatter.

When I spoke to Brody, it felt as if we had been together for years. It was like I knew him somehow. Our thoughts came together seamlessly, creating a twirl of emotions that moved within the depths of our hearts and pulled us together.

The passion that tangled like twining vines between us was intoxicating—a heady mix of desire and longing that left the both of us entirely breathless. It was cliche, but time really did seem to stand still whenever we were together, lost in a pink haze of a world where only the two of us existed. The outside world, the horses, and the trees faded into the back of my mind, as our connection became the focal point of my world. It was an emotional tempest that threatened to swallow us both whole, but we freely yielded to its intensity.

Despite the level of heat between us, there was an over-whelming feeling of wonder. Our relationship, like blazes in the dead of night, offered questions and unknown wants yet to be found. Everything with Brody was unexpected, and I liked it. It was a delicate yet powerful dance of emotion as we passed through the uncharted waters of our feelings for one another, not sure of where this fiery passion would take us.

After Sam, I never thought I could feel the way I was feel-ing. Brody was a breath of fresh air, but he was also the reason I couldn't breathe. He was everything all at once. There was a sense of both exhilaration and fear in the heart of the growing connection that felt so damn right.

We were mindful of the risks that existed if we chose to be together—the danger of our hearts being destroyed by the ferocity of our feelings. It was unlike anything I had ever experienced before. Neither one of us could resist the temptation of it all—the magnetic pull that tugged us closer to each other with each passing second.

The heat that flared between us was both lovely and dangerous, a fine mix of desire and doubt that I still wanted so bad. It was an attraction that went beyond logic and reason, urging me to give in to its intoxicating embrace. So I found myself giving in to the lure of Brody Strauss, knowing that the journey that lay ahead of us would be filled with both pleasure and pain. If I let myself be afraid of being with him, I wondered if I would ever feel right again.

I felt like there would be a missing chunk of me that wouldn't recover from the loss. The desire swirling between us remained an unsure question in my heart, a spark that ignited brilliantly in the deepest parts of our hearts. I didn't feel like it would ever end. It was a connection that was almost too much for me to understand, entangling us forever in its mesmerizing hold.

Brody had a distinctive charm, a magnetic pull that draws me towards him with a confusing sort of power. The two of us seemed to be connected, seemingly set to collide in the delicate dance of existence.

I needed his closeness, the warmth of his touch, and the comfort of his arms around me. But, as much as I wished for Brody's presence, I couldn't ignore all of the challenges that waited for me. The path that led to having him in my life was littered with complications, an intricate system of challenges that threatened to test my faith in him. Sam had been one of those hurdles, making my heart afraid to get close to anyone again.

Despite everything, I felt myself unpersuaded by the problems that might lie ahead of us. I wanted Brody in my life, and I hoped he wanted me in the same way.

Maybe it was the intensity of my feelings that made me so ready to put up with all the challenges that came with him. Love had a way of blurring the lines that existed between emotions and rational thought, pushing me to make sacrifices and continue in the want of that elusive link. I wanted to belong to someone, and I wanted Brody to myself. I didn't know if I could handle seeing him with anyone else. It was as if my heart began to take over, overpowering any rational thoughts that dared to raise fears about the difficult times that might be ahead.

The two of us had already been through so much together. He represented a constant want in my life, an anchor in the middle of the chaos. In a world where everything felt short-term and temporary, he felt completely different.

Having him around brought the safety and security I had been longing for—a place of refuge where I might find hope in the middle of the storm. As a result, I was willing to throw myself into everything and just be at his side. Yes, he was wild like the ocean, but he was also the peace of the blue sky, never-ending and beautiful.

The path that led to having Brody in my life was not without its share of fears and doubts. Maybe it would have been easier to just be on my own, like I was before I met him. I couldn't really imagine being without him now. There were times when I doubted my own courage, wondering if I had what it took to face the things that might happen as time went on.

But when I was in doubt, I would close my eyes and let

my emotions guide me, remembering the unforgettable connection we felt. Just looking at him made me feel so much better. The feeling of love, in all its hidden power, defied rationality and passed the bounds meant to stop it from happening. The most valuable lessons in my life were learned in love. Whether it was love that had been broken or love I felt when I looked at the horses and the shell shop.

In the long run, it was the depth of my desire to have him in my life that was important, not the comfort or the convenience of it. I craved peace, but I would take chaos to have that connection with him. I was determined to face the problems head-on, to battle against the odds, because a life without him close to me seemed unthinkable. I wanted this with him. I wanted him and Corey in my life. This was just the start of something that would change me forever, good or bad.

"What are you thinking about?" Brody's voice rumbled against my ear. "Where did you go?"

"I'm here," I whispered, pulling him back up to kiss me. "I was thinking about us."

His hands were under my shirt, his fingers grazing the soft skin of my breasts. The feeling was enough to make me focus on him and not the thoughts gathering in my head. He pulled my tank top off, and dipped his head to my nipples, sucking.

"I think," he began, closing his mouth over my skin, "you need to stop thinking so hard."

I pulled, my heart sinking. "Sam used to say stuff like that, and he was cheating on me."

He stared at me, his eyes going wide. "Wait, what? Rosa, that's not what I meant. I just didn't want you to worry about anything."

"I told you I was thinking about us, and you told me not to think so hard," I accused him, feeling very exposed at that moment. "What is that supposed to mean? What am I supposed to think?"

He touched his forehead to mine, and my heart fluttered. I was so affected by him.

"Hey," he murmured, his breath brushing my lips. "Stop worrying about everything. I'm here, and I want you. I'm not Sam."

"I don't think that," I let out a shaking breath. "It's just hard to see past everything I went through with him. Do you know what I mean?"

"I understand," he said, nodding. He kissed me again. "I'm not going to hurt you. I want to be with you. I've never wanted anything so badly in my entire life."

"I want you too," I said, as if it weren't obvious by the way we were lying half-naked in the middle of a beachside meadow. "And what I really want is for you to take your shirt off."

He laughed, and the sound warmed me. "Your wish is my command."

Soon enough, we were both bare, our skin slick in the summer heat, and our clothes folded neatly at the edge of the blanket. The horses waited impatiently by the trees, but I could only pay attention to Brody and the way his warm mouth moved down my body.

"Brody," I cried, as he left a line of kisses down my skin.

All I could think about was Brody. I was lost for a moment in his glow; thoughts of him.

"Come back to me," Brody said, breathing a laugh across my belly. "You left again."

"Trust me, I'm here," I told him, breathless.

Brody's mouth closed over my warm center, and I felt sparks fly behind my eyes. He licked and sucked, and my body arched under his touch. I heard my own cries disappearing into the summer wind that ghosted through the trees, and the Spanish moss swayed gently over our heads as he brought me to a climax under his mouth.

"More," I cried, grasping at him with grabbing, shaking fingers. "Please, Brody."

His fingers slipped inside of me, moving in and out and making me cry out. His other hand wrapped around my thigh to hold me in place as I came apart again around his fingers. He moved back up as my whole body shook, and he kissed me, letting me taste myself on his tongue. I reached down and wrapped my hand around his thick, hard length, angling him to push inside of me. When he slipped in, we both let out a gasp, finally getting what we wanted. He touched his forehead to mine.

"Are you okay?" he asked, his voice a hoarse whisper. "Rosa?"

"More than okay," I gasped out.

I wrapped my legs around him and pulled him to me, letting his length fill me up completely. I couldn't help but cry out, and he smiled, kissing the sound away. He began to move, thrusting in and out of me over and over again. I felt my whole body begin to shake around him. My hands grasped at him, and my fingers dug into the skin of his tanned shoulders. One of my hands reached up to tangle in his soft hair and he kissed me as he found his own climax, gasping into my mouth as he let go.

"You're amazing," he breathed as I flopped back onto the blanket, completely spent. "Rosa, you're absolutely amazing."

My heart was beating hard enough to thump right out of my chest, and a golden glow of happiness began to fall over me. I closed my eyes, letting him pull me close to him.

"You know, I think the horses are getting impatient," I said nodding at them as I opened my eyes, smiling and kissing him. "We should head back to the barn."

After what happened with Sam, I felt like falling in love was like poison.

It ate away at my thoughts, ravaged my heart, and broke me down for so long. The grief of betrayal was difficult and painful, leaving scars that seemed to be forever weeping and unable to heal fully. I built barriers around myself and my heart, determined never to let anyone into my inner circle again.

Love became associated with pain and suffering, and I convinced myself that being alone was better than being hurt by someone I trusted again. For me, days grew into weeks, and weeks turned into months. Although time passed, the resentment within me continued to be there, waiting. I stood by and watched while others found joy with the one they loved; their laughter and affection served as constant reminders of what I had lost in my last relationship. I became a bystander in my own life, terrified to take another risk on love.

But as the days passed by in my little bubble of privacy, a voice within urged me to let go of the past and find real happiness again. It convinced me that not all love was poison, that there were people out there who could repair the wrecked pieces of my heart. Slowly, I began to doubt my convictions, wondering whether I had let one person's betrayal define my entire view of love. It was hard not to think that way, but now I was really questioning it.

With fear tangled in my heart, I started trying to open myself to the possibility of love. I even went on a few dates, which all turned out to be duds. I started slowly, allowing myself to trust again and let someone in. It wasn't easy, and there were times I felt overwhelmed by terror. But I refused to let the past shape my present. At the time when Brody entered my life, I had given up once again and decided I didn't even care anymore.

As I tried to let love back into my life, I learned that maybe it wasn't poison after all. Maybe it was my mind that was the poison. Or maybe Sam was the poison, twisting my thoughts into something dark and hopeless. Love was a salve that healed the pain within me, and it would turn out to be a balm for my wounded spirit. I had forgotten that love had the capacity to heal the hurt and to offer joy and happiness.

I understood that not everyone would betray me like him, but it was still hard not to see his lies in everyone else. There were those who would love and respect me, who would stick by my side through good and bad times. Love was about trust, understanding, and progress, not pain, as I thought. It was about finding someone who would accept me as I was, my flaws and all. Brody had his own flaws, and maybe we could learn from one another as we got deeper into whatever this was.

I wanted to be the kind of person who was open to love and who was able to accept her own feelings without worrying about being hurt. I refused to let fear stop me the way it did before. I had been so closed off when I got to the island, and Mr. Perry welcomed me into his life with open arms. I took a page out of his book and chose to trust in love again, to accept the vulnerability it brought with it. And it was because of this route that I found an attachment that was natural, genuine, and free of the poison of betrayal. At least, as far as I knew anyway.

I thought that love was something to be feared, but I don't think so anymore. Maybe it was a gift, a beautiful and glowing warmth that was able to slowly heal even the most awful of broken hearts completely. Maybe the issues I went through were just the path that led me to find Brody in the process. Maybe this was exactly where my life should have been.

BRODY

*R*osa was standing on the beach, waiting for me to start her first surf lesson.

"Brody!" she said, calling to me. "Are you doing this or not?"

She was grinning, and it was warmer than the sunshine above my head. I couldn't help but smile back at her infectious enthusiasm. She was so damn beautiful, looking like a goddess rising from the sands. Her excitement was infectious, and it washed away any lingering doubts or hesitations I may have had about whatever was happening between the two of us. With a nod, I grabbed my old surfboard and made my way towards her. I grabbed her in my arms and spun her around, making her giggle.

"You owe me a kiss," I told her with a grin as I put her down. "I don't do free lessons."

"Oh yeah?" she asked, laughing. "Is that so? I thought we were doing a trade here. Riding lessons for surfing ones."

"You were the one who did the riding yesterday," I said with a smirk, and I was happy to see her cheeks go bright red.

"Just shut up and kiss me," she pulled at the collar of my wetsuit.

"You taste like a cherry popsicle," I told her after our lips met, matching her enthusiasm.

"Mr. Perry had a little market at the shop today. He had a couple of vendors in the parking lot, and the elementary school kids showed up to learn about the turtle nesting season. The nests are close to the shop."

"Sounds fun," I answered, nodding. Although I was a little hurt she hadn't asked me to come. I was sure Corey would have loved it.

"I wasn't sure if you were busy, and I didn't want to assume," she said, as if she were reading my mind. She looked unsure, but my relief unknotted the hurt in my belly.

"Next time I'll bring Corey, and we'll make a day of it," I said, giving her a warm smile.

When I wasn't surfing and making money that way, my dad's insurance left a sizable amount my mom split with me years ago. I always had that to fall back on, and so when I wasn't surfing, I was normally just exploring the island with my son or doing whatever the wind took me to do. When Corey wasn't being homeschooled by his sweet, elderly babysitter, he loved riding shotgun in the jeep, and roaming the beaches.

"I always have time for you," I told Rosa, kissing her once again.

The sound of crashing waves and the salty breeze filled the air, creating the perfect backdrop for our adventure. As I watched Rosa, I couldn't help but revel in the way that the sunlight glittered over her and danced in her eyes, reflecting the joy she seemed to radiate since yesterday. Her warm energy was contagious, and I felt a surge of affection building within me. This was more than just a surf lesson between the two of us; it was a chance to share a special moment with someone who had brought warmth back into my life, doing something I loved to do.

The two of us walked towards the shifting shoreline, the pale sand soft and sliding beneath our feet. I patiently explained the basics of surfing to the woman at my side, the techniques, and the importance of balance for her to stay on the board. Rosa listened to me intently, her pretty eyes sparkling with interest and excitement. It was clear she was ready to dive headfirst into this new adventure. Hell, she rode huge animals on the daily. A wave was nothing.

We both waded into the cool ocean with our surfboards in hand, feeling the slosh of the water embrace our legs the deeper we went. The waves crashed behind us, calling us to join their rhythmic dance. I moved the beat-up board in the water at my waist, showing Rosa how to lie on the one I brought for her and to paddle deeper with me. She grinned, and her excitement was obvious as she followed my guidelines, her bravery shining through as she was ready to get started. I couldn't help but think of her underneath me, writhing and crying out under my touch. I tried to push the thoughts away, focusing on what we were currently doing together.

"Alright, now it's time to catch your first wave out here," I told her. Even I could hear the wild mix of excitement and pride that made my voice higher as I spoke. I moved my board beside her, ready to guide her patiently through the thrill of the ride. As the perfect wave approached, I shot Rosa a bright smile. "Hey, you got this, okay? Just remember to hold your balance and trust your body."

I watched her, and, with a burst of energy, she paddled out to the rising wave with all her might. I felt the small burn of fear as she was lifted up, but I pushed it away. I believed in her. I saw her begin to smile as she rose to her feet, a look of pure happiness spreading over her pretty face.

The moment was an absolutely magical one to watch. It was as if time stood still, and it was just Rosa Rivers, the swell of the wave, and the vast ocean before us. She let herself ride the rising wave with grace and courage, her bright laughter echoing through the briny ocean air. It was a sight to behold, a real show of her bravery and desire to embrace new and exciting experiences with me. I had so many feelings for her and, at that moment, they were intense.

I realized this surf class was about more than simply riding the waves with the woman I had come to care about completely; it was about enjoying life, taking chances with the people I loved, and finding joy in even the most insignificant of situations. Rosa's smile widened as she floated closer to the beach on her surfboard, and she gave out a victorious cry as she got closer to me. I couldn't help but join in, a wave of happiness and appreciation washing over me.

"Hell yeah!" I yelled, laughing happily and whooping. "That was amazing!"

She ran at me, laughing, and threw herself into my arms. I spun her around, and when we stopped, I touched her chin with two fingers, tilting her face up to mine. The grin slipped from her pretty face, and something dark and more sensual took over.

"You're a natural!" I cried, smiling at her.

"Oh yeah?" she asked with a laugh. "Well, maybe I'll enter the surfing competition, too, then. Give you a run for your money."

"Don't put me through that," I said, giving her a kiss. "You wouldn't embarrass me in front of my friends."

"Oh, I would never," she laughed.

"This has been an amazing day," I murmured, holding her in my arms.

It was true. Being with Rosa was like standing in the

ocean, feeling the waves wash gently over me. She was sunlight, and I needed her like I needed the warmth.

"Brody," she whispered, her lips brushing mine. "I want you now."

That sounded like a perfect end to this perfect day. The beach was empty around us, and we tumbled into the sand. I felt hot, burning want coursing through me. Even now, though we had fallen into bed together, I still wanted her more than I had wanted anyone else. This wasn't an itch that needed to be scratched. This was some kind of soul bond that was pulling us into the same circle.

"Don't think you're off the hook just because you're talented," I told her. "You have more lessons ahead of you. We're going to spend hours on this beach."

"Can't wait," she said, leaning up to press our mouths together. "We can spend hours here today too."

"Oh, is that right?" I asked her with a grin, brushing my hand over her breast. "I think I can make time."

My phone began to ring in my pocket, and we both jumped.

"Heather," I said with a sigh. "I better take it. She has Corey with her."

Rosa nodded, sitting back in the sand. I watched her for a moment before turning away.

"What?" I asked my ex-girlfriend.

There was silence for a moment. "I'm going to tell you this once. I want her gone."

13

ROSA

*M*r. Perry was arguing with a customer.

"I heard this place was broken into," a young, cocky voice said.

I had already seen the teenagers when they walked in, shoving each other and laughing. I hoped they would leave quickly, but they were just lingering in the shop.

"Hey, old man, did you hear me? Are you deaf or something?" one of them asked.

Okay, that was it. My cheeks burned with anger, and I stomped over. Mr. Perry was stocking the candy case, filling the wooden shelves with lollipops and chocolates. The three boys were crowded around him, lurking like gangly, annoying little horse flies.

"If you're not going to buy anything, you need to leave," I snapped.

One of them turned, looking me up and down. "Oh, hey, baby. You work here, too?"

"Yeah, that's right. I'm security and you need to leave," I said, staring him down.

He raised his hands, laughing. "You got a bad attitude, huh?"

"Mr. Perry, are you okay?" I asked, ignoring the teenager. I touched the man's arm, looking him over in concern. "Are they bothering you?"

"We're not bothering anybody; we were just asking the man a question. We can't ask questions around here?" The taller boy asked, the look on his face sour.

"You can leave, that's what you can do," I told them all, pointing at the door.

"I heard Logan wasn't doing anything wrong," the tall boy said, his eyes going dark. "I heard you accused him for no reason."

I felt panic flood through me. "You heard wrong. Logan is an asshole."

"Rosa," Mr. Perry warned, patting my arm. "These boys were just wondering what happened to their friend, and now they're leaving."

"Oh, so you can talk?" the first boy said, letting out a huff of rude laughter.

"Christopher," Mr. Perry said, his raspy voice disappointed. "You were one of my best students. What happened to you?"

The boy's cheeks went red, and his friends laughed. "You rode ponies, man?"

"Horses," Christopher mumbled. "Let's just go."

"Yeah, good idea," I snapped, pointing at the door. "Bye, Christopher."

He glanced back one more time before they shuffled out, shoving at each other again. I let out a long, relieved breath. They weren't burglars, and they weren't my ex. They were just dumb, annoying kids with nothing better to do. And I was just glad they were gone.

"Are you alright?" I asked Mr. Perry again, helping him over to the checkout counter and into the chair behind it.

He nodded, and I knelt in front of him. "You worry too much, Rosa. I'm just fine. My shoulders ache, but I'm an old man. It comes with the territory."

"Why don't you take a break?" I asked him. "Go make some coffee in the back and have a little sit-down."

"Now you know if I go back there, I'll fall asleep in that recliner," he said, a smile pulling at his mouth.

"That's the plan," I told him kindly. "Come on, it's been rough around here. You deserve a break. I've got this."

"Rosa, wait," he said, stopping me as we got to the door. "I want you to know that I don't blame you at all for any of this. Problems happen, and we'll be okay here."

"I know," I told him quietly, nodding. I did feel a little responsible, but I wouldn't have been a normal, functioning person if I didn't feel that way.

The back room was just a small, closed-off area with a coffee maker and a TV on a table. There were two thick little armchairs with foot cushions in front of the TV, and the safe was tucked under the table there. There was also a chest of drawers on the other side of the room, by the window, that held extra inventory and little knick-knacks.

"Well, maybe a little sit down might do me some good," Mr. Perry said with a sigh.

I watched him take a seat in the chair, and I walked over, flipping on the TV for him. He had been watching that thing since before I was born.

"Bridge on the River Kwai?" I asked, and he nodded. "I'll bring you some lunch in an hour or so. Fish stew from that seaside place? The owner has a crush on you, after all."

He chuckled, his mood very obviously lifting. "If Maggie starts to look at me the way that young Strauss boy looks at you, we'll be in business."

I felt my cheeks go hot. I gave an awkward laugh, and just nodded. When I left the room, closing the door behind me, I couldn't stop thinking about Brody. It was like he was a part of me now. I shook myself, trying to think about my job instead of anything else. I needed to keep my mind focused on what was going on. I really couldn't afford to let my guard down. I needed to be on alert at all times for the people I loved.

Suddenly, there was a knock, and the door banged open, smacking against the opposite window. I spun around, my mouth open in shock. I was expecting the boys to stomp back in or the visage of my ex-boyfriend to come in like a whirlwind, destroying everything around him. It wasn't Sam standing in the middle of the shop, though, and it wasn't the annoying teenage boys either.

"Are you her?"

The woman was dressed in tight blue jean shorts and heeled ankle boots that made her tan legs look a mile long. Her hair was strawberry blonde, and it fell over her shoulders, nearly covering the tight tank top she was wearing. Flashing blue eyes looked me up and down, and her mouth was twisted into a frown.

"I'm sorry?" I asked, confused. "What are you talking about?"

"Where is Brody?" she snapped, stepping forward.

My heart was pounding in my chest, but I kept my composure. Did Brody have a girlfriend, and he was just stringing me along? Was I about to find out that I was the other woman?

"I think you have the wrong address," I told her easily. "Brody isn't here."

I went behind the checkout counter and pretended to be busy. I shuffled around some papers and checked the computer, even though I was looking at nothing at all.

She leaned against the counter. "Don't play stupid. I know what's been going on."

"Okay," I said finally, turning to her, "who *are* you? Look, if you've been seeing him or you're his girlfriend or his wife, I don't know what to say."

She looked at me for a minute and then she laughed. "Sweetheart, I've been there and done that."

"You're Heather," I said, pausing. I wasn't sure why I was expecting her to be blonde. This was the mother of Brody's child. "You're Corey's mom."

I could see her expression freeze over. "What the hell do you know about my son? I don't want you close to him."

"What is this about?" I asked, keeping my voice calm.

The last thing I needed to do was to meet this woman after going through everything I had been through. She was immediately at my throat.

Despite my best intentions and efforts to be a positive presence in Corey's life, it didn't even matter. Heather was pretty obviously opposed to me being involved with him at all. It was evident to me that she harbored negative feelings and was determined to keep me away from their son. Is that what she was doing in the shop?

"How did you find out where I work?" I asked.

She barked a laugh. "You don't worry about that. The only thing that matters is that I do know where you work. And I know where you live, too. Stay away from my son."

"You can go now," I said flatly. She was no better than the annoying teenagers who were in the shop a few minutes before her. "I don't want any trouble. I don't need that."

"Excuse me?" she asked, her expression flattening. "I'm not going anywhere."

Heather's dramatic reaction to having me in Corey's life made it a difficult and complicated situation. And it was a little ridiculous. I had only known the kid for a little while.

Maybe she saw something serious in what was between me and Brody. It was sad to see how much stress it was going to push onto Brody, who seemed to be looking for a positive relationship for both his kid and himself. But Heather wasn't supposed to be in the picture anymore. He would be caught in the middle as a result of her, divided between his desire to preserve a reasonably calm co-parenting relationship and his need for his kid to have a positive male role model in his life. He wasn't going to let his time with Corey just slip away while his ex decided what she wanted for him.

Despite what I may have thought of her, I decided I needed to try to be respectful of her wishes and not push myself into the situation against her will. I understood that, as Corey's mother, she had the right to make decisions regarding anyone who came in and out of his life, and it wasn't even a big deal to me. I didn't really care about being a stepmom or anything like that, though I did like Corey.

Despite that, it was just annoying to be kept at arm's length by someone I didn't even really know, especially when I genuinely cared for Corey's well-being and really wanted to be someone who could contribute positively to his life. Who even knew if Brody and I were going to last? I mean, I hoped we would in the back of my mind, but there was no telling what would happen. I didn't want to hold out hope that we would work.

Maybe I would just need to take a step back. I didn't want to, though. I didn't want to be cowed by Heather and made to leave Brody in the dust. The more I was with Brody and Corey, the more I wanted them both in my life. I wanted us all to be together.

If the need came up, I could offer Brody parenting advice and support. I would hope that he would take into account my suggestions in his interactions with Corey, but I really didn't even know that much about kids. I was good with the ones who took lessons at the horse barn, but it wasn't like I was some kind of child whisperer.

I figured if I needed to, I would also make a point to keep up a positive and supportive relationship with Brody because it was important for Corey to see the people in his life getting along. I had never let myself hope I would be that much of a permanent fixture in either of their lives.

Now that Heather was acting as if I was going to be around for a while, I was thinking about how it could be smoothed over between them. Despite the fact that Heather obviously didn't like me, I stayed optimistic that her stance would come around over time. I realized her concerns could possibly be based on personal reasons or previous experiences with other women Brody had been with, and I hoped that, with time and understanding, she would see the upside of my involvement in her son's life.

Meanwhile, I concentrated on being a positive influence on everyone around me. Mr. Perry was the chosen family I needed to concentrate on. If there was anyone who needed me, it was him. Eventually, I would figure the hard stuff out with Brody and Corey. If it was meant to be, it would be. I hoped that by fostering close ties with them, I would be able to find some sort of common ground with Heather.

I needed to remind myself to be patient with her. If he was my son, I wouldn't want some random woman coming in either. It didn't matter how much I liked Brody. Hell, maybe she still liked him herself. Heather was Brody's ex-girlfriend, and whether I liked it or not, she was still a part of his life. I was going to meet her eventually if I stayed with Brody.

"You know what?" I said, forcing a bright smile. "I think we just got off on the wrong foot. I'm Rosa Rivers. It's really nice to meet Corey's mom. He's a really great kid."

She stared at me for a moment and then scoffed. "Don't

pull that nice bullshit with me, girl. You're playing bedsheet bingo with the father of my child. Save it. I don't want to hear it."

"You're making this so much harder than it needs to be," I said, trying to hold on to my positive attitude. It was really difficult. "I don't want to take anything from you."

"You couldn't even if you tried," she said with a sneer.

Heather was pretty, really pretty. Corey had her perfect, straight nose. She had one of those faces that you might imagine sculptors in Ancient Greece using as their muse, all soft lines and tilted angles. I had always been called a "girl next door" type of woman. Heather was more the popular cheerleader, always getting what she wanted because of her looks. It was too bad that her attitude ruined it.

"What do you want me to do?" I asked her, feeling myself growing closer to my breaking point. "Do you want me to stop seeing Brody? That isn't going to happen."

"How about I just call up child services and get you both taken away from him? Do you know who I know?" Heather snapped. "How does that sound, huh?"

"Why would you do that?" I asked her. "There's no need for that."

I was really getting annoyed. If Brody's ex-girlfriend was determined to take the dangerous step of contacting child services about him, the effects of that decision would be awful for both Brody and Corey. I could see why they weren't together anymore.

The prospect of becoming the motivating factor for a custody battle and the idea of causing anxiety in their lives weighed heavily on my conscience. I shouldn't have even had to think about that, but I couldn't help it. Brody had already been through a lot, including what must have been an emotionally draining breakup with Heather and then rebuilding his life as a single father.

The last thing I wanted was for him to be drawn into a legal struggle that might potentially rob him of his parental rights. It was obvious Corey was the most important thing in his life. It was a situation that no one should have to have to face, especially when they were doing their best to create a loving and caring environment for their kid. And Brody seemed like a good dad.

The bleak prospect of what could happen if child services became involved, just because Heather was jealous, was terrifying to me. Would they carry out an in-depth look into every element of Brody's life? Would they challenge his ability to care for his son, calling his parenting abilities into question? I had never been through anything similar, and I didn't want to.

I couldn't stand the idea of Brody fighting tooth and nail in order to prove his value as a father. He had already shown immense love and care for his son, going above and beyond to ensure his well-being. To think that a single phone call from Heather could derail all of his efforts was an awful thought. Why would she want to up-end her son's life in that way? Maybe she was just that petty.

Whatever part I played in Corey's life, I felt a strong need to protect Brody and his son from any extra harm. I didn't want to be the reason Heather came after him. Now that I had met her, I could honestly say she was really unpleasant. I knew I had to do everything in my power to keep this situation from escalating. Brody deserved at least that much from me.

I remembered seeing him on the beach when I finished my surfing lesson. He was so happy and proud. I wanted to keep him that way. I was determined to be there for him every step of the way, whether it meant having a heart-to-heart with Heather or meeting her toe-to-toe on the battlefield. In the end, it was important to remember that Brody's son's happiness was the number one priority. Whatever the outcome, he needed to be surrounded by warmth, stability, and a loving environment. I didn't know if I could be that for either one of them, but I was willing to try.

"I'll do what's best for my son, and maybe Brody isn't what's best anymore," Heather said tartly. "Maybe he needs a better male presence in his life. What I know for sure is that he doesn't need someone like you around him."

"Someone like me? You don't even know me," I said, completely flabbergasted.

She was the kind of woman who didn't like other women. I could already tell. She was the kind of person who saw everyone else as competition, and she would never be satisfied. It was crazy how easy some people were to read. She was an open book.

"Maybe I don't know you, but my boyfriend does," she said, sneering at me.

"Your boyfriend?" I asked her, confused.

She pointed to the figure walking through the door. It was Sam. She was dating my ex.

14

BRODY

*P*ounding hooves made me jump, and a big, red horse tore the grass behind me, stopping short.

"Rosa, hey," I said, waving at the familiar figure on the horse's back.

She stared at me. "What are you doing here, Brody?"

"Uh, am I missing something?" I asked her, looking around. "Isn't this my first lesson?"

Her pretty face scrunched up. "I didn't think you would show."

Confusion rattled my thoughts. What had changed between yesterday and today? I thought we agreed I would come by the horse barn after she finished work.

"Well, yeah, we had a deal," I said, shooting her a grin. It fell away once I realized she wasn't smiling back. "Rosa, what's wrong? What's going on?"

"Nothing," she said, climbing off her horse. "Let me tie her to the hitching post."

I was still unsure, but I shoved my hands into my pockets and followed her into the barn. The wooden stalls had metal bars around the top, and she slid one of the doors open.

"Who is this?" I asked her, looking at the round, brown horse with black legs.

"This is Seven," she said evenly, digging out a brush from somewhere. "He'll take care of you. He's young, but he's got a good brain."

"Can't relate," I said, trying to draw out a smile, but she gave me nothing. I leaned against the bars, sighing. "Rosa, what did I do?"

She stopped brushing Seven's shoulder, and she just stared, taking a deep breath.

"I met Heather," she said quietly.

It hit me like a ton of bricks. How the hell had she met Heather? The implications of that were enough to make me open the stall door and come inside with her there.

"What do you mean you met her?" I asked, coming up behind her.

She glanced over her shoulder. "She took it upon herself to come right into the shop. Thank goodness Mr. Perry was in the back. He doesn't need even more stress because of me."

"Wait, she came by the shop?" I said, shaking my head. "What did she say?"

She shrugged. "What does it matter?"

"It matters, Rosa," I told her, reaching out to touch her hip. "What did she say?"

She flinched away from me. I drew my hand back, watching her curiously. What could my ex-girlfriend have said to her to make her act that way? Rosa wasn't someone who was scared easily, so I was sure she wasn't afraid of her.

"Let's just get this horse saddled and get you out there in the arena," she said, her voice turning into the high, polite tone that I knew she used with her lesson kids.

She was pushing her body by me before I even had the chance to talk to her again. She was leaving no room for argument from me. It was hard to believe that this was the same Rosa who had been tangled with me under the wind-bent trees, the same woman who touched me so lovingly on the beach and let me hold her close whenever I could.

"Here, remember how to put your foot in the stirrup?" she asked, coming over but carefully not touching me. "There, just grab the horn and hoist yourself up into the seat."

I did what she asked, and then watched her as she did the same on her horse. She trotted off, but I waited there, determined to get the truth out of her somehow. She stopped under the oak trees, realizing finally that I wasn't following her to the arena.

"What are you doing?" she asked. "You just push your heels into his sides."

"What did Heather say to you?"

Her expression went sour. "I thought you were here for a horse riding lesson."

"I'm here for you," I corrected, putting my heels into Seven's side, as she said. He ambled along, and when we were closer, I could see her mouth trembling. "Jesus, Rosa, it must have been something terrible. Did she threaten to slice your tires?"

Her eyes widened. "Why did you say that so casually? Is that normal behavior for her?"

"Pretty much," I said with a sigh. "So she didn't then?"

"No, she didn't," she said, letting out a huff of laughter that sounded tired. "Look, I don't want to be in the middle of this whole thing. You and Heather need to figure it out."

"Figure what out?" I asked in disbelief. "I don't have any connection to her except for the relationship we both have with Corey. Whatever she told you, I don't have feelings for her, and she doesn't have feelings for me."

"I never said you had feelings for her," she said with a shrug. "We need to get to the arena. I told Mr. Perry we would only be out here for an hour or two. He invited me to dinner."

"Oh, that sounds nice," I nodded.

"I think he wants to talk," she said distractedly. Obviously, there was something else to that, but I wasn't sure how to ask or if she would want to say it anyway. She shook herself. "I have a lot going on right now and a lot to think about, okay?"

"Yeah, I get that," I agreed. "I'm not trying to overcomplicate your life."

I felt like everything was spiraling out of control. I seemed to have lost Rosa as quickly as I found her. Something gave me the impression that she was a runner. Now she was running away from me. She was giving up on me, and I wasn't even sure why that was.

She didn't say anything else. She just patted her horse's shoulder and hopped off, opening the gate. I watched the way her long legs moved in her tight riding pants and boots and the way she flipped her dark hair over her shoulder. She was amazing.

"Okay, so," she said once we were both inside the fenced in area, "we'll start by taking Seven in easy circles. Just pick up your reins and hold them low. Keep a soft hand, and don't pull on his mouth. There you go. Keep a steady pressure with your leg."

Soon, the horse was trotting under me, bouncing me around in circles. I kept sneaking glances at Rosa, but she was in full instructor mode, all business.

I stopped the horse short, making me jolt in the saddle.

"What did I say, Brody? Didn't I say not to pull on his mouth? You're going to make him bit sour," she reprimanded, shaking her head.

"You need to talk to me," I told her. "I'm not moving until you do."

Whatever my ex-girlfriend said to her was enough to

cause her to distance herself from me, leaving me baffled and jilted. The heaviness of the tension between us continued to be in the air, creating an uneasy friction. Maybe she mentioned our son in her talk with Rosa, and she voiced her issues about Rosa's involvement in his life.

She had already made it clear to me she didn't want any other woman around him. I didn't plan on listening to her though. I wondered if she told Rosa the same thing. It wasn't like it was going to be some heartbreaking revelation that Heather didn't want Rosa around our child. What hit me square in the gut was that Rosa might have agreed to it. It was the only reason I could think that she would be trying to keep her distance from me. I couldn't imagine her believing anything else Heather told her. My mind raced with questions as I attempted to make sense of what had happened.

What could Heather possibly have said to cause such a split between us? I didn't even understand why she didn't want Rosa around him. She didn't even know Rosa. Heather was the kind of woman to hate someone just because they were pretty. I knew she was petty, but she had been a good enough mother to Corey. Why wouldn't she want him to have people in his life that cared about him? Did she have any doubts about Rosa's ability to feel compassion for Corey? Was it more personal for her, a reflection of her own unresolved feelings and insecurities?

I had tried for so long to understand Heather, but we just weren't the same at all. The gnawing uncertainty made it impossible to find a resolution. And Rosa wouldn't even tell me what was said.

Rosa, who had seemed like an ever-present source of strength and comfort, was now distant and guarded. For that, I really hated Heather. Rosa had been slowly becoming one of the most important people in my life. Our growing relationship's warmth and affection had been replaced with a visible detachment from each other. It felt as if a wall had been built between the two of us, based on whatever Heather had told her.

The agonizing pain of losing Rosa's trust and connection was absolutely miserable, leaving me longing for a chance to rebuild the shattered parts of my connection with her. Corey, who was just our innocent and unaware kid, was always on my mind throughout whatever this emotional struggle turned out to be. How would this random divide affect him? He liked Rosa, too. Would he notice the conflict between his mother and me, or worse, be divided between two people he loved the most? I just wanted to have an easy relationship with Heather, and I wanted to be with Rosa. The fact that our connection might be ruined now was awful to think about.

"Did Heather say something to you about Corey?" I asked her, watching her for a reaction. I saw her expression shift. "She did, didn't she?"

Rosa finally sighed, and I saw her deflate. "Yeah, she did. She was right. I'm not anything to Corey, and I don't want to come between you two. I want to be done."

"What?" I asked her, nearly falling off the horse in shock. "What are you talking about? Done with what?"

"Done with everything," she told me, looking away.

"You mean you're done with me," I said, sitting back in the saddle. "You don't want to see me anymore."

"That's right," she said, clearing her throat.

I shook my head. "I can't believe you let Heather scare you off like that. I didn't think you were like that."

"Like what?" she asked, her attention snapping to me. "What exactly am I like, Brody? Please tell me."

I heard the sarcastic tone of her voice and knew I should

have backed down. I just felt so hurt and surprised. I didn't have the filter on my thoughts that I normally did.

"Well, I just didn't think you would be scared of someone like Heather," I told her, though maybe I regretted it as soon as I said it. "I thought of you as stronger than that."

Her face went red, and she looked like she was biting the inside of her cheek. She stared at me for a moment, shaking her head. Then she pushed her heel into Cinder's side, making them walk away to the other side of the arena. Despite my limited knowledge and the fact that my lesson seemed to be cut short, I followed her lead and went after her. Yeah, maybe I should have let her be, but I didn't want to lose Rosa Rivers. That was the last thing I wanted.

"Your lesson is over," she said coldly. "You can go now."

"Rosa, I don't understand," I said, trying not to sound pleading.

"Well, apparently I'm just scared," she snapped, taking her horse in circles around me. "Maybe you could take a moment to understand that I don't want to be in the middle."

"In the middle of what?" I asked, throwing up my hands. I quickly grabbed the reins when Seven took it as a cue to walk forward. "Stop, horse!"

"Whoa, boy," Rosa said calmly, rolling her eyes at me, and Seven stopped short.

"If you're not scared, then what is the problem?" I said finally, watching her.

She looked away. "Why don't we let this be? We can just be friends again."

"Again?" I couldn't help but exclaim. "Rosa, we were never friends. I can't be friends with you. There's too much between us now. Could you really just be friends with me?"

Her eyes glittered. "Stop making this so hard on me."

I turned my horse closer to her, and soon enough, we were right beside each other.

"Hey, I'm not trying to make anything hard for you, okay?" I said gently. "I just don't understand any of this. How do you have such a changed opinion of me?"

"My opinion of you hasn't changed," she told me, shaking her head. "I'm doing this for you, Brody. Why couldn't you just let it go? Why couldn't you make this easy?"

"There's nothing easy about losing you," I said quietly, swallowing hard.

She looked at me, those pretty eyes bright. "I didn't want to fight with you."

"Tell me what she said to you," I said, reaching out to touch her thigh gently. "I can't help if I don't even know what's going on."

She swallowed. "She said that if I stuck around, if I got closer to you or Corey, she would make sure that social services gave you a call."

I stared at her in shock, my mouth falling open. Was Heather really that petty? Yeah, she had her moments, but I didn't think she would ever try to destroy the relationship between my son and myself. That was just about the lowest she could ever conceivably go. I had always thought Heather respected me as Corey's dad, if nothing else. I dropped my hand from Rosa's thigh, and my anger at Heather's words was palpable.

"She said that?" I asked her, my voice coming out tight and controlled.

She nodded, and I squeezed the reins in my hands until they hurt.

"So, I can't be with you," she told me quietly. "I can't be the reason you lose your son."

I shook my head. "Heather doesn't get to decide who I spend my time with. It has nothing to do with her. If she goes that route, I'll fight anything she tries to say."

"It doesn't work like that," she said, sounding defeated. "Judges normally side with the mothers, don't they?"

"Not necessarily," I said, though she was right. "Corey is normally with me, and Heather is all over the place. She never has a stable place to live."

"Does she date a lot?" she asked hesitantly.

"Uh, I guess so, yeah," I said, confused. "Why do you ask?"

"If she doesn't care about you, then why does she care if you date someone?"

I looked at her. "She doesn't care about that. She cares about getting even, and she cares about the pettiness of it all. That's what I'm realizing."

"How has she tried to get even in the past?" she said, petting Cinder's neck distractedly.

"Why do you ask?" I wondered. "What does it have to do with anything?"

The sun gleamed through the oak trees, and the light flickered over Rosa's tanned skin. The horses stomped their hooves, bored. I wasn't paying attention to anything but her.

"You need to know something," she said, letting out a long breath. "Heather is dating Sam. Your ex is dating my ex."

"What?" I asked, and I felt my eyes go wide. "What are you talking about?"

"It's true," she said, shaking her head. "It's crazy, but it's true. They both came by the shop. I think they were trying to intimidate me, but I made them leave. Unlike what you seem to think of me, I'm not scared. I also don't like drama, though. I like peace."

I did know that about her. She had already told me she ran from the turmoil of Sam to her peace on the island. She was a runner, and I didn't want her to run from me. This was all almost too much to deal with. How the hell had Heather even gotten with him? I mean, they had met once or twice, but that was it. Was she really that childish?

"I know—" I began, but Rosa's phone began to ring, stopping my words.

"Hello?" she asked. A minute later, she looked at me, terrified. "Mr. Perry had a heart attack!"

15

ROSA

$\mathcal{M}$y heart was beating out of my chest, and my head was throbbing.

"He's going to be okay," Brody said, shushing me gently. "Sitting here worrying isn't going to help anyone."

"I can't do anything else," I told him, shaking my head.

The hospital waiting room was deathly silent. The low hum of the vending machine was like a constant buzzing in the back of my mind. I tapped my foot on the linoleum floor.

"You can hope for the best," he said as he reached out to squeeze my hand. "The old man is strong. He can get through this, and they found him just in time."

"Thank goodness the stable hand ran out of alfalfa and went to find him at the shop," I said, my voice trembling. My hands were still shaking, just like my whole body.

The sudden and unexpected situation of someone close to me getting hurt or dying was something that shook me to my core. Truthfully, up until that point, I had been happy and fortunate enough to lead a relatively sheltered and easy life, shielded from the harsh realities of loss and pain. Besides what happened with Sam, most of my life had been positive.

Despite that, Mr. Perry's heart attack completely shattered the haze of invincibility I had unknowingly built around myself and the ones I loved. The jarring nature of what happened was overwhelming to me because it forced me to confront the fragility of the lives around me and the unstable balance of the world we lived in. It was hard for me to grasp.

It was as if the ground beneath me had sunken in, leaving me disoriented and wondering where to go next. What happened to Mr. Perry sent a shock wave of fear through me. At any moment, someone I loved could be snatched right out from under me without a goodbye. It was so horrible to think about.

My lack of past experience dealing with something like the loss of someone I loved made it even more difficult to understand. The feelings that surged over me were a chaotic mix of horror, grief, shock, and uncertainty. I battled with myself to try and make sense of the unexpected emptiness that might have been created in my life if Mr. Perry had passed. If he had died, there would be a hole in my heart, and it wasn't something I had ever faced before.

His having a heart attack also acted as a real wake-up call for me, reminding me of the short jump of life and the real importance of cherishing every minute spent with the people around me. This happening made me realize what was actually important. Petty fights meant nothing when it came to the people I cared about. It wasn't worth it to go back and forth when they could be here one minute and gone in the next.

In the aftermath, I found myself navigating a whole new wave of emotional territory. I tried to fight the wave of sadness that swept over me. It was a process of healing and growth. I eventually might be able to accept the reality of loss and find relief in memories of the love I felt and the support of the people around me.

Mr. Perry lived a full life, but I wanted him to keep living that life. I tried to calm myself, but it was hard to see that there was hope through the shock of it all. Despite what happened with Brody, I was glad I had him by my side. I really believed that life was so short and we needed to make the most of everything we did.

I realized I wasn't going to let the things Heather said to me make an impact on how I felt about Brody. Or even Corey, for that matter. Life was too short to give up so easily on something I knew could make me happy.

"You can go in and see him now," one of the nurses said, coming out of the double doors. "You're his daughter?"

I was going to correct her, but Brody put his hand on my shoulder, squeezing gently.

"Yeah, she's his daughter," he said, nodding. He looked at me. "I'll wait out here for you."

"Don't you need to go pick up Corey?" I asked him. "You don't have to stay."

After all that had happened between us and the way I had treated him, I wasn't going to ask him to wait in a dreary hospital room for me to come back. He smiled ruefully at me.

"I'm sure Heather would love some extra time with him," he said, shaking his head. "Maybe it'll soften her up to the idea of you and me. Sam is with her anyway, I'm sure."

The Sam and Heather issue wasn't important to me at the moment. I wanted to focus on seeing Mr. Perry and making sure he was going to be okay. Nothing else mattered.

"You can go ahead and follow me back here," the nurse said kindly, gesturing at me. "Now, he is sleeping but it should be okay to have a little company."

"Thank you," I told her as she showed me to the correct door.

I hesitated outside the hospital room, my heart nearly pounding out of my chest. Even knowing he was okay and just behind that door, I still couldn't shake off the worry that had consumed me since I received the news.

I took a long, calming breath, pushed open the door, and stepped inside. I swallowed as the sterile scent of antiseptic filled the air around me, the smell mingling with the faint beeping of machines monitoring Mr. Perry's vital signs, letting me know he was alive.

The sight of him lying there in the hospital room, pale and frail on the sheets, sent a hard pang of sadness through me. My boss had always been more than that to me. He was a strong and easy presence, the backbone of his businesses, and seeing him so vulnerable was hard.

I made my way up to his bedside cautiously, my soft footsteps muffled by the polished tile floor. I didn't want to wake him up, but I needed to speak with him and know he was really alive. I needed to know everything was going to be okay. His wrinkled eyes were closed, and I could see the lines of pain etched across his weathered face. I reached a hand out and gingerly took his fingers in mine, hoping to offer some comfort for him, even with the small gesture of touch. I waited for him to see.

"Hi, Mr. Perry?" I whispered, my voice barely audible, even in the hushed room. "It's me. It's Rosa. I'm here, okay?"

I waited for a moment and watched him as he shifted in the crisp, white sheets. His eyelids fluttered open, revealing tired but bright eyes that held a glimmer of recognition in them for me. A small smile tugged at the corners of his mouth, and I felt a warm surge of pure relief wash over me at the sight. It was a great feeling to see him conscious and moving a little, to know that he was fighting. I had been so worried.

"How are you feeling?" I asked, my trembling voice filled

with real concern. "Are you in any pain? I could call the nurse for you."

I didn't know how to act or what to do. I had never had to deal with someone in the hospital. I once visited my great-aunt in the nursing home for Halloween, but all I could remember was candy and mothballs. This was nothing like that.

He let out a raspy little chuckle at that, his voice barely rising above a small whisper. "I feel like I've been hit by a rogue wave and then stomped on by a horse," he said to me, his words laced with the smallest touch of humor. "But don't you worry about me. I'll be alright. I just need a little time to recover from this."

I nodded, trying to hide the strain of worry that still pulled at me. "The surf shop will be fine for however long it takes, but I'm going to miss you," I said, my voice tinged with sadness. "I was so worried. When I found out you were okay, I was so relieved. You have no idea. I have everything under control."

His eyes softened at that, familial care shining through the sleep in his eyes. "Thank you so much for being here. It really means a lot to me to have such a wonderful young lady to look after my well-being."

The two of us sat in silence for just a moment, the weight of what had happened hanging in the air of the dimly lit hospital room around us. I squeezed his hand gently, offering what little comfort I could. I wanted to be there for him, as he had always been there for me. He had been like a grandfather to me. I sat with him as the sound of the machines continued their steady rhythm, a reminder of the softness of life and how easy it was to lose everything all in one go.

"Well, my young Rosa, it seems I'll be retiring earlier than I planned, doesn't it?" he said, giving a tired little laugh. "But, I suppose I was ready to hang up my sandals anyway."

"What are you talking about?" I asked him, confused. "You'll be fine in a few days. You can go back to light work and being around the horses, right?"

"Oh, I don't think I'm going to be doing much of that," he answered.

"Did the doctors say something?" I asked him, leaning forward. "I meant to ask them, but I never got the chance—"

He held up a hand. "It wasn't anything those doctors told me, Rosa. It's in my heart to take a step back."

"What will happen to the surf shop then? What about the barn and the horses?" I said, feeling my voice rising frantically. "Mr. Perry, you can't be serious. Not yet?"

"Well, I wanted to talk to you about that," he said, clearing his throat. He gave me a proud, kind smile. "I want you to buy me out, Rosa. I'm damn proud of you, and I couldn't think of a better person to take over. Those horses couldn't be left in better hands."

I sat in my chair, frozen. I thought I would have more time to figure out how to get the money. There was no way I could get enough to buy the shop from him or anything else, for that matter. Right now, I barely even had enough to buy the feed that Cinder liked.

"Mr. Perry, I don't think—" I began, my throat aching.

"Tell me about those horses," he said, his mood lifting. "How are they doing?"

"The stablehands are watching over them," I told him, faking a hollow smile. "They're all doing just fine, but they miss you."

"How did you get here, my dear?" he asked me suddenly, looking at me.

"Oh, Brody drove me," I told him, my cheeks going hot.

He gave me a tired grin. "You tell that boy he has my approval," he reached out to pat my hand. "As you know, I don't have any children of my own. I have a niece in

Michigan who I see a couple of times a year, but that's it for me."

"I know you don't," I said quietly. "But you've done well on your own."

"I just don't have it in me to take care of it all anymore," he said with a sigh. "My young years are far behind me. These are my golden years."

"Are you leaving?" I asked him, confused. "Moving away?"

"Oh no, of course not," he said, but he didn't elaborate further.

I was hoping it was just his traumatic experience talking, and maybe he would change his mind. Maybe this was just his pain medication coming through. I really hoped he would reconsider. I didn't even want to think about what might happen if I wasn't able to take over for him. I was terrified of what the places I loved would become if I couldn't be there. Would the surf shop fall into ruin, or would it be demolished to turn into some cheap beachside outlet mall? Would he sell the trails and land to the highest bidder and let some auction take the horses?

"I'm feeling very tired, I think," he said around a big yawn. "Could you convince that nurse with the kind eyes to give me an extra Jello, Rosa dear?"

I couldn't help but laugh. "I'll see what I can do." As I got ready to leave the room, I leaned in closer to my boss, my voice barely above a whisper. "Take care, Mr. Perry. We'll all be here waiting for you when you're ready to come back."

He nodded at me, his eyes filled with determination. "I won't let this keep me down for long. You can count on that. I trust you to take care of things for me. When I'm back, we can talk about you taking over."

I felt my stomach flip. With a final squeeze of his fragile hand, I made my way out of the hospital room, my heart heavy with concern but also filled with a sort of anxiety. I felt better knowing he was okay, but I wasn't ready for what was to come.

"Hey, are you alright? How was Mr. Perry?" Brody said, hurrying up to me. He had two cups of coffee in his hands. He handed one to me.

"Thank you," I told him, taking the hot cup gratefully. "He was doing good. I think he's going to make a full recovery."

"Rosa, what's wrong? Did something else happen?" he asked, brushing my cheek with his thumb.

"I need to sit down," I let out a shaky breath.

I felt as if the whole world was spinning like crazy around me, swirling in a kaleidoscope of dizzying color. I sat down heavily in the seat.

"Hey, are you okay?" Brody asked, putting his coffee down as he kneeled in front of me.

I didn't know if I was the kind of person who could shoulder that much at one time. There was so much going on, and I didn't know what to do. There had to be something, though. I wished so badly I could have been someone else, someone with more money.

I looked at him, my mind reeling. "Brody, I'm about to lose everything."

16

BRODY

I was dreaming of Rosa Rivers.

I woke up suddenly to the deep sound of crashing waves and the golden rays of the morning sun glowing through my bedroom window in my little house. It looked like it would be a perfect day for surfing, and I couldn't help but feel a bright burn of excitement coursing through my veins about the day ahead.

I really needed the practice anyway. The fact of the matter was that the annual surfing competition was just a few days away, and I should have been training relentlessly for the moment. I had been all over the place lately and this would be perfect to get my head in the game and fine-tune my skills.

I found myself on the beach, close to the surf shop. I knew Rosa would be there soon, but I also knew she was taking care of the horse barn. I hurriedly slipped into my wetsuit, feeling the familiar tight fabric that always made me feel almost invincible when I was out in the water.

Grabbing my surfboard, I made my way down to the beach, the sand shifting warmly beneath my bare feet. The briny breeze caressed my face, and I couldn't help but grin. The ocean was my sanctuary, my full getaway from the chaos of life. As I reached the shore, I saw a figure in the distance. I had been so deep into what I was doing, I didn't hear anyone pull up.

Squinting my eyes against the morning sun, I realized it was Heather in her bright, tight tank top. My heart sank, and a knot formed in my stomach. I knew she was about to ruin my good day. She had a way of making things harder than they really needed to be. I didn't understand why she couldn't just be kind, at least in front of our son.

"Corey, buddy, what are you doing here?" I asked my son, watching him walk happily toward me with his hand in Heather's.

"Don't talk to him," she snapped. "I heard something really interesting. Apparently, he almost drowned in the water. If you remember correctly, I forbade him from going out there."

"What are you doing here?" I asked, my voice laced with a mix of anger and concern. "Hey, bud, could you go sit down over there for a second? Daddy's phone is right there, and you can play that horse game you like. Do you remember the passcode?"

When he nodded, I turned him in the direction of my things. Heather tried to protest, but I ignored her. Corey went and sat down happily in the sand, picking up my phone.

"I'm here to make sure you never see Corey again," she spat, her words like venom in open wounds.

"He didn't drown, Heather, and if you had let him take more swimming classes like I wanted, there wouldn't have been the possibility of him going under at all," I said, though I regretted it as soon as the words left my mouth.

Her face went red, and then purple. "Are you really blaming me?"

"I'm not blaming you," I said, letting out a calming breath. "I'm just saying we've both made mistakes."

"No, don't drag me into this," she scoffed. "You're the one bringing your little girlfriend into the mix."

"You're dating my best friend," I said, trying not to sound too sarcastic. "I think that's a little closer to home, don't you?"

She shrugged, turning up her nose. "Well, I just don't think you're able to take care of my son anymore. I think you're too distracted by that girl."

My heart was thudding painfully in my chest, and I fought to find the right words. "What the hell are you talking about?" I asked, glancing at Corey, who waved at me. "He's my son too, you know. You can't just take him away from me like that."

Her eyes narrowed, and she tightened her hand into a fist. "What do you think this is, Brody? You think you can just come in and out of his life whenever you want to? You're never around. You're almost always chasing your idiotic dreams, leaving your son behind in the process."

"What the hell are you talking about?" I asked. "You know that's not true."

She smiled, slow and deliberate. "Does it matter? Let's see what the judge thinks about it. With your history and what happened to your dad, they'll see my side. Like father, like son."

Her words cut deep, and I felt a surge of anger wash over me. She was someone who knew so much about me and tried to use it against me for that exact reason. She would do whatever she could to get what she wanted. I had no doubt about that. She was always jealous of the surfing and never even wanted to watch any of my competitions.

I couldn't help but compare this piece of my past to the woman I hoped would be my future. Rosa was learning to surf. She was miles above this bitter, petty woman in front of me. In some part of my mind, I had hoped we might all be friends, but Heather wasn't going to let that happen. I had always believed that my dreams would provide a better life for Corey, a life I never got to have with my own dad. I always planned to be there for my own son.

"Look, Heather, I don't want to fight with you. I know you don't approve of what I do, but you know I love our son more than anything in the world. I have to be a part of his life," I all but pleaded with her, my tone filled with a soft sort of desperation. "Don't do this to him."

In the back of my mind, I already knew what she was going to say. Platitudes and things of that nature didn't matter to Heather. When she was set on something, nothing was going to change her mind about it. And for some reason, she was set on this.

She scoffed at me, her face pinched with bitterness. "You know love isn't enough, Brody. My son needs stability, and he needs a set group of people around him. He also needs a father who will be there for him, not just when it's easy. I plan on giving that to him."

"What is that supposed to mean?" I asked, my voice rising. She couldn't mean Sam, could she? After what I knew he did to Rosa, I didn't even want to look at him.

"Don't worry about it," she sneered. "See you around, Brody. Or maybe not."

The soft sand flew up and burned my eyes as I watched her turn away from me, pulling our son along behind her. The dark weight of her words hung heavy in the air, and I felt a sense of helplessness begin to fall over me. I couldn't stomach the thought of losing my boy, of never seeing him grow into the man he was meant to be, and of never being the one to be there for him. If I didn't have him close to me, I wasn't sure what I would do about it.

"Damn it," I muttered, wiping a hand over my face.

As they disappeared into the distance, I waded into the water. I felt the most calm when I was there. The rush of the ocean was cool against my skin. The waves around me crashed, mirroring the turmoil that swirled within me.

ROSA

"*C*an you come over? It's an emergency," Brody's voice was tense when I picked up.

I dropped the dish I had been washing, letting it clatter loudly in the sink.

"An emergency?" I asked him frantically. "What kind of emergency? Is it Corey?"

After Mr. Perry suffered his heart attack, I couldn't stop thinking about it. A cold dread, one that had been there since I got the call, began to settle deep within my chest, covering me in a strong sense of unease that made me constantly worried. It was as if an ominous cloud had floated over me and descended on my mind, constantly telling me something awful had to be waiting in the wings.

Every passing moment seemed to make this feeling even more urgent, leaving me forever on edge, my senses on high alert for any signs of coming doom. The weight of the uncertainty seemed to push heavily on my shoulders, making my mind move with worried thoughts. Just thinking about it made my heart beat frantically.

The once familiar peace of knowing I had Mr. Perry was

tinged with the unsettling knowledge that anyone could be gone at any time at all. It was as if the very fabric of my mind had been ripped apart and shaken by the near-tragedy of it all. The normal, simple act of stepping outside my front door became a hard task for me, and a terrible fear consumed me that something awful would happen to me or to those I held dear. Each passing day only served to deepen this sense of foreboding as news of Mr. Perry's slow recovery trickled in, leaving me in a constant state of apprehension. The world around me seemed to lose the once-vibrant colors it had held, replaced instead by a gray cloud of panic and anxiety.

I found it hard to sleep and had so much to think about and worry over. Sleeping through the night became a luxury I couldn't even remember. It had been a few days since everything happened, and I hadn't seen Brody. He went radio silent.

It felt like my whole body was on high alert. And his silence didn't make it any better. My nights were becoming one big struggle. I couldn't stop restlessly tossing and turning in my sheets, haunted by horrible nightmares that revealed my deepest anxieties. I would dream about losing Brody or Corey going into the waves and never returning to us.

The once-familiar sights and sounds of the beach and the shop now seemed distorted to me. It was like they were mere illusions clouding my vision, covering a hidden danger waiting just beneath the surface. Nearly every phone call or knock on the door from my mail lady sent my heart thundering in my chest, my mind racing through a complicated mix of worst-case situations.

The weight of what had happened felt almost suffocating, and it was an unknown I was trying to figure out. I struggled to find my way in the middle of the chaos that had taken over life for the foreseeable future. If it wasn't Mr. Perry's accident, it was Heather or Sam. I needed a break, or at least my mind did. It was as if I hadn't had a chance to calm down for days on end.

I was hoping that my mind would settle soon enough. The fact that Mr. Perry's condition had begun to improve had given me a small amount of comfort, but I kept thinking it wouldn't have happened if I had been there. I tried to tell myself it wasn't my fault, but it was hard to imagine I wasn't at fault. It wasn't about Mr. Perry being there alone; it was about me wondering whether Brody thought this whole thing was important enough to keep it going. If he didn't, I left Mr. Perry all on his own for nothing at all. That would have been my fault, for sure. I tried not to worry too hard over it. With each day that passed by, the frozen dread in my chest began to thaw out, replaced instead by a leery optimism that told of easier days ahead compared to the ones that were behind.

"It's not Corey, but can you come over?" Brody asked once again, and any sort of resentment I had for him seemed to melt away.

"Right now?" I asked him quietly, but I was already gathering my things to leave.

There was silence on the other end, and then, "I need you, Rosa."

The sound of Brody's deep voice on the other end of the line sent a sharp rush of anxiety and excitement through my body. I could very clearly hear the urgency in his voice, so without really thinking about what I was doing, I grabbed my keys and headed straight for his house.

As I drove through the familiar streets, the ocean whooshing back and forth to my right, quick flashes of our time together flickered around in my mind. Brody was so much more than I hoped anyone could be. He had his faults, but I did too. It felt as if he had been avoiding me, and it was understandable.

After all that had happened, the two of us felt like parts of the same soul that were meant to be one whole piece, spending every waking moment aching for the other. It was clear there was something more that was burning and flickering between us, as much as I tried to pretend it really didn't mean anything to me.

I turned the headlights off and stared at the familiar door. Strangely, it felt like this night would change everything. It felt like *this* night was going to be the catalyst. If I walked through that door now, I would never be able to turn back, figuratively at least. This would be the deciding moment between us. I could just feel it, like the electricity in the air before a storm.

I finally reached his house and was at his doorstep. I took a deep breath, trying to calm the butterflies fluttering around in my stomach. The man had been all over me and in my heart, but I was still nervous. What did he want? I went up and knocked on the door, my heart thumping with the anxiety of it all.

My hands were shaking for some reason. I wondered if Corey was with him. I wondered what all of the urgency was about. I hadn't seen either of them in what felt like ages. There was the sound of footsteps and I sucked in a breath. When Brody opened the door, his bright eyes met mine, and I could immediately see the open vulnerability in his gaze. Without a word, he pulled me right into his tight embrace, and I melted in his warm arms.

"I made some coffee," he said, speaking into my hair. "I'm sorry, I know it's late."

"Coffee sounds good," I told him, squeezing him gently before pulling back.

He nodded, shoving his hands into his loose linen

trousers. He wasn't wearing a shirt, and his tanned torso was ridiculously distracting. His warmth under my hands made my whole body ache for him. I pushed it aside though. This seemed too serious.

I waited at the entrance to the kitchen while he quietly poured two cups of coffee into beach-themed mugs. We moved to the living room and I assumed Corey wasn't around.

The air was heavy with unspoken tension, and I wondered what this was about. Sitting on the couch with our bodies inches apart, I couldn't help but feel the electricity that always seemed to spark between the two of us. I was holding my coffee between my thighs, letting the warmth calm me. I watched as Brody's hand reached out to brush mine, and as our fingers curled together, a surge of heat spread through my whole body.

"Brody," I said quietly, using my other hand to put my coffee on the table, "what's going on?"

He took a drink, sighing. "Heather found us at the beach yesterday. We had a little chat while he played in the sand."

"I'm sure she had a lot to say," I replied bitterly.

"Oh, she made sure to speak her mind," he told me, and I hated how defeated he looked. "She wants to take Corey away from me, like she told you."

"She can't do that," I said, shaking my head, though I felt my stomach sink.

Of all of the terrible situations I had imagined, this hadn't been one to cross my mind. I didn't think Heather would take it this far. Actually, realistically, threatening to take Corey from Brody was disgusting when he tried to do everything he could for his son. He was a wonderful father and was doing his very best.

"I'm putting you in the middle of all of my issues, and you

never asked for this," he said with a sigh. "The last thing I want is to make your life difficult. Especially now."

"I'm happy to help if I can," I told him, squeezing his fingers again. "I can't say that I'm well-versed in dealing with situations like this, but I've dealt with really tough customers. I'm not some fainting damsel."

"You also nearly kneecapped two teenage burglars," he pointed out, grinning sideways at me. "I don't think fainting damsels know how to do that. I would trust you with anything at this point."

I shrugged off the compliment, giving him a small smile. "Well, you know. All in a day's work."

"I still can't believe she would do this," he said, looking sad and years older than he actually was. "I mean, she's been terrible before, but not like this. This is about the lowest she could go."

"I feel like it's partly my fault," I said, clearing my throat. "I mean, Sam came here to see me and met her, right? She hates me, and that's why she wants to take Corey from you."

I had been thinking about it since I met Heather in the first place. Sam found out where I was and wanted to come see me. Heather lived here, somewhere on the island, I assumed. They must have met at some gas station or coffee shop. I imagined him charming her the way he did me, giving her that million-dollar smile. It made me feel bad for her before I realized who I was thinking about. Heather didn't seem to be any better than Sam had been.

"No way," Brody said, shaking his head. "None of this is your fault. She just wants to get back at me because she's jealous. I didn't want to be with her, and she always resented me for that. She thought we would get back together for our son's sake."

"But taking Corey?" I asked. "That's low. Where is he anyway?"

"He went to dinner with my mom. They have a sort of tradition. At least one night a week, they go out and have fish and chips with ice cream on the side."

I wrinkled my nose. "Well, I can't say I'm jealous of their dinner."

He chuckled. "It was what she and my dad ate the night I was born. I think it makes her feel closer to him. She says that Corey reminds her of my dad."

"That's sweet," I let go of his hand and took a sip of my coffee. "Did you tell her about what Heather said? What did she have to say about it?"

"I didn't tell her anything," he said, clearing his throat and looking embarrassed. He sat forward, resting his elbows on his knees. "I didn't want her to have to worry about it."

I was starting to get a feel for Brody and his mom's relationship. He avoided telling her anything too personal or important, and she kept Corey from any of the drama because of it. I assumed his mom was a woman who had been given a hard hit and came back with a few bumps and scars because of it. I couldn't imagine losing a husband.

"We'll figure this out," I told him quietly. "Everything will be okay."

Suddenly, my mind flashed to myself, going back to the hospital, and my heart raced.

"I'll do it, Mr. Perry," I told the man resting in the hospital. "I'll take it off your hands."

"Well, I can't tell you how happy that makes me," he said with a smile. He didn't even need to ask what I was talking about. "I can't imagine better hands to take care of the shop and the horses."

"It might take me a minute to come up with the money—" I began, my words stuttered.

He waved a weak hand. "Oh, you take your time. I know you won't let me down."

Mr. Perry was part of a generation that thought nothing

of a little money between friends. They would trade back and forth without thinking about it. When he was my age, he would have had enough to buy two of his stores. I knew he probably assumed I had some money put aside, and I didn't want to admit that I had pretty much nothing.

"What are you thinking about? Where did you go?" Brody asked me, touching my knee.

"Mr. Perry wants me to buy him out," I said, and I couldn't think of any other way to say it. "He wants me to have the shop, and the horse barn and everything with it."

Brody raised his eyebrows. "He wants to retire?"

I nodded. "I think he's wanted to for a long time. This has been coming for a while."

"Well, what did you say?" he asked me, and I could feel him watching me.

"I told him I would take it off his hands," I said, and my eyes began to burn. I looked at him. "Brody, I don't know why I did it. I don't have that kind of money. I just couldn't stand the thought of losing the place to someone else or having it torn down by developers and the horses sold off."

"Hey, it's okay," Brody told me, sliding closer on the couch. He reached out, pulling me into his arms. "It's going to be okay."

"I'm not trying to make this about me," I said into his shoulder, suddenly realizing I had turned our conversation into a crying session about my problems.

He pulled back to wipe gently under my eyes, where tears were sliding down. I just felt so hopeless. I wanted to help with Heather and Corey, but I couldn't. I wanted to make Mr. Perry proud and take some of his stress away from him, but I didn't know if I could.

"You're important to me, Rosa. I'm glad you trusted me with this," he said gently, his big hand rubbing up and down my back as he watched me.

"Maybe I could sell some of my great-grandma's diamond earrings," I said dully, letting out a breath. They were one of the only things of importance that I owned. "Or maybe my Bronco." My heart wrenched at the thought.

"No, no," he said quickly, pulling me back into his embrace. "We'll figure this out together. We'll figure all of this out, Rosa."

I nodded, letting him hold me tight. It felt nice to have someone to lean on, figuratively and literally. His breath touched my skin. He kissed my neck gently, making me shiver.

"I need you," he whispered, echoing his words from what felt like ages ago, his voice barely audible.

I felt like the two of us were just bobbing in the water, barely holding our heads above the waves. At that moment, I knew what I felt for him was the same as what he felt for me. If I had any doubts about him, the way he touched me was enough to quiet those thoughts quickly. It wasn't the first time he held me, but it was the first time it felt like forever might be in the cards for us. We were two of the same kind. The connection shared between us wasn't something I could deny any longer, and I was willing to do just about whatever it took to be there for both him and little Corey.

What I felt for Brody was an unexplainable and deep connection that went beyond the limits of normal relationships for me, and I had never felt anything like it before. Our souls were closely entwined and held together by an unexplainable power that seemed to go against what I knew about logic and reason.

What was between us went beyond just friendship or romance; it was a cosmic bond that seemed to have been formed deep inside the universe itself. Yeah, maybe my thoughts were colored by how I felt for him, but I wasn't seeing him through rose-colored glasses. I had seen the man in almost every situation, and I still wanted to be with him. I felt comfort every time I looked into his eyes, as if I had known him for a lifetime and not for less than a month.

It felt as if the two of us had been looking for each other across time and space, eventually finding peace of mind in each other's company, despite what the both of us had been through. Our bond was so strong and magnetic, it felt as if we were two sides of the same whole, bound to find each other in this lifetime and every other.

The time we spent together felt like it was filled with an unexplained sense of rhythm and connection. No, we didn't always get along, but it would have been strange if we did. Our wants appeared to easily match up most of the time, and our talks moved with a naturalness that was so different from any other person I had ever been around. If I had met him earlier in life, I wondered if we would be inseparable by now. It was as if we were able to connect without even using words, just touching and understanding each other's deepest desires, fears, and dreams without using anything else. I felt a sense of wholeness and fulfillment when I was around him, even when we were fighting, that I had never felt before. It was as if he held the missing piece to my puzzle, his sheer presence filled the emptiness that lingered in my mind. Our relationship was more than just physical attraction or common interests; it was a deep meeting of minds, hearts, and souls that went beyond the surface parts of human connection.

Our relationship was marked by that intense attraction and overwhelming emotion of awakening from within that I had felt even on that first day when he came from the waves. To me, it seemed like maybe we were twin flames. We lit a fire in each other's souls, igniting a passion and feelings that burned forever brighter than any other flame ever had. It made sense that there were so many issues between us and that we needed to figure them out together. We were supposed to be together, or it felt like it to me. The way he touched me and held me, I knew Brody felt it too. I wanted to think we were going to be unbreakable, but all of the problems in my past made me think twice. I wanted forever, but I would be okay with just today.

Brody was a kindred spirit—the one whose presence gave me peace of mind, understanding, and unrestrained affection. Even when we weren't getting along, I could still feel it from Brody. There was always a look on his face when he was around me that made me believe he wanted to stick around. Our connection to one another reminded me there was an even greater level of connection that existed outside of the hurt that I had seen so far in my life, a bond that was so much more than the limits of what I felt before I met him.

"Brody," I said softly, my voice just a whisper.

Without hesitation, he leaned in, covering my lips with his in a firm, passionate sort of kiss. The touch of his mouth to mine was filled with a mixture of want and tenderness between us. It was as if he was trying to show all of the emotions we had been holding onto for what felt like so long. We had been together before, naked bodies twined like growing branches of a wind-bent oak tree, but this was different. What burned between us was a moment of pure bliss and need, a confirmation of the feelings that had been lingering between the two of us. As we pulled back, our foreheads resting against each other, I could feel the weight of our unspoken words hanging in the air of Brody's living room.

I wanted more, and Brody swept me into his arms, carrying me to his bedroom.

BRODY

*R*osa was warm and pliant in my arms, moaning my name into my ear.

There was a long hallway in my house that led to a familiar, lamp-lit bedroom. She wrapped her hand around mine, squeezing tightly, as we made our way to the end. She pulled in a soft breath as we stopped at the bed, but we moved past it and headed out to the balcony. I wanted to see the look on her face when she saw the amazing view. The house was perfectly set over the water, but it wasn't a good surfing spot. She looked out at the ocean rushing across the white, sandy shore. She let go of my hand and leaned against the chipped, white railing. The never-ending peaks of the cresting waves seemed to stretch forever out into the night, and the fog from the slow rain drifted like ghostly fog over their shifting rise and fall.

Rosa was heartbreakingly beautiful, all pink cheeks and soft skin, and I couldn't keep my eyes off of her, despite the view that spread out before us.

"You grew up here, right? It's so beautiful," she said to me quietly. "I can't even imagine. Where I lived in Daytona, the house was in the middle of the suburbs. After I moved here, I was happy to be closer to the ocean."

I ran a hand over the long, dark braid down her back, and she shivered under my touch. Her hair gleamed in the moonlight, and the surf shop t-shirt she was wearing caught in the wind, making her curvy, attractive form very obvious.

"I didn't grow up in this house, but yeah," I told her, and when I moved my body to stand behind her, pushing her petite body into mine, she didn't try to protest. Her curves felt amazing as she pressed back against me. "The beach isn't always this beautiful."

She appeared hesitate for a moment, but turned slowly into my arms, warm against me. Her thin hands pressed against my skin, easy on my chest. My whole body was aching to pull her in even closer.

"Well, it's like they say, beauty is subjective," she said to me, and I could hear the smile in her voice.

"No, that's not true, at least not for me," I told her, tipping her face up with my fingers under her chin. Her mouth met mine. Her breath was soft over my lips. "I think I know something beautiful when I see it."

I leaned in further, turning her completely to push our mouths together in a slow, sound kiss. Rosa melted into me like the summer rain falling over the shore that slanted across the darkening horizon.

She ran the tip of her tongue over my bottom lip, and I gripped her round hips, digging my fingers into her skin. The low, sweet sound that fell from her mouth was covered completely by the kiss, but I could feel the murmur of it in my bones all the same.

Her slender, nimble fingers dipped down, catching on the waistband of my trousers, and then there was just a hint of a whispering touch over the front of my tight briefs. That was enough to light me up from the inside out. It felt like there was always a tension between us, an unspoken bond just waiting to find its way to the surface level of our relationship.

I could feel her round, soft breasts pushing against my chest, her nipples hard and tempting as the rain soaked our skin in the cooling night air. She brushed against me, and I was aching for her.

I slipped my hands under her thin t-shirt and she moaned in that soft, pretty voice, burying her face in my neck. Her mouth touched my skin in an open-mouthed kiss as I pulled her closer, and I held back a moan of my own. I could feel her fingers trembling against me, and it was an act of strength not to have her right there on the balcony.

"Brody," she said, her voice unsure. "Thank you for asking me to come by."

If something was bothering me, Rosa was the first person I thought of calling for support or advice. Now that she was in my life, I wanted to keep her there. I was always there to listen and hear her perspective, and I knew I could trust her to provide a comforting presence, and I wanted to do the same for her.

She had a way of making me feel peaceful and validated, and her easy care and empathy made her the perfect person to turn to in times when I felt I couldn't take the world around me. I wanted to have her that way forever. She was going to become my go-to person for help and encouragement, whether it was a personal problem, a professional issue, or just a terrible day, I could feel it.

"I trust you, Rosa. I know I haven't really been around, but I figured you wanted some space. You seemed okay about Mr. Perry, but I just wasn't sure," I told her, brushing a hand under her chin.

"I've never really known a man like you, not like this," she said, her cheeks going red. "I've never had someone like you."

"Neither have I."

She was the first woman to ever have a real connection with myself and my son, other than his mother and our elderly neighbor. She was everything I needed and so much more. A primal sort of desire for her rose up in me. I wanted her today, tomorrow, and every day after that. The notion of *her* being mine and of making her my girlfriend and then my wife pressed at the forefront of my mind. Yeah, I had fallen hard for her. I didn't want another man to ever touch her again. I wanted to be her one and only, for a lifetime. I could see it very clearly.

"Rosa, tell me what you want," I told her, dipping down to mouth at her soft, pretty neck until she moaned under my touch. "Tell me."

She pushed her breasts against my chest, looking up at me with lust-dark eyes. The sound she made was like every wet dream I'd ever had pushed into one, real-life beautiful woman. I almost couldn't believe that I was getting her all to myself once again.

"I want to be with you," she told me at the end of a sharp pull of air. "I need this. I need you, Brody. Please."

For a moment, I forgot that the two of us were standing at the edge of the balcony, on the edge of the ocean and the impending storm. It almost felt like we were standing on the edge of forever together. The slant of a sharp rain moved its way across the waves, drenching us.

She grabbed my hand, and we turned back, heading into the house before we turned into rain ourselves. Her fingers intertwined with mine, burning against my skin where we touched. My bed was soft and warm, full and overflowing, with throw pillows on the thin quilt. Heather left them behind, and I had grown to like the annoying, embroidered things.

"Pillows," Rosa said, looking perplexed.

"Some men have pillows," I told her, grinning. The rain thundered over the roof. "But not all men have Rosa Rivers on their pillows."

"You're a lucky man," she said, taking off her shoes.

"Oh, I knew that already."

A soft sound came from her mouth, and she crawled over into my lap, digging her fingers into my hair and tangling it in her grip. I moved her hips up and pushed down gently, grinding our bodies together.

She was obviously a little jittery, trembling against my touch, but this wasn't our first time. She was like a flower in the sunshine, blooming and slowly opening above me. She was the most beautiful woman I had ever seen. I pulled her t-shirt over her dark hair to reveal the soft, creamy warmth of her skin.

Her supple breasts bounced as she let her thin, lacey bra fall away onto the bed. Her pretty, round eyes were like the warmth of a summer day, burning bright in the darkest storm. She was holding herself there like she wanted me to touch her even more than I already was. I looked up at her and she was looking at me, bare and gorgeous, warm in my lap.

There was a heat, a burning behind her eyes. And it was just for me. She wrapped her hand into my hair again, and I couldn't help but grin as she pulled me in to suck on her hard nipples. I slid a hand up her thigh, squeezing gently, and I could feel myself growing hard under her, hard enough to hurt, I wanted her so bad.

"If we're doing this again," she began, sounding unsure, "we need to be clear about what this is between us. I don't mind some casual fun, but this doesn't feel like that to me. Does it to you?"

I hated that hesitancy in her voice. "I feel the same way you do. Stop doubting this, Rosa."

"You're always so sure of everything," she whispered, touching her forehead to mine. "I wish I could be that way sometimes."

"I just put on a good show of confidence," I said with a sigh. I ran my fingers over her cheek, brushing a thumb across her plump lower lip. "But I know what I feel when I look at you. This isn't temporary for me."

"It feels like forever to me," she answered, and then blushed as if she had just blurted out something that she never meant to actually say. "I didn't mean that in the way that it sounded. I know that sounds crazy—"

It was such a relief to hear her say the words out loud. She wanted this just as badly as I did, and she wanted it for as long as she could have it, just like I did.

I couldn't help but feel giddy at her admission. It was nice to know I wasn't crazy for thinking I could have her. Something had been building between Rosa and me for what felt like ages. The hot, burning tension between us was entirely palpable, and it was simmering just beneath the surface of our conversations, waiting for the perfect moment to burst into flame and take us with it.

The two of us had so much going on, but it was still the most important thing at this moment to have her in my arms. It seemed to me the universe was whispering constantly to bring us together, weaving a tunnel of web-like desire that neither of us ever wanted to try and resist.

It was like the elephant in the room, though. Because of Heather and Sam, I knew we both knew that giving in to our desires was always going to be a dangerous game to play. As much as I didn't want to base my life around either one of them, it was important to try and keep the peace for Corey's sake.

We had both been down the path of relationships and romance before, and what remained after the fallout had left us both emotionally abused and bruised. Despite that, the pull between us was undeniable. It was obvious it was only a matter of time before the dam burst between us once again, and we found ourselves wrapped up in each other's arms.

The anticipation was becoming a familiar feeling. It was both exhilarating and terrifying. The two of us moved each other, forever testing the bounds of our self-control, but the feelings between us were too bright and undeniable to ignore. Every encounter, every stolen moment, good or bad, only seemed to throw fuel on the fire that was smoldering within us. Rosa and I were walking a tightrope of romance and dread, teetering right on the edge. We both knew one wrong move in this game could send us falling and spinning into a world of bright passion. The night had turned into that breaking point, and it had been hard to even look at Rosa without wanting to lay her down.

Once the tension between us had reached its breaking point, and all of our other thoughts were pushed aside, it was inevitable. It was hard not to surrender to the overwhelming pull that had been growing between us in a storm of need and longing, like the storm that swirled outside.

Technically, we had met in a storm, when the waves tried to take me under. She was there waiting like a beacon in the night, the lighthouse in the dark.

The world went away as we lost ourselves in one other. I couldn't wait for the moment when our bodies would be moving in perfect harmony, our hearts thumping together in sync.

"It didn't sound so crazy to me," I told her evenly, curling the same hand over her cheek and then moving it down to cup her breast. "It sounded like you were reading my mind." I slid my tongue across her nipple, making her shiver.

"That's nice to hear," she whispered, but I could tell she wasn't really paying attention anymore. "Brody."

I knew I would never get tired of hearing my name on her lips.

"Rosa," I answered, kissing her cheek and moving to the crest of her ear.

She reached down, plucking at my trousers, until she slid her hand under the waist band and squeezed, making me gasp. Rain thundered over the clear, balcony door, and the storm watched our frantic movements. I reached over and pulled her into me, pushing our tongues together. She made a soft little sound of want, pressing her body against mine, and it was hard to let go of her. I had to though, so that we could be even closer.

"Let's get these off," I said, my voice breaking.

We slipped out of the rest of our clothes, and she was naked under me, pushing her hips into me. I wrapped my hands around her waist as her mouth pushed into mine.

"Please," she whispered, and I was so hard, aching with want for her so much more than before.

"I have somewhere I need to be," I told her in a hoarse whisper, smiling a little. She looked confused until I moved down her body, kissing as I went.

"Oh," she said breathlessly. "I want you *in* me," she murmured, but I could tell she didn't mean to say it out loud. Her cheeks went pink. She leaned away from me, her eyes squeezed shut, "Please pretend I didn't just say that."

"Rosa," I said as I kissed my way down her belly. "I would spend all night and all damn day in this bed with you if I could. Don't take anything back. Don't regret anything."

She swallowed, and her face went soft and slack with want. A sweet little breath left her mouth, and she nodded, digging her fingers into my hair and holding me down to her.

"Brody, please," she begged, her voice strained.

I couldn't help it as I leaned over to her, licking into her as the thunder crashed outside and the windows rattled with it. She tipped her head back, and I slipped my hand up her thigh, squeezing the soft skin, and then moving down to dip my fingers inside her wet warmth.

She was throbbing gently against my hand, opening her legs to me as I moved my tongue expertly. I wanted so badly to pull up and bury myself inside of her, but I wanted her to feel good. I wanted her to think about me in the dark when her body was aching for the warmth of my mouth.

I licked and flicked my tongue as I curled my fingers inside of her, and she seemed to choke on the gasp that left her mouth. Rosa was panting under my touch, and she squeezed her eyes shut, crying out as she felt her release fully. I curled my fingers again and she was shaking, trembling.

"I want you in me," she said again in a breathless voice, and this time she didn't seem embarrassed. She was sure of herself.

I nodded, coming back up to kiss her. I held my length, and she reached out, stroking a few times with that soft, smooth hand. She looked up at me, her eyes dark and hot.

"Let me do it," she murmured, and we both watched as she angled my shaft, setting it perfectly to slip inside of her. "Brody," she said, pushing closer.

I slid into her, filling her up and entwining our bodies, and we both gasped in relief.

"Brody—" she began, digging her fingers into my shoulders.

The doorbell rang out, violently bright and annoying in the darkness.

ROSA

"*I*'m *sorry*, Rosa, okay? I didn't know my mom was going to bring him back so late," Brody's voice said, pleading. "I just assumed he would spend the night there."

I was holding the smooth surfboard in my hand, squeezing the wood under my fingers. I had been so annoyed the night before, but I knew it really wasn't fair to Brody.

"Yeah, I get it," I said with a shrug. "Her power went out because of the storm."

He nodded, and I could feel him still staring at me. I just wanted to start my lesson.

"Do you want to talk about it?" he asked me, his voice sincere. "We don't have to keep things from each other. You can tell me if something is bothering you."

I looked at him, trying to be subjective. The sun was bright and golden, lighting him up where he stood in the sand. The storm the night before had torn up the beach, making fewer tourists want to come and frolic in the dirtied ocean water. It was better for us. As we got closer to the weekend and the surf competition, I knew the beach would be full.

"Can we just do this?" I asked him, nodding at the surf shop on the hill. "I need to get back to work. I don't want to leave Mr. Perry alone for too long."

I planned on using the beach showers and getting back to work right away. I felt a little dumb for being embarrassed that we *almost* had sex again, but I was trying to let it go. The connection between us was strong, and I felt heady just being near him.

"Yeah, we can do that," he said, letting out a sigh.

"Look, I'm sorry. I really do understand, and I'm not trying to make things difficult for you," I said, giving him a small smile.

Some of my resentment was melting away, and I felt better about the whole thing. We would have plenty of time to make up for that night, I could just feel it. I had hope for us.

He wrapped an arm around my shoulders, kissing my temple. "Let's hit the water."

There was crunching in the sand behind us. I turned quickly to find Heather stomping across the beach, her hair perfectly pulled into a slick ponytail and her clothes tight on her curvy body.

"Well, how cute," she said, giving me a grin that had way too many teeth. "Look at you two."

"What do you want, Heather?" I couldn't help but blurt out.

I was tired of her butting in when she wasn't welcome. She was like a fly at my ear, continuing to buzz and aggravate me.

"Oh, you think you can just talk to me however you want, huh?" she asked, spitting the words at me.

Brody's arm dropped, and I felt cold.

"Is Corey in the car?" he asked her, sounding tense. "By himself?"

"No, he's not by himself," she snapped. "He's with Sam. They get along really well. He's a good dad."

"A good dad," Brody repeated, stepping forward. "You're ridiculous, Heather. Just go get back in the car and have a good day with my son."

"See you," I said, turning towards the water.

"We're busy," Brody said, agreeing with me.

"Busy, huh?" she asked, grinning. "Kinda like how we were busy the other night?"

I felt my stomach sink. I felt nausea fall over me like a wave.

"What is she talking about?" I asked him, trying to keep my voice even.

Brody shook his head. "She's full of it. Don't listen to her."

The salty wind blew my hair into my face. I felt like the world was spinning out of control. I knew exactly what she was implying, and I felt sick.

"You're lying," I said, my voice shaking. "I know you're lying."

Heather grinned. "I saw you slip out the back, sweetheart. After that, he slipped in my front."

"Heather," Brody warned, his voice a low growl.

I couldn't find it in me to believe it. The revelation of the betrayal hit me like a ton of bricks, leaving me reeling with a strong combination of heartbreak, anger, and distrust. I felt so twisted up inside. The person I trusted with my deepest emotions and past issues with men had possibly hurt me in the worst way.

The ground beneath my feet seemed to shift, and the once-stable foundation of our relationship had begun to crumble away before my eyes. How could he have done that to me? It didn't make any sense. Maybe it really was a trick set up by Heather. But no, how would she know I slipped out the back when Brody's mom brought Corey by when her power went out? She wouldn't know unless she was there.

"Brody, what is this?" I asked him, my whole body trembling as I stepped back from him.

"Look, it's not what you think," he held his hands up in surrender.

As the shock began to settle in, a mix of horrible emotions threatened to consume me. It was such a sharp turnaround from how I thought about him. I was getting flashbacks of Sam and how he had hurt me so badly. I should have known his best friend would be just like him. Birds of a feather and all that. Maybe I was naive for trusting him, or maybe I was jumping to conclusions. I wondered if my previous experiences with men were clouding my view and my opinion.

Questions came flooding into my mind, and each one was even more painful than the last. Had he been seeing the mother of his child all along? How long had whatever it was between them been going on? Was it just a one-time thing with them or some sort of pattern of infidelity that could never be broken? I didn't care to try and figure it out. I didn't want to be with a man like that. Did he ever truly care for me, or was I just a placeholder to keep on the roster until someone who had more history with him came along?

I stood on the bright beach, but it was almost as if the entire world around me seemed to lose all of its vibrant color, as if the trust and happiness had been drained away and all that remained was a feeling of hopelessness. The once-familiar moments, sights, and sounds became distant and warped to me, like I was trapped in a dull, continuous nightmare that I couldn't escape. My mind was racing. I was trying to make sense of the situation, but the pieces of the puzzle just wouldn't fit together right.

"We've always had a connection," Heather said, smug. I could barely hear her over the whooshing sound that roared through my ears.

Brody was calling my name, but I didn't want to look at him. The hurt of his lack of loyalty cut me deeply, leaving an unfading mark on my heart. It felt like a sharp knife had been plunged right into the tenderness of my chest, ripping apart the closely woven emotions of our relationship and leaving me floundering and gasping for air.

The heavy, pressing weight of the betrayal pushed down on me, choking me and making it difficult to breathe, to think, to function without that painful thought in my head. In the middle of the turmoil, I really couldn't help but question my own worth. Any woman would have, especially if she had been through what I had been through. What was it about her that was better? Was I really not enough for Brody, even after all we had dealt with together? Was it that I failed to meet his expectations in a partner?

It was maddening that we had been just about to have a wonderful day, and Heather took it away with only a few words. She was good at that. The weight of the self-doubt gnawed at my soul, eroding my confidence and leaving me feeling less than when compared to Brody's ex.

I wondered if I had missed any hints, any little quirks that could have warned me about him. I hated that I had to doubt I knew him at all. Maybe it had all been a lie. The uncertainty and self-blame only added to the overwhelming sense of despair.

Despite my pain and confusion, a spark of rage ignited within my mind, making my head throb. How could he break my faith so blatantly? How could he disregard what we shared for a quick night with Heather? The anger sparked a fire within me, a desire to restore my sense of self-worth and find the strength to move ahead without him, if it came to that. With Brody, it was a series of very high highs and very low lows. As the world swirled around me, I realized that healing would take time, and, though I thought I was over what happened with Sam, this brought the pain to the surface. Deep down, maybe I really was hoping Heather was just lying to cause trouble between us.

"You don't believe me?" she asked, raising a perfectly shaped eyebrow. "It wasn't his mother at the door. It was me. Are you that naive?"

I stared at her for a moment, and I couldn't think of one damn thing to say. Was I that naive? It was feeling more and more like the answer was yes.

"Brody, tell me she's lying," I said, finally glancing over at him. My stomach sank. I saw it on his face.

"It was Heather at the door," he admitted carefully, watching me like I might bolt.

I felt like I might vomit into the sand at my feet, but I didn't want Heather to see me so vulnerable. My heart felt like it was cracking in two inside of my chest. I hoped my pain didn't show on my face, but I could feel my cheek ticking from the restraint it took to hold back my tears. I felt like such an idiot. I had been so happy, and he was going behind my back the whole time.

"Well, I hope you two are happy," I told them, spinning quickly on my heel and tossing the surfboard down into the sand.

"Wait, Rosa!" Brody called, and I could hear him running after me, sounding frantic. "Where are you going?"

"Yeah, run off with your tail between your legs!" Heather called after me.

"I'm going to the shop," I said, ignoring Heather's jab and hoping she didn't hear the crack in my voice. "I have work."

In the parking lot, I could see Sam sitting in the front seat of Heather's car, staring at us. I tried to ignore him. He was on his phone and I was sure he was talking to another woman, stepping out on Heather like he had probably done to all the women he dated. A darker, pained part of me whispered that maybe I just attracted the kind of man who did things like that. Maybe it was a *me* problem.

"I didn't sleep with Heather," Brody called after me, and I could hear her laughing as she headed back to her car. She was thriving in the chaos she had created between us.

"I don't care," I said over my shoulder, trying to ignore him and also trying to sever whatever connection remained between us. A clean break.

"You do care, Rosa. Don't do that," he said, and I felt an irrational anger at that.

"Don't do *what*?" I snapped, rounding on him and staring up into those glittering blue eyes. "You don't get to tell me what to do."

He stared at me. "Look, I know this all looks bad."

"No, I understand completely," I said, digging my fingers into my palms. "You guys have more in common. You have Corey, too. You should be with someone like her. I'm not the woman for you."

Every insecurity I had about being with a man with an established one-time family came rising to the surface. Some part of me would have always wondered if the two of them would reconnect. That always seemed to happen with parents. They found their way back to each other by the end of it all.

"Rosa," he said, but I acted like I didn't hear him.

Heather's car rolled out of the parking lot and, she honked when they left. Brody wrapped his fingers around my shoulders. I flinched back from him. I wondered if Heather liked how long his fingers were or how soft his touch was. I wondered if he touched her the way he did me. Was it the exact same? I felt so damn sick.

"I'm not her," I told him, gritting my teeth.

"What?" he asked me, pulling back. "I don't want you to be her. What are you talking about?"

"I told you what happened with Sam, and I should have known that because he was your best friend once upon a time, you would be just like him," I said, letting out a shaking breath. "I should have known."

"There is *nothing* going on with us, Rosa," he said, stepping in front of me when I moved so that I couldn't leave. Above us, the lone oak tree's branches swayed in the cool wind. "You have to believe me here."

"No, I don't have to," I said with a shrug. "Tell me this. If you didn't sleep with her, what was she doing there, and why exactly did you lie?"

"I was wrong to lie," he said, pleading with me. "I'm sorry about that. The only reason I did, was because I thought you might get upset."

"That's a stupid reason," I told him, still feeling ridiculous. "I'm upset right now. I'm not some delicate flower that you have to keep from snapping in half. Why was she there?"

"Okay," he said, seeming to let out a relieved breath, "my mom's power really did go out."

"What does that have to do with your ex-girlfriend?" I asked, getting impatient. "I mean really, Brody. Do you expect me to just blindly believe anything you say?"

"No, but I need you to trust me."

"Trust is earned," I snapped, rolling my eyes. "You actually devolved as a human in my mind."

"Rosa, I didn't sleep with her," his gaze was intense.

I felt weak. "Okay then. So what happened?"

I didn't know why I was asking him anything. I just wanted for this to be a bad dream. I wanted him to be the man I trusted again. I wanted to be able to take what he said to heart, but I was sure I wasn't able to anymore. That seed of doubt had already been planted, and the roots were spreading like wildfire through my mind.

He let out a sigh. "My mom's power did go out, okay? I told you I wasn't lying about that. But she took Corey to Heather's house instead of mine. Heather brought him over because it wasn't her time to have him."

"And so what then? She stayed over after that?"

"No, she didn't stay over. She just left, and nothing else happened."

"She saw me leave," I said, my teeth gritted. "She knew everything about that night, and I was in the dark. I wasn't important enough for you to tell me the truth."

I realized that whether I believed Heather just left his house or not, that wasn't what I was really upset about. It was like Brody had treated me like an outsider, or just someone he wanted to fall into bed with, and he was willing to say or do anything.

I wanted to be more important to him than that. Heather was the one who knew everything. He had gone to the front of the house, seen her, and rushed me out of the back like a dirty little secret. The thought of it made me feel sick. I thought it was okay to sneak out of the back door when it was his mom; of course neither one of us wanted to explain to her why I was there in the dead of night. Heather was a different story. I thought he would have been strong enough to ask me to stay, to have me by his side. Though, really, it made sense, didn't it? Pushing me out to let Heather in?

"It wasn't like that, Rosa. I just knew that Heather would try and start something if she saw you, and I knew you would think badly of me if Heather was there at night."

"So, you thought you would just trick me then?" I said, my hurt leaking into my voice. "You know, I really thought better of you, Brody. I really did. I thought you were different."

"I didn't sleep with her!" he said, his voice rising in a panicked sort of way.

"I don't care!" I said in the same pitch. My eyes were burning. I heard the tiny, high-pitched squeak of the curtains in the shop, and I knew Mr. Perry was watching from inside. "I don't care, Brody. You thought I wouldn't ever find out, and you didn't care."

"I didn't think it was that big of a deal, and I didn't do anything bad," he said, his voice going quiet. "I'm sorry. I really am."

"You can go be sorry somewhere else," I said, looking away.

I saw his expression crumble. "Rosa, please don't do this. Don't let Heather come between us. This is exactly what she wanted. Don't let her do this to us. Not now."

"You did this to us," I told him, shaking my head. "It wasn't Heather."

I didn't actually know if it was true or not, but it felt like what came out of my mouth was the right thing to say. I couldn't be worried about this right now. I had too much on my mind with buying the shop and the horses.

"Rosa, just think about this, okay?" he said, raising his hands. "Don't do this."

"You need to leave," I told him, my voice dull and flat.

All I could think about was the pain of his breach of trust. I had lost faith in him, and I didn't know if I wanted to trust him, or anyone, again. If he was capable of lying so easily about something so mundane, what else was he capable of lying about? I felt so damn sick.

"Rosa—" he began, stepping forward.

The door to the surf shop creaked open.

"Get on home, son," Mr. Perry said gently but firmly, shuffling out. "Go on now."

Brody looked back and forth between us, and I stepped

back to my elderly boss's side, solidifying my stance in the conversation. Brody's expression went slack and dull.

"Right then," he said, looking away and shoving his hands into his pockets. "I'll see you around."

I stood there on the welcome mat, watching the oak tree shift overhead. My eyes were burning, and my whole body was trembling. There was a painful lump in my throat.

"Rosa, what happened?" Mr. Perry asked me, but I didn't know if I could speak. "What did he do?"

"He—" I started, my voice choking in my throat. I watched Brody get in his vehicle and leave, disappearing down the curvy road, and I felt myself break.

"What is it?" my sweet old boss asked, meaning well.

Mr. Perry helped me inside, letting me sit down in the back room on one of the chairs. The sun was warm on my face through the window, and I closed my eyes for a minute. I thought about Brody and how our souls felt connected. I could almost see the string that stretched between us fraying as he drove away. I could feel the pain in my chest like it was tangible. I put so much faith in one person, and that would always be my downfall.

I opened my eyes and looked at Mr. Perry. "He's gone. It's over."

20

BRODY

$\mathcal{I}$ sat at the dimly lit bar, tapping my fingers against my bottle. The place was cool in the early morning, but I knew it would be stuffy and smelling of beer and stale peanuts by mid-afternoon. I had only been there once before, but once was enough.

The door opened behind me, swinging shut with a sharp scrape across the floor.

"A little early for a nightcap, buddy," a familiar voice said.

"Sam," I responded, nodding. I tapped my bottle. "It's a root beer."

He chuckled. "I think I'll have the real stuff. Dan?"

The hefty, tattooed bartender nodded, swiping the bottle of good whiskey off the top shelf. Sam sat heavily beside me, shifting and nearly melting down into his uncomfortable bar seat as if he were in his recliner at home. It was obvious he spent a lot of time here. I tipped my bottle up, trying to keep myself calm and even.

"Thanks," Sam nodded when Dan slid over two fingers of whiskey. He looked at me and drained the whole thing in one go. "Good for the soul."

"But not for the liver," I finished, unable to stop my small smile.

The mantra had lasted us through two years of community college, gluing us together amid beer and women and way too much bravado. He had been my constant companion, the two of us coming as a package deal on most days. When he moved to Daytona, we slowly lost touch. I had a pregnant Heather in my life, and he had the women who followed him around like he was the pied piper. Then he had Rosa, and I never, not in a million years, thought that woman would become so damn important to me.

I cleared my throat. "You never let me meet Rosa."

"What?" his eyes narrowed. "Is that why you called me here? You want to talk about her?"

"I don't want us to be on bad terms," I said, letting out a breath. "We were close once, weren't we?"

The fan clicked on overhead, and the breeze ruffled my hair into my face. I heard Sam shifting in his seat. When I finally looked over, he was watching me with curious intent.

He tilted his glass at me. "What do you want to know about Rosa?"

It surprised me. I expected some sort of argument, or maybe even him taking a swing at me. I was starting to think Heather was the one who was orchestrating most of the discord between all of us. With her track record, it made the most sense.

"Why didn't I ever meet her?" I asked him, resting my elbows on the bar. "I mean, you knew about Heather, and I knew you had a girlfriend, but I didn't ever meet her."

He shrugged. "I don't know, man. We weren't even serious. She blew the whole thing out of proportion. She's crazy."

And there it was. I tried to stay calm, but my blood was all but boiling in my veins.

"Didn't you live together?" I said, keeping my voice normal with herculean effort. "That seems pretty serious to me, *man*."

"She's putting all kinds of ideas in your head," he said, waving a hand. "I tried the girlfriend thing with her, and it didn't work out."

"You're not pissed like you were before," I pointed out. "You accused Rosa of seeing me behind your back."

I saw something dark flash across his face. "I don't care anymore. I have Heather. I figure we're even now, don't you think?"

"This isn't some stupid game, Sam," I said, my cheeks burning with barely restrained anger. "We're grown now. I have a kid. You can't mess around with people like this."

His bottle clanked against the bar. I saw the bartender look up, his eyes narrowed.

"You got a lot of nerve calling me here and then accusing me," my old friend snapped, giving me a dark chuckle. "You always got everything you wanted, didn't you? Grades? Girls? I mean, hell, even when your dad died, you got my dad, didn't you?"

"Sam—" I felt a lump in my throat. "Your parents were divorced. It wasn't like my mom broke up their marriage. C'mon, man, that's ancient history now."

"You and Heather are ancient history," he replied, turning to me. "She's mine now."

Talking to Sam felt like whirling in circles, unsure of where I might land. My previous friend had always been quick to anger and drinking, made him even more volatile.

"I don't care that you're dating Heather," I said patiently, struggling to keep my composure. "I don't give a damn about Heather beyond what relationship Corey has with her. I do need you to tell her to take a step back, though. She's causing trouble."

"She's not the one causing trouble," he said, giving me a careless shrug.

"What are you talking about?" I asked, watching the bartender watch us. I gave him a slight, nearly unseen nod, and he let his shoulders drop, turning around. "Look. I don't know what Heather has been telling you, but she's making my life a living hell."

Sam's chair scraped across the linoleum floor as he jumped up from his seat. I flinched back in surprise. He always worked himself up for no good reason, but it had never been directed at me until recently. I remembered holding him back at smoky bars when the midnight hours rolled around and he decided he wanted to throw some punches. I never once thought those punches might be thrown in my direction. He had that rowdy gleam in his eye, as if he were just looking for a reason.

"Sam, he's my son and she's trying to take him from me," I said, putting my bottle down. "Do you think that's right?"

"From where I'm standing, she's not the one twisting up his life," he said, swiping his hand over his face. "After years of being friends, I never thought you were like that."

"What?" I asked, completely confused. "You don't know what you're talking about."

"I know I'm going to step up once you're out of the picture," he said, giving me a wide, malicious grin. He threw his hands out wide, stretching his stained green t-shirt. "I'm going to take care of Heather too, like you never did."

"Heather? You were coming after me about Rosa the other day. Make up your damn mind," I said, and I regretted the words as soon as they were out of my mouth.

I looked down deep and realized I really didn't care anymore. For years, I had brushed off Sam's bad attitude, mostly because it was always directed at other people. I pretended I didn't see the way he treated those around him, and now it had come back to bite me in the ass. I didn't care about pushing down what I really thought any longer. Sam always thought he could say whatever he wanted, no matter the situation.

"I don't give a damn about Rosa," he said, spitting her name like it was a bad taste in his mouth. "You can have whatever leftovers of mine you want. Everyone always liked you better, and you had the perfect family, but you screwed it all up."

"I didn't screw anything up," I told him, my voice low and dangerous. "Stop this before we both say something we don't mean."

"I mean every damn word that comes out of my mouth," he said, punctuating the words by jabbing his finger in my face. He must have had a few drinks before I got there because his voice was beginning to slur. He gave me a slick grin. "You know what? I'm Corey's dad now."

I saw a haze of red cloud my vision. Apparently, that was my breaking point. That was the shove that pushed me right over the edge. Anger pulsed through my body, and I shoved myself from my seat, knocking my barstool to the floor. Sam gave a laugh before it was choked by my body slamming into his. I knocked him to the floor and landed a punch. Blood sprayed from his nose as my fist smacked into his face.

"Hey, whoa, no!" I heard Dan say as he tried to come around the counter. "Get that shit outta' my bar!"

I ignored him, and so did Sam. He was excited now, and I heard a wild laugh come from him as we twisted and fell into a table, our bodies rolling across the floor.

Sam had been in jail many times, more frequently during our college years, and he just seemed to have a knack for getting himself into fights over nothing at all. He was volatile and used to getting his way, especially when it came to women. It was why he was so brazen about cheating. Maybe

I never realized before, or maybe I realized and wrote it off because he was my friend.

BUT SAM never shied away from an argument, whether it was at a party or on the streets. It was almost as if he lived on the adrenaline rush that came with each clash. His reputation as a troublemaker followed him wherever he went, and I usually had to be the peacemaker. People would mutter about his confrontational attitude and his knack for finding himself in the middle of trouble. It was both fascinating and disturbing to see the speed with which he could turn an apparently calm situation into a violent conflict.

DESPITE HIS RIDICULOUSLY NORMAL run-ins with law enforcement, my once-best friend never seemed to learn his lesson from his mistakes. The man always wore his arrests like little badges of pride, telling everyone about the way he was able to hold his own in a real fight. It wasn't really something to brag about if you were a well-adjusted human being, but he obviously wasn't. It was like he thought that physical fights were the only way to assert his dominance and gain respect from other people, especially other men.

HIS DAD WAS a hard guy to be around, and Sam gained an amount of emotional damage from him. He was stunted and constantly trying to prove himself to his dad. Maybe that was why I tried so hard to excuse his issues. But I wasn't that young, naive kid anymore. I couldn't deal. Maybe this whole thing really was my fault. Maybe I was looking for a fight too and some way to work out the emotions tumbling around in my head.

. . .

As a close friend, I was often split between pride for his bravery and worry for his well-being. There was also a small amount of anger at him, though now there was more. I couldn't help but wonder what drew him to these violent interactions. Was it a deep-seated resentment or a desire to prove himself? Or maybe it was just a method for him to get away from the dull reality of everyday life.

I couldn't help but be thankful I had a good dad and a mom who always tried. If my dad had been alive when my son was born, he would have been a great role model. Sam's dad always seemed to like me, favoring me over his own son at times. But he was never a man I looked up to. My stomach flipped, and more hot anger filled me when I thought of Jack Wesson having an influence on my son. No, I couldn't let that happen.

I should have seen it sooner and left Sam in the dust. Instead, we just drifted apart over the years. Maybe I was a coward for not confronting him about his behavior. There was a fragile and tortured soul underneath his strong demeanor and propensity for violence. I discovered his passion for fighting was only a coping technique for him, a method for him to hide his fears and disappointments. I thought that once we graduated from college and went our own ways, Sam would find healthier outlets for his feelings, but it seemed I was wrong. I was done making excuses for him. I hoped he'd find a sense of purpose that didn't involve violence or breaking the law, but instead, I was only adding to the fight.

"I knew you wanted to beat my ass," he said, spitting a laugh through his split lip.

He rolled us over and landed a punch to my jaw, rattling my teeth and making me bite my tongue.

"He's my son," I bit out, shoving him. "You're an ass, and Rosa is better off."

He just laughed, and it pissed me off even more. I was on him again, smacking a blow to his ribs, and he coughed raggedly. I felt hands pulling at me from behind, and I shrugged them off. Nails dug into my shoulders and yanked at my t-shirt.

"Brody! What in the world are you doing?" I heard a familiar voice shriek, and I slowed my assault. Even Sam looked up, his eyebrows raised in shock and a little guilt.

"Mom?" I said, pushing away from my former best friend. "What the hell are you doing here?"

"Language," she said sharply. "Your son can hear every word."

My mother was standing there, her mouth pinched in disappointment and her thin face pale. Corey was holding her hand, watching me with wide eyes.

"Why did you bring him to a bar?" I asked her, feeling embarrassed at my son seeing me on the floor.

I got up, straightening my clothes, my face was aching something fierce.

"Heather told me where to find you," she said, her voice tense. "She said you were getting a late breakfast here."

"A late breakfast?" Sam asked, coughing a laugh. "Yeah, something like that."

"I told you she's a liar," I grunted as Sam spat blood from his busted mouth.

"Why don't we go back outside?" my mother said, smoothing her dark hair back over her shoulder and blatantly ignoring me to look at Corey. "I think there's a nest out there in one of the trees you might like. Do you want to see some baby birds?"

Corey was staring at me though, paying his grandmother no mind at all. He looked over to Sam then, and I could see that his eyes were glistening with unshed tears.

"Uncle Sam?" he asked quietly. "Why are you bleeding?"

My mom saved us, coming to the rescue and taking Corey out into the parking lot. Just for spite, I gave Sam another shove before running out behind them, and he tumbled into a table. Behind the counter, I caught sight of Dan calling someone, most likely the cops. Being arrested was the last thing I needed, especially with Rosa's dismissal hanging over my head like a leaden weight and my son seeing me all beat up in a stinky bar.

"Mom!" I said, tripping out into the sunlight and covering my eyes.

The smell of the ocean hit me, and I felt instantly calmer in the briny wind. My mom stood at the curb with Corey's hand in hers. She looked back at me and sighed.

"You're not this man, Brody," she said, and disappointment radiated off of her in waves. "Your father would have been ashamed to see you that way— and Corey."

"Are you okay, Dad?" Corey asked, turning to look at me with big, bright eyes.

"I'm okay, buddy, it was just a little disagreement, that's all," I said, trying to give him a smile and failing when pain radiated through my face. "What are you guys doing here?"

My mother sighed. "Corey left his blanket in the jeep. He wanted it to sit on the beach for a picnic. Do you have it?"

I nodded slowly. "Corey, buddy, why don't we go put you in Grandma's car? I'll bring your blanket to you after me and Grandma have a chat."

Corey nodded, and I kissed the top of his head, thankful

he didn't see even more. We put him in the car, and he settled in, picking up one of his books from the seat.

My mother was waiting for me at the back of the car, leaning her hip against the tail light with her arms crossed. She didn't look up at me as I approached. My face was pounding, and my knuckles were throbbing. I felt like a little kid getting in trouble.

"Mom, I can explain," I said, raising my hands in my defense.

"I'm waiting," she told me, finally glancing over with dark eyes that could cut me open. "What happened, Brody? Why are you and Sam arguing like this? He's your best friend. Is it about that Rosa girl?"

"She's not just a girl, Mom," I said, my chest constricting. "I can't explain it, but this whole thing spun out of control. I was looking for Rosa the entire morning. She was avoiding me, I guess."

"You need to straighten this out before Corey gets caught in the crossfire," she said. She turned to me, her thin hands on my upper arms. "If he hasn't already. You need to go clean yourself up."

"Mom, I'm going to figure everything out, I promise," I told her. I hoped it was the truth. Rosa's rejection hurt more than I cared to admit, and I just wanted to talk to her. I looked at my mom. "Do you think you could convince Dan not to call the cops? You know he has a crush on you, *Mrs. Elizabeth.*"

She shook her head, grinning. "I'll see what I can do. Let me grab the blanket, and then I'll go smooth things over."

I followed her over to the jeep in the parking lot, and she looked wistfully at my father's old vehicle, like she always did. She opened the door and dug around, pulling the plaid blanket out and tucking it under her arm. She stopped, looking at something in the seat.

"Brody? Someone is calling you, and you already have five missed calls," she said, concern in her voice.

I hurried over, snatching up my phone. Mr. Perry.

"Hello? What's wrong?" I asked him, frantic. There was static over the speaker.

Was it about Rosa? My heart sank when his voice, tired and worried, answered me.

"Rosa put your number in my phone when I was in the hospital," he said, hesitating. "Have you seen her by chance? She was feeding the horses, but that was over forty minutes ago. She was supposed to pick me up from the doctor's office, and she would have texted me to let me know about the horses by now."

"Do you need someone to come and pick you up?" I asked, but I was really only thinking of Rosa.

"I'll take the bus; my house isn't far," he said. "But, please find her. This isn't like her."

He hung up, and my heart was in my throat. My mother nodded solemnly, and I jumped in the jeep, cranking it up, and hurrying out of the parking lot in a blind panic.

21

ROSA

*A*voiding Brody Strauss was becoming like a sport that I was in no hurry to win.

I walked into the center aisle, taking in the smell of fresh hay and molasses-covered feed. The horses shifted in their stalls, waiting to be let out after their meal. My heart was heavy as I thought of this place going under, lost in the chaos of the world.

As I stood there in the horse barn, the familiar smell of hay and manure wafted through the air, covering me in a comforting, loving embrace. I heard the soft clomp of hooves against the barn floor echoing through the space around me, creating an easy rhythm of sound that resonated deep within the warmth of my soul.

I let my gaze scan each stall in turn, taking in the sights and sounds of the easy-going horses snuffling and shuffling within. The animals, with their sleek, smooth coats and gentle brown eyes, stood magnificent and proud, their manes long and shifting. They were so much more than just horses in my eyes. They were the ones I went to when nothing was going right in my life, my constant friends, and my peace in a world that often seemed too much to handle. Cinder chomped on her hay and then looked up at me, her coppery ears perking up. I gave her a smile, watching her.

As I watched them finish their meals, their ears flexed back and forth, and their eyes stuck on me standing in the aisle, eagerly awaiting any signs of more food in their buckets. I couldn't help but laugh and feel a little bit lighter. My whole chest felt like a leaden weight had been dropped on it, and my mind was whirling with what-ifs and possibilities that might never come to pass. If I couldn't trust him, I didn't know if I could ever see him the same again.

I tried to focus on the horses and make them my primary focus. It was in moments like this that I realized the huge and important responsibility I held as the person taking care of them. They trusted me just as much as they did Mr. Perry, and I was honored. There was a burn in me that wanted to keep them happy and safe. I cared about them as much as I did any of the people in my life, and I was determined to always stick around to keep them safe and sound.

These horses were more than merely a means of getting around or a hobby; they were a part of my very being and who I was. They had seen me through the worst of times, giving me ease and peace when the weight of the world threatened to crush me under it. Their soft nuzzles and warm breath on my cheek reminded me I was never alone.

But it wasn't just during the difficult times that the horses made a difference in my life. They were also there to be at my side through the good days, to share in the times of happiness and excitement. Their presence brought an indescribable sense of happiness and contentment, their playful antics and spirited gallops filling my heart with pure bliss.

For a while, Brody meant just as much to me, and I thought he would be what the horses were. He turned out to be something of a disappointment. I was still hoping he would come around and be what I wanted, but maybe my hopes were just too high.

Horses never let me down. Even on their bad days, they still managed to come through and redeem themselves. Horses always tried their best to do their job. I wished people cared enough to do the same. Once again, Mr. Perry proved he was the only person who would never let me down. With everything going on, I just wished so badly that things could be different. I didn't want to have to worry that the horse barn would fall into someone else's hands or that Brody was with someone else. What if he was with her right at that moment? I shook myself and tried to chase the bad thoughts away. Thinking that way wouldn't do me any good.

When I was in the horse barn, time always seemed to come to a standstill. The place was a sanctuary, a sort of refuge where the worries and troubles of the outside world just seemed to melt away. It was like a port in the storm. The horses in the barn, with their easy movements and graceful nature, had a way of grounding me where I was. They reminded me of the simple things in life and maybe even the importance of living in the current moment instead of dwelling in the past.

It was hard not to think about Brody, but I needed to take care of the animals, and it was enough to keep me busy. I couldn't help but be overwhelmed with feelings of gratitude as I stood there, surrounded by these amazing horses. I felt so damn grateful to be able to see them and the lessons they taught me about patience, perseverance, and unrestrained affection. I wanted to take that affection into the relationship with a certain surfer, and I tried hard not to think about what we could have been.

"How about a turn out in the pasture, huh?" I said as I approached one of the stalls and opened the latch. I patted the forehead of the big, black mare there, grabbing her halter to lead her out. "Come on, Magic. Ready for some grass, girl?"

The horse tossed her head, making her eagerness clear. She ran off into the big paddock, and I made my rounds, turning out the rest of the horses until only Cinder was left. The dark, ominous storm clouds that had been rolling over the ocean finally crested above the trees, sending sharp stabs of lightning to the ground, much too close for comfort. Once all of the horses were out in the paddock to graze, I was going to pick Mr. Perry up from his follow-up appointment. After that, the couch in the cottage and some Chinese takeout were waiting for me. I was ready to drown my feelings in hot lo-mein.

"Well, Cinder girl, you ready for a good run?" I asked the coppery red horse, giving her a warm pat on the shoulder.

To my surprise, she flew back and nearly collided with the wooden wall. I had never seen the horse look so terrified. The whites of her eyes showed as lightning flashed. She had never once been afraid of a storm, and it was as if she didn't want to leave her stall. I took a step forward, putting my hand out to her.

"Hey, whoa! It's okay, girl, don't worry. It's just a little storm," I told her. Cinder snorted, jumping back again. I reached out for her. "It's okay. You can trust me."

The big horse seemed to calm down after a moment, but she still seemed wary. She settled enough to let me get into the stall with her and wrap my fingers around her halter. Then she jumped back again and seemed on edge the entire time I pulled her along. It was almost as if Cinder didn't want to leave me in the barn. She was hesitant to go out into the paddock, even though she usually took off running into the thick, soft grass. I figured she just didn't want to go out into the storm, but it was much safer for the horses to be outside than stuck in the barn during a thunderstorm anyway. There was less of a chance of them getting scared and hurting themselves, or God forbid, something falling on them and trapping them inside their stalls.

"Go on out, pretty," I said, letting go of Cinder's halter and unclipping it. "It's okay now. You can go."

She took off running, but then stopped just before she got to the other horses in the field. The trees swayed above her, shifting Spanish moss. She looked back at me and snorted, giving me a look I would have called "regretful" if she were a human. I watched her, and she finally turned, running off to graze with the other horses.

I headed back into the barn to straighten everything up, and my traitorous mind conjured pictures and snapshots of Brody as I went by the dim, winning ribbon covered office. I remembered him finding me there and wanting to talk, and I wanted nothing more than to see him again. I tried very hard to push down the feeling. I had been ignoring his phone calls all morning. I didn't know if I could stomach a conversation with him, despite how badly I wanted him.

Thunder crashed somewhere nearby, and I was reminded that I was completely alone. The stablehands were all sent home by Mr. Perry after I assured him I was fully capable and he didn't need to do the work of ordering them around. When I was a little girl, I was terrified of storms. Standing in the now empty horse barn, with the horses all turned out and the storm pushing down on me, that fear was coming back.

The dark clouds that punctuated the sky loomed overhead, casting an eerie, creeping shadow over the once bright barn. The place no longer felt peaceful and safe. The sound of the violent thunder rumbled closer than before, getting louder and even more awful with each moment that passed by. The sharp wind howled through the cracks in the wooden walls of the barn, and I couldn't help the sense of unease creeping up within me, making me feel choked.

I was suddenly assaulted with memories from my childhood, reminding me of the many sleepless nights I spent hiding under my covers in Daytona in my childhood home, trying to find safety and solace from the raging storm that plagued the world outside. The storm seemed to echo the thoughts whirling in my head, and it was all too much.

All I could think about, under the thoughts of Brody, were my fears as a kid. The vibrant flashes of lightning would light up my room, making eerie shadows dance across the pale walls, and the thunder would rattle the very foundation of our home. It was in the middle of those moments that I felt tiny and weak, at the complete mercy of the storm's wrath.

When I grew into an adult, I had learned to face my fears and overcome them, even facing down an asshole boyfriend and making my way out. But, standing in that empty, yawning horse barn, with the storm closing in on me from all sides, it felt as if time had turned back. Suddenly, I was all but transported to that scared little girl hiding under the covers. I wished I had some to hide under. The familiar knot seemed to get even tighter in my belly, and my heart raced with fear and anticipation. I just needed to get to the Bronco and get back home.

I looked quickly around the darkened barn, once filled with the peaceful presence of the snuffling, shuffling horses. Now, it felt strange in the electricity of the storm. The absence of the animals only amplified the sense of isolation and terror I suddenly felt. It was as if time were standing still. There was anticipation in my belly, like something was about to happen.

The quickly approaching storm seemed to mirror my inner turmoil, making it worse with each passing second. Heavy raindrops began to slant against the tin roof above me, creating a whirl of sound that all but drowned out my thoughts. Maybe that was a good thing. I took a deep breath and reminded myself I wasn't that scared little girl anymore.

I was safe, no matter how I felt. With everything that had happened recently, I had grown stronger and even more brave than before. I had faced down many, many challenges and come out at least partly victorious. The storm around me was just another test, it was Sam and Heather and my feelings for Brody in another form, and it was another moment to prove that I could make it through.

"You're okay," I told myself, taking a deep breath and letting it out again. "You're fine. Get to the car and leave."

With a newly formed determination sitting heavy in my heart, I stepped forward, closer to the opening of the barn. The cool wind whipped through my hair, yanking at my clothes, and it was as if it was trying to push me back inside the barn. I stood my ground, refusing to let fear dictate the way I lived my life. As the first droplets of rain touched my skin, I closed my eyes and figured I should just run right into the storm. I let the thunderous sounds and the electrifying lightning fill me, though I dreaded it. I would be home and safe before I knew it.

Oh hell. I had forgotten to put Cinder's bucket away.

"Damn it," I said, hissing the words.

I huffed, turning and running back into the dark barn. I reached Cinder's stall and slid in, grabbing for the bucket. It was hung on the hook, and I tried hard to pull it away.

I stopped dead as lightning burst to the ground.

There was a sickening crack and snap from outside the stall, and my heart dropped. The world came crashing down around me, covering me in darkness.

I screamed, and my throat ached by the end of it. A tree must have been hit by lightning, and the force of the entire thing had been dropped on top of Cinder's stall. Thank God she wasn't inside. It was too bad that I was. I was completely trapped under the twisted, broken wood and snapped trunk and branches. There was a hot burn in my side, and I reached down with one shaking hand to touch my skin.

"Oh God," I said, my voice trembling as I brought my fingers up to reveal bright red.

A broken off, sharpened limb had punctured my side, sending shooting, burning pain through my body. Tears burned my eyes as I realized I could barely move. I had no way to bind my wound and no one knew I was there. There were still two whole hours until Mr. Perry's morning would include me, and I was all alone until then.

Rain pelted down through the huge hole the tree made, and I was soaked after just a few moments. I could only see the swirling clouds in the darkened sky and I wondered vaguely if I would die under the ruins of Cinder's stall, trapped under the crashing storm. And to think, she had tried to warn me of what was to come.

The thought of never seeing Brody again broke my heart.

"Please," I begged any deity that was listening. "Please don't let me die here."

I couldn't tell how bad the stab into my side was, but I needed to try and move. I wasn't going to sit there and fade away without a fight. I shored myself from the pain and tried to gather my arms up to my chest. I pressed my fingers against the heavy wood that covered me, and I pushed as hard as I could, feeling my body throb painfully in response.

Tears streamed down my cheeks, and I felt the piece of the wooden stall wall shift a little. I tried to slide my body back. My limbs were shaking, and it seemed to be forever before I finally moved it halfway. It was just enough to scoot away and lean my upper body against the one part of the stall that remained standing. It didn't matter though. I was still trapped under the rubble and this one pocket of space was all I had. I couldn't believe this was actually happening to me.

Pain that ached down my side.

I finally looked down, and my hands were shaking. There was a hole in my side and a red rose was spreading down my hip and pants leg. A sob shuddered through my lips, and I pressed a trembling hand to the fiery pain in my side. I tipped my head back, squeezing my eyes shut. My phone was in the Bronco. I was completely alone.

"Please," I said again, and maybe I was begging now. I didn't care much for pride.

My mind kept flashing to Brody. My heart ached as much as my body, and my head was throbbing. From somewhere outside, I heard Cinder whinny shrilly. It might have been my imagination, but she sounded terrified.

Maybe she saw someone. Maybe she was trying to tell them.

"Hello?" I asked, calling out in a weak voice.

There was silence but for the storm, and my chest felt heavy again. Then, there were footsteps across the ground outside.

"Hello? Help! Please, I'm in here!" I called, my throat aching from the effort.

I slumped back against the wall again, completely spent, and trying to force my body to keep me awake and aware. It was a huge effort, and it took a lot out of me to stay up.

"Cinder?" I heard a familiar voice ask, though the wind tried so very hard to carry the sound away from me. "Where is she, girl?"

I coughed a wet laugh. Only Brody would treat my horse like Lassie.

"Brody!" I cried out, forgetting everything I had been thinking about him and all of my doubts. I trusted him with my life. "I'm here!"

There were more hurried footsteps. I heard them inside the barn, smacking on the concrete of the center aisle. My breath was coming in ragged gasps, and my hand was barely strong enough to press against my side.

"Rosa? Oh fuck," Brody said, his voice ending on a sharp gasp. "Are you under there?"

"I'm here," I murmured weakly.

"I'm going to get you out of there, okay? Oh god, are you okay? I can't see you, Rosie," he said, his voice frantic. "The rubble is too deep."

"I'm okay," I told him, but I was fading fast. I was losing too much precious blood, and I felt so tired. "But— there's blood."

"What?" All of the shuffling against the broken stall stopped short. Brody's voice was low and intense. "Rosa, what are you talking about? Are you hurt?"

"I'm—yeah," was all that I could say. "I'm sorry, Brody. I'm so sorry about everything."

I wanted to tell him before I couldn't anymore. I wanted him to know what he meant to me. All this time, what I felt for him had been building, and I didn't want it to collapse too.

"Don't do that, Rosie," Brody told me, choking up. "Don't you dare say goodbye to me."

There was a new round of shifting, and something snapped. A beam of light broke through, and over the raging of the storm, I heard movement close by. Brody must have somehow pushed through the rubble. I was terrified for him, and I would have stayed under that mess for a lifetime if it meant he stayed safe on the other side.

"No," I whispered, but it was weak.

Suddenly, he shoved under the wood and crashed into the little space I was sitting in. Behind him, the rubble crashed back down, covering what must have been his escape route, though it did leave a little more room where we were squashed together. He didn't pay it any mind; he didn't even look back at all. He was getting soaked where the rain dripped in, and his dark waves were so familiar and endearing. It reminded me of the stormy day we met. Bright eyes looked at me, and he was frantic.

"So blue, like the ocean," I mumbled with a cough as I watched them flash down my body.

"Rosa," he whispered, cupping my cheek in one warm hand and brushing his thumb across my cheekbone. He pressed his mouth to mine, kissing me gently, and I tasted saltwater tears on his lips. "Baby, stay with me."

My whole body warmed at the endearment, but the warmth was fading fast from me.

"It hurts," I whispered, and I saw him look down at my side.

"Jesus," he hissed. He touched me gently as he ripped a strip from his t-shirt and pressed it against the wound.

I cried out, and he pressed his forehead to mine. A sob caught in his throat, jolting his body, and I realized he was trapped with me. A new dread began to form in my belly.

"You shouldn't have," I told him, nodding at the broken down stall around me.

"I couldn't leave you. I could never leave you," he whispered, cradling my face in his hands. "I love you."

I blinked at his warm, handsome face, wondering if I had imagined the words. The way he said it, so full of warmth, meaning, and longing, it had to be real.

"You said not to say goodbye," I told him tiredly, my voice aching in my throat. "You think I won't make it if you're saying goodbye to me."

"I'm not leaving you, and you're not leaving me," Brody said firmly, kissing my temple with a mouth that was trembling. "I just needed you to know."

"I would rather die here alone than have you stuck here like this," I told him, swallowing. I looked up at him, my eyes bleary with tears. "I love you, Brody. I've never felt love like this before. I didn't want to feel it."

The last words came out slurred, and I knew it wouldn't be long before the darkness would overtake me and Brody would be alone.

He huffed a shaky laugh, pushing my hair back. "Well, I'm glad to know loving me was such a bother to you."

"I'm sorry," I told him, wincing as my side throbbed.

"No, I'm sorry for everything, Rosa," he whispered, and I could feel him trembling as he tried to hold back his tears.

"Meeting you was worth all of it," I whispered, pressing a soft kiss to the underside of his jaw. "I would do it all over again."

He pulled me into his lap, and I slotted perfectly against his warm chest, feeling my body growing heavy. I couldn't feel the pain any longer, and I was warm and fuzzy. The longing in my soul for Brody was the only thing I could feel. It was never quiet in the first place, and now it was the only thing in my body that was burning bright.

"Baby, please don't," I heard Brody sob brokenly as he held me close. I felt the darkness pulling me down, down, down, into the depths of nothingness. "Please," he begged me, or maybe it was the universe he was begging, down on his knees, but I couldn't see him clearly in the bleary edges of my vision.

The last thing I saw was the sky and the storm itself, ripping the world into dark oblivion.

22

BRODY

*S*am's heavy hand was on my shoulder. He was holding cups when he came around.

"You look like shit."

"You look like the guy who looks like shit punched you in the nose," I countered, rubbing a hand over my sore face and ignoring the ache. "Thanks for the coffee."

He let out a strained chuckle. "Mind if I sit?"

I nodded, waving at the chairs beside me. It felt odd and awkward, but my old friend sat down heavily. He cleared his throat, and it felt less tense between us. A day ago, we had been beating each other with rage in our bellies, and now we were sipping coffees, and sitting in uncomfortable waiting room chairs. What a week.

"I hate hospitals," he said, his voice gruff.

"I remember," I nodded. "You hate the people."

"It always seems like everyone is in mourning," he said, "and like everyone here is just waiting to die." I winced, and he shifted awkwardly. "Sorry, man."

"Thanks for answering the phone," I said quietly, though I knew he had only answered because he thought it was Rosa calling, as much as he pretended not to care. "Yours was the first number I could remember."

"I was surprised as hell to hear you screaming on the other end," he said haltingly. "I was scared too, man."

"Yeah, join the club." I said with a scoff.

As much as I had scrubbed, I could still feel the phantom sticky blood on my hands where I had tried to hold Rosa together. The terror was still in my heart—the absolute fear that had crawled its way up my throat when the woman I love went limp in my arms.

Sam shifted, making his seat creak. "We need to talk."

In my experience, Sam wasn't good at talking. He was good at fighting and he was good at arguing, but he wasn't a big talker. That was pretty evident by my bruises.

"Yeah, shoot," I said, feeling more tired than anything else.

"I shouldn't have hit you," he said, and I could almost hear the wince in his tone.

"I think the hitting was pretty mutual," I said, resisting the urge to let out a painful cough.

I had never been in a fight like that before. It was strange that the first real, violent fight I had ever been in was with my once-best friend. I had wanted so badly to knock my fist into him as hard as I could, but now I was just thankful that he was next to me.

"I wanted to tell you," he began, sounding hesitant. "I broke up with Heather. I left her."

That actually surprised me. "Is that right?" I asked.

He looked uncomfortable. "I don't know, man. I think I was still trying to prove myself. I wanted to be better than you as a father. I wanted to be better than my dad was to me. It wasn't my place, though."

"Where is all this coming from?" I asked him, confused. Yesterday morning, he wanted to beat me black and blue.

"It's two in the morning," he said with a shrug. "This is when the truth starts pouring out, right?"

"What happened?" I really was just curious.

He shrugged. "She picked me up after the bar. She was pissed and left her phone to go talk to Dan about dropping any charges. Her phone was on the seat, and she got a text." He shrugged again. "I read it."

"Well, what did it say?" I asked, not even hiding my obvious interest.

"I guess she's been seeing some other guy or something," he glances at me with a small, bitter smile. "That's karma for me, for sure."

"What did the other guy say?" I asked.

"I read the whole text thread, and everything I needed to know was in there," he said, wincing. "The guy works for CPS. I sent screenshots to my phone. You have what you need for a custody battle if you want them."

"So that's why she was so sure of herself," I answered with a scoff.

"She was pissed about being caught," he said. "She kicked me out of her car, and your mom saw me walking and drove me home. She told me I was being a dumbass," he said, smiling a little. "Once I got home, I got your call."

"It's been a hell of a few days," I said, letting out a long breath.

"Rosa is going to be okay, man," he said quietly, and I just nodded. He kept going. "For what it's worth, I did love her. It meant something to me too. I'm just an asshole. She always deserved better, and I knew that. You're better for her, Brody. You've always been better."

Hearing all of that out of Sam's mouth was shocking, to say the least. I didn't know what to say. Maybe he really was just a lost soul looking for an anchor.

"Thank you," I said, putting my hand out. I looked over his bruised and battered face. "And sorry about the split lip."

"Don't be," he told me, grinning as he vigorously shook my hand. "I didn't know you had it in you, Brody boy."

I couldn't help but laugh. "Yeah, me neither."

The reality of the situation came flooding back, and I felt heavy with fear. My mind was flashing back to holding Rosa in my arms and her telling me that she loved me. Now, I was in the cold waiting room, wondering if she was even going to make it. I had spent way too much time in hospitals lately, and I was so ready for everything to be okay.

"I've never seen you like this with a woman," Sam said quietly.

"I've never felt this way about any other woman," I answered, my chest aching.

He nodded, but just as he was about to say something, the doctor came rushing down the hallway. My heart jumped into my throat as soon as he stopped in front of us.

"Doc?" Sam asked, standing quickly. "How is she? Is she going to be okay?"

I was on the edge of my seat, and my fingers ached from gripping the plastic armrests so hard. The doctor finally nodded, and relief flooded through me like a rushing wave.

"She's going to make a full recovery," the gray-haired man told us, a small smile on his face. "The branch didn't puncture anything substantial, but she did lose a lot of blood. You can go in and see her if you'd like."

I stood up so fast, my head spun, and the doctor smiled warmly. Sam nodded at me.

"Follow me," he said, waving a hand. "She may be drowsy, but she's okay."

I nodded my thanks and went quietly into the room, pushing open the heavy door. Rosa was pale, and there were dark circles under her pretty, luminous green eyes. Her dark, chocolate hair was dull, an inky smudge against the creamy pillows. She looked up at me and something crossed her face that I couldn't decipher. Her big eyes watched me, nearly glowing in her pale, drawn features. She was otherworldly, heartbreakingly beautiful, even under the heavy sheets of the hospital bed.

"Brody," she whispered, a slow smile spread across her face. "Hey."

I couldn't help it when I rushed to her side, collapsing into the chair next to her bed. I wrapped my fingers around hers and kissed her palm, holding our hands there as I looked at her. I had almost lost her, and it was gut-wrenching.

"I'm okay," she said, using her other hand to run thin fingers through my hair. "Hey, it's okay."

Those same fingers brushed over my cheeks, and I realized that hot tears were sliding down my skin. I couldn't help it.

"I was so worried about you," I whispered against her skin, shaking my head.

"You told me you loved me," she said quietly. She sounded hesitant. "Or did I dream that?"

I coughed a laugh. "Only if you dreamed that you said it back."

She looked at me for a moment. "Your face. Why do you have a black eye? Was that from the barn?"

"Uh, no," I told her, clearing my throat. "It was Sam."

"Sam?" she asked, her eyes going wide. She sat up quickly and then cried out.

"Hey, no, it's okay," I said, standing up and putting my hands on her shoulders. I pushed her down gently. "Everything is okay now."

"He hurt you," she said, her eyes blazing. "That's not okay at all. How can you say that?"

"I hurt him, too," I told her. I sighed. "I asked him to the bar to talk, and it got tense for a minute."

"You got into a fight," she said, making a face.

"Yeah, we got into a hell of a fight." I shook my head. "He broke up with Heather after."

"What? Are you serious?"

I shrugged. "That's what he told me. We sort of worked everything out."

"Why did he break up with her?" she asked, watching me carefully as I sat back down, content that she wasn't going to hurt herself.

"It turns out she was seeing another guy who works for Child Protective Services. Sam read all of their texts and found out about her lies, I guess," I told her with a shrug. "I didn't want to ask too much."

"I can't believe he had the nerve to hit you," she said, color returning to her cheeks as she seemed to grit her teeth. She was stuck on the punching, and it was adorable.

"Rosa, he's the one who drove us to the hospital," I told her gently, and she looked at me in surprise. "I called him from your phone. His number was the only one I could remember off the top of my head, and because of the storm, neither one of us could get through to emergency services."

"I can't believe it," she said, sounding unsure.

"There's some good in him," I told her, knowing it was true.

"Maybe so," she yawned. "Nearly dying takes a lot out of a girl."

My heart wrenched. "Don't say that, okay?"

"Come here," she said, looking at me.

I nodded, leaning over her to press my mouth to hers. Her lips were cold and dry, and my whole body seemed to relax into the kiss. I sat gingerly on the bed at her side, cradling her pretty face in my hands. Under the sheets and the hospital gown, the wound that nearly took her from me was hidden beneath heavy gauze. I glanced down at her side, and she swallowed hard, her eyes glimmering.

"I was so scared," she whispered, looking haunted. "I was terrified, and all I could think about was you."

"Rosa," I whispered. My voice was choked through the ache in my throat. I felt like I had been screaming for centuries. "Yesterday was the worst day of my life. If I had lost you, I don't know what I would do. I've waited for you my entire life, and you've been worth every minute."

Her eyes were glassy, and a tear slipped down. She blinked quickly, and I thumbed away the warm saltwater that streaked down her skin. I knew I loved her because it broke my heart to see her hurting. I knew I needed her because every waking moment was spent thinking of her.

"I do love you," Rosa told me, her cheeks pink. She smiled a little. "It wasn't just the blood loss. I'm in love with you, and I tried to hide it from myself for so long."

I touched my forehead to hers. "I want you. I want you forever."

In spite of all of the bad that had happened in our lives since we found one another, Rosa had become one of the biggest parts of my heart. She made her own space there and had taken up residence next to my mother and my son. The love I felt for her was something that I couldn't deny, and I found that I didn't want to anymore. I just needed her to understand how much she meant to me and how much it would hurt me if she decided she didn't want me. This wasn't like what she had with Sam. I wanted her to feel safe with me, knowing her heart was in good hands.

All this time, every single moment I was able to spend with her was like a burst of sunlight into my being, and her presence brought with it a sense of peace and beauty. Her laugh and that pretty, radiant smile had the power to brighten even the darkest of bad days and make them so much better. It was like she had the distinct ability to make the world a better place just by existing.

She was a light, and she was beautiful. What I felt for her was as deep and unknown as the ocean, making me feel warm and exhilarated all at once. Despite that, it wasn't just her outward beauty that held me under her sunny spell. The depth and warmth of her soul were just as beautiful, and that truly had me mesmerized. Rosa Rivers had a distinct way of seeing the world with such brightness and curiosity that it made me want to look at it differently. She was the kind of woman I wanted in my son's life and in my life. Just by existing, she made me a better man.

I watched her and she was getting tired, slipping softly into the cradle of my hands and letting herself rest against me. I felt a rush of warm love for her. I wanted desperately for her to know I would always be there for her, ready to protect and love her through whatever came at us in life.

"Stay with me," she murmured, the words barely loud enough to be heard over the beeping of the machines. "Don't leave me."

"I'll be right here when you wake up," I whispered, pressing a soft kiss to her lips. "I won't leave you, never again."

She sighed, curling into me as much as she could without hurting her side. Soon enough, there were little snores against my neck, brushing over my skin.

There was a soft knock against the door, not loud enough to wake the woman sleeping in my arms.

"Come in," I called as quietly as I could. "Oh, Mr. Perry. How are you?"

"I'm just fine, my boy. How is our Rosa doing? Should I come back later?" he whispered, looking at her sleeping form.

"No, it's alright, I don't think she'll wake up anytime soon," I told him, nodding at the chair I had vacated.

"I had the stablehand drive me," he said, making a face. "He's not the best student driver."

I laughed softly. "At least you made it here. Is Sam still out there?"

"He was half asleep in one of the chairs," he nodded. "But why is he here? Why is he anywhere near Rosa?"

I winced. "He drove us to the hospital."

"So the worries are over, then?" Mr. Perry asked.

"I'm not sure about that, but at least we don't need to worry about him anymore," I said with a sigh.

"I wanted to tell you that I know she doesn't have enough to buy the land and horses and the shop off of me," Mr. Perry said, watching Rosa as she slept peacefully. "I planned on keeping it for as long as I could and helping her. I won't offer it to anyone else until she has what she needs to take over. I didn't tell her because I knew she wouldn't want any charity."

23

ROSA

*B*rody was kissing my neck, and my heart was thumping out of my chest.

Two days lying in Brody's bed without him had been much too long.

"Tell me if you want me to stop," he said, his breath ghosting over my skin.

"I'm fine; I keep telling you," I answered, nodding to the thin bandage on my side. "It wasn't deep, it was just a lot of blood."

"We're taking this slow," he said, but I could hear the breathless want in his voice. "I almost lost you, and I'm not doing that again."

"You didn't almost lose me," I said, pulling him up to kiss me. "I'm sorry, I know it was scary, but I'm okay, and I want you. I'm naked in your bed; isn't that proof enough?"

He grinned at me, his gaze soft. "You're beautiful is what you are."

"Brody, you're getting distracted," I said, nodding at him. "Weren't you doing something?"

"Oh, I'm distracted, am I?" he laughed, curling back into

his previous position to kiss down my belly. "I'll show you how distracted I am."

Soft fingers slid over the bandages on my side, barely touching me. He kissed across my thighs, and he moved down, licking into me and drawing a moan from my throat. The pink rays of sunlight burned across his tanned shoulders, flickering over the freckles that dotted his skin. Early morning and late night found us sleeping peacefully, curled into each other. Brody's touch was too much, and we were both aching for it.

"Brody," I cried out, my voice catching, and I was glad Corey's room was on the other side of the house.

Long fingers wrapped around my thighs, holding me down. He licked and swept his tongue passionately over my center, gathering warm wetness and making me moan again. Hot, overwhelming pleasure burst over me quickly, and Brody pushed his fingers in, curling gently as I writhed under him. Pleasure covered me again, and I *screamed*. I scrambled to quiet down, even the neighbors would have heard that one.

"He's a heavy sleeper," Brody murmured, kissing the crease of my thigh. "You can be as loud as you want."

"I need you," I said, pulling him up to kiss me.

His tongue tasted of me, and he was smiling against my mouth. I reached down, rubbing my hand over his naked chest and then his belly, wrapping my hand around his hot, hard length. He gasped, watching my movements as I stroked back and forth. He reached for my hips, pulling me up higher on the bed, and I angled his heavy hardness to press against my warmth.

"Rosa," he breathed, leaning down to kiss my neck again. "I love you," he said as he slid into me, filling me up.

"I love you," I gasped, digging my fingers into his shoulders.

The rising sun burst even hotter through the window, golden rays illuminating the tanned body entangled with mine. My side twinged, and Brody must have sensed it. He stopped, looking me over, and I nodded once the small pain had fled. I wanted him, and nothing was going to stop this from happening. I felt relief as he rocked his hips into mine, and the bed shuddered underneath us. The ocean crashed outside, falling over the shore, and Brody's thrusts picked up speed, harder and faster than before.

He was golden, sun-bright, and filling me up perfectly. Our bodies were as close as two people could be, and we were the same tanned, tangled creature for just a few moments in time. He cried out, letting go and letting me hold him limp against me as he reached his pleasure just in time for the sun to completely crest over the horizon.

"You're amazing," he whispered, warm lips at my ear. "You're the best thing to ever happen to me, Rosa Rivers, to me and my son."

"I'm the lucky one," I said, trying to slow down my breathing. "Come here."

He pressed his forehead to mine, kissing each of my cheeks in turn. His fingers touched my skin, caressing gently and reaching the bandage at my side.

"Are you hurting?" he asked, watching me carefully.

"Not even a little," I assured him, kissing his cheek. "Though I am starving."

He chuckled. "Bacon and eggs in bed? How about orange juice? Coffee?"

"You're a very thorough waiter," I giggled. "A girl could get used to this."

"Oh, I'm all about your pleasure," he said, licking at my chest and closing his mouth over my breast, making me writhe. He grinned, standing up and stretching. "I'll get started on that breakfast."

I laughed, shaking my head. "You're a monster."

He bowed low as he reached for his pants. "I'll take that as a compliment."

The smell of food was wafting through the house when I made my way into the kitchen, dressed in one of Brody's big t-shirts and my shorts. He looked up at me, surprised.

"You're supposed to be waiting for me to bring it to you," he said with a frown. "Corey even made you coffee."

"Corey?" I asked, and heard footsteps behind me.

"Good morning, Rosa," Corey said, giving me a bright smile where he stood in his pajamas. "Dad says we're going to the pier. I'm happy!"

"The pier, huh?" I reached over to ruffle his hair. "Are we?"

Brody served the plates up, putting them on the kitchen table at our seats. He wiped his hands on a kitchen towel and put it over his shoulder. He grinned at me.

"Yeah, I thought we could go check out the dolphins and get some ice cream," he said as we sat down. "Let's eat and get ready to go. Does that sound good?"

"That sounds perfect," I told him, digging into my delicious food.

We got ready quickly, and I slipped my feet into my sandals, following the two of them out to the jeep. About thirty minutes later, I sat relaxed on the smooth wooden bench. The warm, balmy breeze gently caressed my skin as I watched the waves crash against the edges of the pier. The sound of the seagulls flying and ducking into the water filled the air, their bright cries mingling with the playful laughter of children and the distant hum of conversation from down below on the beach. It was a perfect day, and I couldn't have asked for better company than the people that I had come to love.

Sitting beside me on the bench, Brody held two ice cream

cones. Dripping lines of ice cream ran down his hands. The sweet scent of vanilla and chocolate wafted through the air and he looked excited, and also more calm than he had in days. He glanced over and handed me one with a bright smile, his eyes sparkling with glee. He glanced down, looking at my side, bandaged under my tank top. I gave him a nod, letting him know I was fine.

"There you go. The best ice cream in town," he grinned.

I took the cone, the coldness of the ice cream sending a shiver down my spine. I licked it tentatively, savoring the creamy sweetness of the treat. "Wow, you were right about this. This ice cream is amazing. I can't believe I never thought to get it from the gas station."

He laughed, and the sound of it was infectious. "Told you so. Now, let's enjoy this gorgeous day. I don't want to think about anything but you and Corey."

"Not even the competition the day after tomorrow?" I asked.

"Not even that," he said, putting his arm around me.

We sat in an easy sort of silence, but I could feel there was something he wanted to say. We had been through so much, and I was happy to let him tell me when he was ready. If it was something truly bad, he would make sure I knew. I couldn't help but steal little glances at him where he sat beside me, his wavy, soft hair tousled by the wind and his pretty eyes filled with warmth and sentiment I was used to seeing. Being with him always felt so natural, like we had known each other for a lifetime, though we had only met weeks ago. Our souls recognized each other, and they found something they liked in the confines of our hearts.

As we enjoyed our ice cream, I noticed Corey standing at the edge of the pier, his eyes fixed on something in the water. I followed his gaze to the calm ocean and gasped in delight as

I saw a group of glittering blue dolphins leaping through the crystalline waves.

"Look at the water, Rosa!" Corey exclaimed in his high, bright voice, his tone filled with excitement. "There's the dolphins! They're so cool!"

I grinned at his eagerness, his enthusiasm. "They're so beautiful, aren't they? Nature's wonders never cease to amaze me. Maybe we could make a habit of doing this."

"I think that's a great idea," Brody said, kissing my cheek. He turned his attention to his son, a proud smile on his handsome face. "You're so right, buddy. Dolphins are incredible creatures."

Corey turned back to where we were watching him, his eyes shining with anticipation. "Dad, please, can we go closer? I just want to see them up close. Mom never lets me do that."

At the mention of Heather, we both prickled with dislike. Brody recovered quickly, hiding his reaction from his son easily enough. I pushed down my resentment, giving him a smile.

"Well, maybe we should change that," Brody said as he glanced at me, his eyes filled with a mix of glee and uncertainty. "What do you think we should do, Rosa? Should we get closer?"

I felt warm that he was already starting to include me in his decisions, especially when it concerned Corey.

I nodded at him, my heart pounding in my chest. "Absolutely. Come on, then, let's go! We don't want to miss them."

Brody held my hand as we followed Corey and made our way to the very edge of the pier. The wood was firm and thick, and there was no need to hold Corey back from the secured edge. The sound of the waves grew louder and more prevalent with each step. Corey's excitement was easy to see. His small hand tightly gripped my fingers as we leaned a little over the railing, watching the swirl of the dolphins as they swam gracefully beneath us.

As we stood happily staring at the sight below us, Brody turned to me with intent, his eyes filled with a mixture of apprehension and resolve.

"Rosa, can we talk? There's something I've been wanting to ask you for a while now." He wasn't fidgeting, but he might as well have been.

I looked at him curiously, my heart skipping a beat. "Yeah, of course. What is it? Is something wrong?"

He took a slow, deep breath, his voice filled with a sincerity that made my heart swell with warmth when he did finally speak his mind.

"You mean a whole hell of a lot to me. I've been lucky enough to get to know you, and I can't imagine my life without you now. Corey loves you, and you're good for us. Would you be my girlfriend? Officially, I mean? What do you think?" he said, staring at me with bright eyes.

My heart soared with delight, a smile spreading across my face.

"Yes, Brody," I said, nodding enthusiastically, and I didn't care how crazy it made me look. "I would love to be your girlfriend. I would love to be yours, and I want you to be mine."

His handsome face lit up with triumph and joy, and he pulled me into a tight hug, his mouth finding mine in a sweet, lingering kiss. It seemed as if the whole world around us began to fade away, and at that moment, it was just the three of us there by the water, surrounded by the wonder of the ocean and the love that had grown between us. Corey broke us out of it.

As we pulled apart, Corey's happy voice filled the air. "Yay! You guys are officially together now! Can you stay with us, Rosa?"

"I need to head into the surf shop," I told him regretfully. "And your dad needs to get in some time in the water, don't you, Brody?"

"Is Mom going to watch me?" Corey's little voice asked, completely unaware of anything going on, good or bad, with Brody and his mother. "Or Grandma? I want Grandma to watch me!"

"You want Grandma to watch you because she lets you watch movies all day," Brody said, chuckling as he ruffled his son's hair. "But alright. Let's head on out and drop Rosa off at work."

Corey sighed, slumping a little. "Okay, I guess," he said, dragging out the words.

"I'll see you later," I told him, giving him a warm smile.

Brody drove me to the surf shop. There were already people waiting in the parking lot, and I saw Mr. Perry's decrepit car there, sitting like an old friend. When I got out, Corey was playing with a racecar, but he waved goodbye to me. I was starting to think this was what my life could be, and I loved every minute of it. Brody walked me to the door. We stood outside in the warm sunshine, and I felt like I must have been glowing with the happiness I felt inside. I was so unsure of being with anyone again after what Sam did, but Brody was a hard man to doubt.

"How early can you be there to watch me at the surf competition?" Brody asked me, and the golden spell was broken.

My stomach flipped. Suddenly, the surfing competition seemed very real. I wasn't sure why it felt as if it wasn't actually going to happen for so long, but everything was just so chaotic that it was sent to the back burner. I thought of Brody in the waves, and I suddenly felt a rush of terror so strong that my side began to ache. I put my hand to where the bandage sat, and Brody noticed right away, as attentive as he ever was.

"Are you okay?" he asked, questioning me again, even though I hadn't answered the first time he asked me something.

"Brody, can I ask you something?" I cleared my throat. The good feeling from before felt something like fear now, and all I could think about was the man I loved being swallowed up by the waves.

"Anything," he nodded, reaching out and wrapping his fingers around mine.

"What if you didn't do the competition tomorrow?" I asked, hurrying to get the words out before I turned too chicken to say them. "I mean, maybe me, you, and Corey could take the Lion's Bridge into St. Augustine and explore the old town or something."

He dropped my hand, and his face flickered with confusion. "What? What are you talking about?"

"It just seems dangerous," I said quietly, my heart hammering. "I mean, you have me and Corey to think about."

Even to my own ears, it sounded ridiculous. I was just suddenly hit by the awful fear of losing him, and this was the only thing I knew to do. I was hoping maybe he would reconsider. After everything, I just wanted some peace, and I didn't want to have to worry about Brody drowning or being knocked into unseen rocks in the water.

"I hope you're not serious, because that is completely unfair," he said, taking a step back. I hated the way he was looking at me. It was like he couldn't believe what he was hearing.

"How is that unfair, exactly?" I asked, watching him. "Wanting you around and safe is unfair?"

He scoffed. "It's unfair of you to ask me to give up something I've wanted for so long just because you think I should.

What if I asked you to give up horses? I mean, being at the horse barn could have killed you too, but I haven't said I don't want you there, have I?"

It was a good point. Maybe I was being unfair, but maybe not.

"After what happened to your dad, I just thought maybe…" I trailed off, wincing. I shouldn't have said it.

Brody looked as if he had been slapped. "Yeah, that's too far. I'm leaving now. Come tomorrow, or don't. I won't beg you to support me."

He turned on his heel and hurried across the parking lot. I watched his wide shoulders as he got into the jeep. Corey waved at me again as they drove away, and I felt my stomach flip. How had this amazing day gone so sour?

"I think you need a nice, cold Coke," Mr. Perry's voice said, and I saw him leaning out of a window I didn't notice was open.

"Mr. Perry," I said weakly. "So you heard everything?"

"Everyone in the store heard everything, dear Rosa," he told me sympathetically. "Come on inside. It's too hot out to sulk in the parking lot."

I sighed, catching one last glimpse of the retreating vehicle as I trudged in. Mr. Perry was checking someone out. He bagged their items, and the older couple gave me a look of pity as they passed by with their goodies.

"We're due for a chat, you and I," Mr. Perry said as I went behind the counter with him.

I leaned against the window and glanced over at the couple of people shopping through the store's selection of beach items.

"I don't think this is the right time," I said, my cheeks going hot and red. "Are still okay to take me home?"

"They heard everything, and it's fine," he said, waving a hand and ignoring my attempt to change the subject. "Now, why did you start that argument? Are you not feeling well? Is it your side?"

"What?" I asked him, my eyes going wide. "I didn't start anything."

"You did, and I could see it was out of fear or pain," he said sagely. "If it's not your wound, are you afraid of losing young Mr. Strauss?"

I sighed. "I don't know. I just felt scared. I thought about how dangerous surfing really is. I know I shouldn't have brought up his dad, and it was out of the blue, but I couldn't stop thinking about it."

"Well, perhaps it wasn't your place, but that isn't for either of us to decide," he said gently.

"I know," I told him, feeling sadness begin to make my body heavy.

He sat down with a groan in the office chair. "Rosa, I think there's something I should tell you."

"Okay," I said slowly. "What is it?"

I didn't think I could take another hit right at that moment. I didn't want to feel even worse than I already did. I couldn't just brush Mr. Perry off, and I wanted to hear what he had to say.

"Well, I knew Brody's father," he said, looking terribly sad. "He was a good, good man. He shopped here often. The only thing was, he cared more about those waves than he did anything else. I used to watch him from my window here and wonder what he was looking for in the swell. When I saw Brody that day, I could see his father in the same position, though he never came back."

"I don't want that to happen to Brody," I said, swallowing hard. "I don't want him to be his father."

"I think that's the thing," he said, nodding. "He wants to prove that he's *not* his father. He wants to show you he will come back. I'm sure he wants to prove it to himself too."

"What am I supposed to do?" I asked. "Just act like it doesn't bother me? I start sweating every time I think about what's going to happen the day after tomorrow."

"Wear extra deodorant," he said with a wink, "and just support him as much as you can."

"He's a good man," I said, letting the words fall from my mouth and knowing they were true. "He doesn't need to prove anything."

Behind us, the door to the surf shop jingled open.

"Are you Rosa Rivers?" said a voice I didn't recognize. I turned and saw a tall woman standing there, watching me. "I'm Elizabeth Strauss. I'm Brody's mother."

BRODY

*M*y mother was standing on the porch, staring at me like she was trying to figure me out. Her long, glowing dress whipped in the briny ocean breeze, and her glittering dark hair was in a thick braid. She pulled it over her shoulder, tipping her chin up to watch us approach.

"She looks mad," Rosa said, sounding unsure.

"That's just how she looks," I told her. I turned to her, feeling regret pool in my belly. "Look, Rosa, I'm sorry about yesterday. I shouldn't have snapped at you like I did."

"It's okay," she shrugged. "It was none of my business in the first place."

"No, it is. I want you to know everything, and I want you to be in my life. I mean *really* in my life." My gaze roved over the tanned curve of her toned shoulder. "And you look beautiful, by the way."

"Thank you," she said, softening. She glanced over at me, pushing her wavy hair back over her shoulder. "When your mom came into the surf shop yesterday to ask us over, I wasn't sure what to think."

"She might seem intimidating, but she's the best person I know," I said honestly.

I had grown up with my mom hovering over my shoulder and constantly helping me through hard times. Sometimes, when I was young, I felt like she was smothering me, but not now. She had gotten me through some of the toughest situations, and, though she wasn't outright warm and welcoming, she was fiercely loyal to the people she loved. If you were lucky enough to be in her circle, she would always be there for you. I knew why she invited Rosa to dinner. She wanted to feel her out. She wanted to see for herself who her son had been allowing around her only grandchild. She didn't wait for us to come up; she just went inside.

Soon enough, my mom was across the table from us, helping my son spoon out creamy mashed potatoes. I sat nervously at the dinner table, stealing glances at Rosa as she delicately picked at her food. It was a big step for me, letting her get to know my mom, and I hoped everything would go smoothly. Even though my mom had made the first move, I wanted to be the one to keep things easy and simple. Mom had never liked Heather, but it would be different with Rosa. She was no Heather.

"So, Rosa, tell me," my mom began, her voice filled with warmth, though I could hear the seriousness behind the seemingly innocent question. "How exactly did you and Brody meet?"

Rosa looked up quickly from her plate of roast and potatoes, her eyes bright with what must have been a mixture of anxiety and excitement.

"Well, we actually met at the surf shop," she replied, her voice soft. There was a hint of strain there, and I hoped she wouldn't tell my mother how she actually met me. "I was sitting at the checkout counter, reading a book, and Brody came inside when we were about to close. We just clicked instantly. He was my last customer that day."

I couldn't help but wince at the memory. That rock had really done a number on me, and I could still feel the pull of skin where it had healed. I did get to meet Rosa though, and that was a plus. It felt like that day, fate had brought the two of us together, and I had been ridiculously grateful for every moment since, good or bad.

"That's lovely," my mom said, her eyes crinkling with a smile I knew all too well. She had always been smarter than everyone else. "Brody was out in the waves, wasn't he? Surfing late again? His father loved that same spot."

Rosa's cheeks turned a bright shade of pink as she glanced at me. "Uh, yes, he was. He fell off—"

"She bandaged me right up," I told my mom, and Corey looked at all of us, eating his food.

"You fell?" my son asked me, his eyes wide.

"I'm okay, bud," I told him easily, nodding across the table at him.

"It's alright, you two," my mother said with a sigh, looking at me and then at Rosa. "He is his father's son. Thank you for taking care of him."

"It was really no problem," Rosa answered, her voice filled with warm affection now. "Time has flown by between us since then. It's strange, really. It feels like we've known each other forever, though we met a month or so ago. I'm just glad we did meet."

I reached out and gently squeezed Rosa's hand on the table, silently reassuring her, and I knew my mom saw it. I knew my mom could be a little intimidating and hard sometimes, but I also knew she had a good, honest heart and truly only wanted the best for me and Corey.

Mom nodded approvingly at Rosa's confession. That was a good sign.

"And how do you feel about Corey?" she asked, her gaze slanting towards my son, who was now sitting quietly beside her with a small, unsure smile on his face.

Rosa's gaze seemed to soften as she looked over at him.

"I absolutely adore him," she said in a tone that sounded sincere. "He's such a sweet kid. He's a very smart little boy. I've loved being able to get to know him and being a small part of his life the way I have been."

Corey, who had been listening to what she was saying, looked up at her with a bright smile. It was pretty obvious they had become fast friends, and I was glad to see it. Knowing it warmed my heart, and it was nice to see them forming a sort of bond, even with everything going on with his mother. I hadn't told my mom about that, and I didn't plan to. There was no need to stress her for no reason, and we could handle it. I knew that Rosa being in our lives had been a positive thing to happen out of the whole ordeal.

"That's good to hear," my mom told her, the tone of her voice filled with genuine happiness. "You know, family is important to us, and it's important that Corey has a positive influence in his life. Especially with the negativity he's had."

She was talking about Heather. Rosa nodded, her eyes filled with sincerity. Mom always thought Heather was a bad influence on our son, constantly telling me how awful I was as a person.

"I understand completely," Rosa said, nodding. "I really want to be there for Corey if I can, to help support him and Brody, and to help him grow into the amazing person I know he's already going to be. You've both done a great job with him."

I sat there preening with pride for her. I really couldn't have asked for a better response. Her words let me know she was really serious and committed, not only to me, but also to my son and his life. Knowing she cared that much was a weight off my shoulders. It also felt nice knowing my mom was able to see the same goodness in Rosa that I did. She was good for both of us.

"Well, I'll help clear away some of these dishes," Rosa said. She stood, putting the empty plates together.

"Oh, you're a guest," my mom said, standing up and wiping her hands. "Brody and I will get them together."

"I don't want to be just a guest," Rosa said, clearing her throat. "I want to help."

Mom stared at her, raising her eyebrows. "Okay then. Let's get these dishes cleared away. I appreciate the help, Rosa."

Yeah, she had fully won my mom over, and I stood to help them, smiling without restraint.

"Why don't you and Corey go watch a movie and get ready for bed," Mom said, trying to sound casual. "The ladies will handle the dishes."

That wasn't something she usually said. She liked equal distribution of chores, and she always made me work the same as she did. She obviously wanted to talk to Rosa alone for some reason.

"Yeah, we'll do that," I said, getting Corey out of his chair. "C'mon buddy, let's go pick out something to watch."

We made our way into the living room, and Corey ran over to pick a movie from my mom's ancient DVD collection. I dug through them, and my son did the same, holding out his choice.

"I want to watch zombies," he said excitedly. He had that big grin on his face he always did when I knew I wasn't going to persuade him away from what he had chosen.

"Zombies," I repeated, raising an eyebrow.

"They're funny," he said with a shrug.

I couldn't help but laugh. "You're a wonder, kid."

A wave of curiosity hit me, and I found myself standing

behind the wall of the kitchen, eavesdropping like a small child. Corey was distracted on the couch by the movie, and I listened hard. I glanced around the corner. Rosa was putting coffee on, and I could smell it brewing. My mom was washing dishes, looking over her shoulder at the woman I loved.

"Rosa, I have to tell you, I've never seen my son look at anyone the way I saw him looking at you," she said, and even I could hear the smile in her voice. "You know, after the other one, I never thought I would see him as happy as he seems to be right now."

"Thank you," Rosa said, and I could hear her smiling too. "He's an amazing person. I'm lucky to be a part of their lives."

I slunk back into the living room when Mom began to ask Rosa about the accident at the barn and the work being done to restore the storm damage. I couldn't stop smiling as I sat down. I watched the movie with Corey until I heard the two of them emerge.

"Hey, Rosa, I want to take you somewhere," I said, standing up from the couch. "It's somewhere close, don't worry," I told her, taking her hand, and my mom nodded. She knew where we were headed.

The sun was beginning to set over the ocean, haloing a warm golden glow over the whole of the backyard as Rosa and I walked hand in hand to the very edge of the perfectly wild property. My mom loved to let the flowers go without cutting them, and there was a deep path through the sea grass leading to the white fence by the blue ocean. I took a deep breath and let it out, listening to the sound of crashing waves. It was a smooth, soothing melody that always brought me a sense of peace when I heard it. I took another breath of the brine, and the salty ocean air filled my lungs as I got myself ready to share a very personal part of my life and myself with Rosa.

"Brody, what's going on? Where are we going?" she asked me, her pretty voice filled with curiosity and maybe even a touch of nervousness. I wondered if she could feel how serious this was.

I looked at her, a little smile beginning to start on my lips. "I just want to show you something," I told her, and I could hear my own voice filled with a mix of anticipation and brittle stress. "This is something that really means a lot to me."

We kept walking, and her eyes sparkled with interest as she nodded at my words, her fingers wrapped around my hand tightening slightly as she did. She was solid and dependable, and I knew I could trust her. She also trusted me, obviously, and that trust meant the absolute world to me. We finally reached the edge of the moonlit backyard, where the thin path led down to the sand and the beach. I led Rosa down the path, the crunch of our footsteps on the sand twisting in time with the crashing of the waves. As we walked, I couldn't help but feel a mix of emotions begin to swirl within me. I began to think about what I was doing. This would be the very first time I had ever brought a woman, a girlfriend, to this important place. It was the final resting spot of my father, though his body had been laid to rest at sea when the water took him under. We never saw him again.

We reached the small clearing that was ghostly in the moonlight, with the fog from the ocean rolling in. There was a simple wooden cross there that stood tall, overlooking the vast push and pull of the ocean. I looked out, and the sight of the ocean always took my breath away. It was a harsh reminder of the fragile dealings of life and the beauty, like that of the ocean, that could be found even with the reality of loss. The loss of my father when I was young had been a horrible thing for me, but this was the perfect place to appreciate my father's life.

"Rosa, this place is sacred to me. This is my dad's grave," I said softly, my voice barely rising above a whisper. "The man loved the ocean more than anything else, and this is where he would want his grave to be, I know it."

"Oh, Brody," she said, glancing up at me as she squeezed my hand.

Her eyes filled with understanding and empathy as she stared down at the cross stuck deep in the sand. She knew the story; of course she did. Most of the island did. I knew nearly everyone had heard it from others, from friends and family, but I had never shared it with her directly, and I thought it was overdue. It was past time for Rosa to hear the truth from me. What happened changed me, and it made me who I am.

"He lost his life surfing out there in the waves," I continued, my voice beginning to shake slightly. I walked to the cross. "You know, I was waiting for him on the beach, just sitting in the sand, when the storm hit. It was a freak accident really, a rogue wave made more aggressive by the storm knocked him off his board and into the water. He never came back out."

Rosa reached out to me and gently squeezed my hand again, her touch grounding me to the moment, keeping my thoughts in line with what I was doing. I took in a deep, calming breath, gathering my thoughts before I continued. I wanted to tell her everything. I wanted her to know about every part of my life.

"I want to be completely honest. I have never brought anyone else here to visit the grave," I said, my voice filled with an open vulnerability I hadn't really ever felt before. She made me feel like I could be that way with her. "I mean, this place has always been too much of a secret, and just too personal. But with you, I feel like I can tell you this part of my life. I trust you with this, and I know I can."

I saw her eyes glittering with unshed tears as she looked at me, her affection and her obvious love shining through as she looked at me.

"I can't tell you how much this means that you decided to show this to me, Brody," she murmured. "I'm sorry. I know how much your dad meant to you, and how much he still means to you. I'm really honored that you would trust me enough to let me be a part of this. I'm really happy."

I reached out to pull her into a tight hug, holding her close as the heaviness of my own emotions threatened to take over at that moment. Right then, I felt a deep sense of gratitude for the woman standing at my side. Even after what she had been through, she offered me her unwavering support and affection. I was a lucky man.

"I do trust you so much, you know," I told he. "I trust you more than you know."

"I know, and I feel the same way," she said, nodding.

We stood there together as the sinking sun slipped gracefully below the purple horizon, casting a warm pink glow over the crashing ocean. I knew deep in my soul that I had made the right choice when I decided to bring Rosa here to my dad's final resting place. I loved her, and she was important enough to show it to. The sacred place in front of us, the only connection to my past with my dad, was now a part of our shared thoughts, and I was so glad she could understand now.

At that moment, as we stood by my father's grave, I began to feel a sense of peace wash over my entire body. I knew, almost instinctively, that my dad would have loved everything about Rosa. He would have been proud of me for finding such an amazing woman. I knew he would be proud of the man I had become in his absence—the man who had found happiness and love even after it seemed like it was out of the picture for good.

"Your mom started a fire," Rosa said, pointing.

Up by the house, orange flickered from the fire pit. I could hear Corey's infectious laughter bouncing off every nearby object as he no doubt consumed way too many burned marshmallows.

"She always lets him have too many s'mores," I said with a sigh. "I should go play bad cop."

"I think you should let this one get away, officer," she told me with a smile. "A little sugar never hurt anyone."

"Oh, is that right?" I asked, grinning as I pulled her in for a kiss. "Because I need a little sugar over here."

"I might be able to help you with that," she said with an adorable giggle, kissing me back just as passionately as always.

I wanted to spend the rest of my life with Rosa Rivers.

ROSA

*B*rody was pulled under by the waves, and his board was lost to the ocean.

My heart was absolutely hammering in my chest, and fear threatened to choke me. Elizabeth was squeezing my arm so hard it hurt, and her eyes were trained on the ocean, desperate to see that dark head pop up out of the water. I was staring so hard, my eyes began to burn in the salty wind. I could feel tears prickle, and I gasped.

"There he is!" I shouted, my voice breaking with my relief. "Oh my god, he's okay!"

"Dad!" Corey called, her little voice high.

Elizabeth told him to wait, to stay put, and she pulled me along behind her. She didn't have to, I was running just as fast as she was down the beach. The crowd behind us was murmuring, and the other surfers had come in from the water. Brody stumbled from the foamy surf, coughing as he struggled up to the shore. He waved away the life-guards and paramedics who were on standby and made eye contact with us. I couldn't help but watch the way the water rolled off his naked, tanned torso and into his surf shorts. He was such a beautiful man. I couldn't imagine losing him.

"That was my fault," he said, scraping a hand through his soaking-wet hair. "I should have been watching better for the waves. What a rookie mistake. Damn it."

"Brody," Elizabeth tsked, shaking her head at him.

"You're not going back out there," I said quickly, my voice shaking. "You can't."

I was absolutely terrified he was going to go out, and I was going to lose him. I had just found him, and I was going to lose him just as quickly. I couldn't let him do it.

"The competition just started, and it's not storming," he told me, breathing hard.

Elizabeth winced. "Just because your father drowned in a storm, doesn't mean it can't happen in the sunshine too. She's right. You have Corey to think about."

"You lost your board and you went down, aren't you out of the competition anyway?" I asked. I was hoping he would be disqualified, and he'd just go back with us.

He shook his head. "We each get one wipe-out and our best waves are counted on a ten-point scale. I need a new board though. I have to hurry up and paddle back out."

"Do you have another board?" Elizabeth asked, sounding stronger than I did.

"That was my backup," Brody said, and I knew he broke the other one that night we met. "I don't know what I'm going to do if I don't have a board to surf with."

"I think I can help with that," called a familiar voice, and I turned to see Mr. Perry hobbling down the sand towards us, a kind smile on his face. "I hope you don't mind, but I asked this young man to help."

Behind him, Corey bounded towards us with a shiny new surfboard in his arms, nearly toppling over in his excitement. I recognized it as one of the brand-new boards at the shop.

They were expensive, much more expensive than we could afford, and I smiled.

"Mr. Perry, you're amazing," I said, reaching out to hug him as he went by.

He laughed. "Happy birthday, young Mr. Strauss."

"It's not my birthday," Brody said, wrinkling his brow.

"Just take the gift, son," Mr. Perry told him, letting out a guffaw. "Win for us, and let me know the drive here wasn't for nothing."

Brody grinned and thanked him, nodding. He ruffled Corey's hair as he grabbed the board, and Elizabeth kissed her son's cheek as she took her grandson back up to the crowd. Mr. Perry gave me a warm smile and followed after them. I was so thankful.

"Be my good luck charm?" Brody asked, giving me an excited smile.

"Just come back to me," I murmured, leaning up on my tiptoes to kiss him. "Please, please, come back to me, Brody."

"I'll take that as a yes," he said, curling a hand into my hair. "I'll be back soon."

With that, he was gone again. The panel of judges at the table was looking at him hard.

I stood on the pale, sandy beach, my gaze fixed on the vast spread of the ocean before me. The breeze smelled salty as it tousled my hair, and I anxiously awaited the finishing rides of the competition. My heart was pounding in my chest, assaulting my ribcage fiercely, and matching the splashes of the crashing waves. At least it was a clear, sunny day. That was one mercy. This was Brody's one moment, his last chance to win an amount of money that could set him up for life, and I couldn't help but feel a mix of anxiety and excitement for him. I was still afraid, though.

"Come and stand by us, sweetheart," I heard Elizabeth's voice say, and her fingers wrapped gently around my wrist as

I followed her back. I realized I had been far away from the crowd, watching Brody with single-minded obsessiveness.

The sun was hanging high and hot in the sky, making a golden glow over the sloshing water. The crowd was absolutely vibrating with anticipation, and they all wanted their favorite to win. Their murmured voices began to blend into a sort of hum behind me. I was looking out at the ocean, scanning over the sea of faces out there, searching for Brody in the middle of the barrage of surfers gliding over the water.

Finally, there he was, sitting tall and confident, his board tucked under him like a lifeline. My heart all but skipped a beat as our gazes met over the water, and he shot me a quick little wink before he began to paddle farther out into the water.

I watched as he went out, his movements on his new board fluid and effortless. He gracefully made his way through the waves, his body becoming one with the rocking of the ocean.

The other surfers and the people in the crowd seemed to fade into the background as my gaze and my entire focus remained solely on Brody Strauss. I knew the competition would be hard to bear, but I had faith in what he could do and that he was going to stay safe. He wasn't his father.

As the last heat began, I felt my hands clench into fists, and my nails dug painfully into my palms. I stared at where he was rising on his board. The strained tension in the warm air was easy to feel, and I held my breath as Brody went ahead and caught his next cresting wave. He rode it with agility and strength, looking like an ocean deity as he carved through the water. The crowd behind me broke into bright applause, their cheers echoing in my head. I was cheering too, and couldn't help but smile. My heart swelled with pride.

Then, it felt like disaster almost struck again, and I

wanted to leap into the waves with him. He tried a daring little twist, pushing the limits of what he could do. The wave crashed down over him, looking as if it had just swallowed him whole. A scream was choked back. Hot, burning panic surged right through my veins as I watched him and his board disappear beneath the crashing water.

Time seemed to stand still as I waited for him to come back to the warmth and the sunlight, my heart caught painfully in my throat. And then, like a phoenix rising from the ashes, he emerged from the depths, miraculously still on his board. He wouldn't be taken out of the competition. He shook off the water like it was nothing, and the pure determination was obvious on his face.

"Please, please, keep him safe," I begged whoever was listening. "I can't lose him."

I watched some of the other competitors take hits, and the final heat arrived with only a few people remaining. I could feel that the tension in the air almost making it hard to breathe. Brody held himself perfectly on his board, his eyes focused solely on the horizon.

Suddenly, the most anxiety-inducing thing happened. A humongous wave rose from the deep dark of the ocean, and the sheer power and beauty of it was amazing. I almost couldn't believe Brody was about to ride it. He paddled with all his strength, holding himself just right to grab the crest with his board.

As the wave got closer to him, Brody jumped to his feet, his body moving with the water. He slipped through the wave with perfect precision, the movement of his body effortless. The people waiting behind began to cheer in a sort of frenzy, their cries blending with the hard crashing of the wave as he balanced on it.

I almost couldn't believe it as I watched him ride. I realized why he loved it so much. The rush was intoxicating.

Then, as if by some kind of divine twist of fate, the wave also wiped out what was left of his competitors.

They flipped from their boards and crashed into the whipping water, their surfboards scattered like fallen leaves in an autumn breeze. Brody, grinning broadly on his board, stayed completely upright, his balance never faltering. The man I loved rode the cresting wave until the very end, and his victory was about to be a sure thing.

The beach burst into a bright din of cheers and applause for Brody Strauss. I just couldn't keep my excitement inside any longer. I shot towards the water, and my feet sank into the soft sand as I ran. Brody made his way out from the water, his handsome face absolutely beaming with his win. He had triumphed, and I was so damn proud of him. I ran up and threw my arms around him, my heart throbbing with love.

"I'm your biggest fan," I told him, grinning.

He laughed, and when he kissed me, it was like sunshine on my skin after a long, cold day.

"Well, I think we have a clear winner!" I heard one of the judges call out. "Number seven, why don't you come on up here and claim your check!"

I went to move, grinning, but Brody grabbed my hand and stopped me.

"Wait," he said, still panting and holding his board. "Before we go up there, I wanted to tell you something."

"What?" I asked, watching him and wondering what could be more important than his win. "What is it?"

"Rosa, listen," he said, dropping his board and holding my shoulders. "With this money, I'm going to buy Perry's place for you."

I stared at him in shock. "You're... what?"

"I talked to him this morning, before you got here. I told

him if I won, I was going to use the money to buy it for you. He cut me a good deal. Do you know what he said?"

"What?" I asked him, tears pricking my eyes as I stood there in disbelief.

"He said 'no ifs, son, I know you'll win for her'," Brody leaned down to kiss me. "He was right."

EPILOGUE

BRODY

"*D*o you have lessons later?" I asked Rosa, wrapping my arms around her from behind.

She turned, smiling as she kissed me. I would never get used to those sweet kisses, and I never wanted to. She had her long, chocolate hair twisted into a braid down her back, and I ran my fingers over the soft strands.

"More kids are coming this year than any before," she said, sounding so pleased. I was happy to see her happy.

"Have I told you how proud I am of you?" I asked, smiling down at her.

Sunlight streamed in through the kitchen window, and it was amazing to see how much Mr. Perry's old, dusty house had transformed in a month under Rosa's capable hands. Corey was off picking out his room.

"Well, you've said it once or twice," she said, kissing my cheek. "But this is all thanks to you. I wouldn't even be able to start the lessons again if you hadn't bought this place."

"Mr. Perry seems a lot happier in the cottage," I said, agreeing with her. I was glad to have the chance to do it for her.

"It's closer to the shop, that's why he told me to just live there when I first got to the island," she told me. "He likes being able to run the shop without the stress of still owning it, I think. Now that falls on me, I guess," she said, laughing.

"We'll figure it out together," I told her, brushing my nose against hers.

"I found one!" Corey said, and I heard his quick footsteps echoing down the stairs. He tumbled into the kitchen, his hair wild and his smile bright. "My room is the one with the ocean on the wall!"

"Mr. Perry painted that himself," Rosa said, looking warm and happy. "I'm sure he's about to become quite the artist in his retirement. He deserves some peace and quiet in his life."

"He's a good man," I agreed.

"Have you heard from Sam?" Rosa asked, looking up at me.

"Uncle Sam!" Corey cried, dashing by us to go watch TV in the sunroom.

"Uncle Sam is back and settled in Daytona," I said, letting out a breath. "After everything, I hope he's finally happy there. It's probably the best place for him."

She nodded, content. "You know, you still haven't picked out your room in the house, though there's a particular one I hope you'll pick."

"Oh, really?" I asked, and I couldn't help but grin. "And what room would that be?"

"The one with the barn view," she said with a sly grin. "I think you're pretty familiar with it."

"Oh yeah, that's your room, right?" I teased. "I think I can find it on my own."

She stepped back. "I really need to get out there and get the horses ready. Do you want to help?"

"I need to help Corey unpack," I let out a sigh. "You have

an hour until the kids start showing up, right? Are you excited?"

"I'm over the moon," she said, her smile was bright and beautiful.

Suddenly, the little box in my pocket felt terribly heavy, like it was burning a hole through my jeans, as bright as the morning sun.

"Will you come with me?" I asked the woman in front of me, feeling emotions swirling like a storm in my gut. "Corey, play down here for a minute, okay?"

Corey nodded, and I waited for Rosa to answer.

"Uh, sure, where are we going?" she asked, looking confused but letting me take her hand anyway.

"I wanted to show you something out on the balcony," I said, hoping my voice didn't sound as shaky as I felt. "I think you'll really like it."

"What is it?" she asked as I led her up the stairs. "Is it the nest in the oak tree? The one with the Spanish moss? Corey showed me already."

I didn't answer as we stopped at the door to her room. It creaked as it opened. Inside, the big, soft bed was covered in her familiar green comforter, and her dresser had both piles of our clothes folded there. The sight of it made me smile.

"It's not a nest," I said quietly as I slid the door to the balcony open. "Here, come on out with me."

Early autumn was turning the barest amount of leaves at the top of the numerous oak trees that stood sentinel around the property. The balcony looked over the dark green horse barn, and work on the back corner was going well. The horses were turned out in the big pasture. They stomped and snorted, eating from a hay bale. Rosa's favorite horse, Cinder, looked up as she heard us, neighing happily at the sight of Rosa.

She grinned, leaning her hands on the wrought iron railing of the small balcony.

"I can't believe this place is really mine," she said, smiling out at the view. "I still can't believe it. All thanks to you."

"I know you have stuff to do, but I just need you here for a minute," I said, suddenly feeling sweaty and nervous in my jeans and t-shirt.

Should I have been down on one knee already? How did that sort of thing work?

"Brody, what's going on?" she asked, turning back to look at me. "Are you alright?"

I opened my mouth, hand in my pocket for the little velvet box, and my phone started to ring loudly.

"Uh, give me a minute," I said, fumbling to get my hand out of one pocket and into the other that had my phone. "Uh, hello? Heather?"

Rosa looked sharply at me, making a face. The last thing I needed right then was for her to be mad at me for talking to my ex-girlfriend. I tried to focus on what Heather was saying. The words were fast and jumbled, and they didn't really make sense, but she didn't give me a chance to process them.

Neither one of us had heard from her for the whole month since the surfing competition. I told Corey his mom was just busy, but since we didn't have a legal agreement, I didn't have to go through a lawyer with Heather. It was a wonder she thought she was going to get full custody despite that fact in the first place.

"What are you saying?" I asked the woman over the phone, struggling to hear her. "Heather, you're not making any sense."

I put her on speakerphone so Rosa would hear, just in case I needed some kind of witness.

"I *said,* I'm going to live in Europe. It's where I belong and

I can be free there without anything to hold me back," Heather said loftily. "Jacque says his parents have a place in the south of France. We're going to stay there, but they don't like kids. Corey can stay with you."

"What are you saying?"

"Corey is yours," she said, and now she sounded bored. "I'll call him when I get settled. He'll understand. Got it?"

I stared at the phone, not daring to believe it. When Heather scoffed and hung up though, Rosa stared at me and I knew I must have echoed her amazed look, my features slack.

"Did that really just happen?" she asked, and I could see the smile spreading over her face.

"I can't believe it's really over," I breathed, and then I laughed, feeling relief like I had never felt before.

I swept Rosa up into a hug, swinging her around. Whatever came next, we would worry about it later. For now, there was a diamond ring in my pocket with Rosa Rivers' name on it.

THE END.

If you enjoyed Forbidden Wave Rider you will *LOVE* Billionaire's Secrets.

Muscle-toned, sexy billionaire's heart is captured by the runaway bride working on his vineyard. Be prepared to be mesmerised and craving for more as you immerse yourself in the opening chapter on the following page!

Access Billionaire's Secrets by clicking here

SNEAK PEEK

BILLIONAIRE'S SECRETS

**I ran from a glitzy New York wedding into the arms of a
magnetically hot billionaire.**

From the altar to a quaint Californian town.
I fled the chaos for simplicity.
Finding refuge working in a charming vineyard.

It was love at first sight.
His fit physique and rugged charm left me weak at the knees.
His blue-eyed allure unraveled my defenses.

Behind closed doors, passion electrifies.
A fire that engulfs us completely.
His touch propels me into blissful oblivion.

But as my feelings for him deepen.
So does my fear of another liar in my life.

Little did I know, he's the town's mayor, and owner of the
vineyard.

When the truth about his identity is revealed.
My trust is shattered.
He's deceived me all along.

My ex-fiancé's return only adds to the chaos and confusion.

With the secrets out, the stakes are high.
Doubts linger about trusting him.
I may have to return to New York and forget this dream ever happened.

Access Billionaire's Secrets by clicking here

Chapter One
Paisley

"Oh, *this* is not what I expected," I mumbled to myself as the car rolled into Valle di Sole. The picturesque Californian town was a stark contrast to the towering skyscrapers and busy streets of New York. Rows of colorful houses, quaint boutiques, and sunflower fields as far as the eye could see were spread out before me.

Taking a deep breath, the smell of fresh-blooming flowers and ocean salt welcomed me. The memories of the last week in New York seemed to belong to another lifetime: the frenzy of the wedding preparations, the fights, the constant media attention because of my fiancé's billionaire status, and the weight of expectations. Every detail about the wedding was plastered on tabloids and whispered about in social circles.

However, nothing had made more headlines than my dramatic escape from the altar. It was a culmination of the facade I'd been wearing for so long. The dress, the guests, the spotlight—none of it felt right. On the outside we were the golden couple, but, deep down, it felt as though I were drowning in a life I didn't choose.

After my "runaway bride" moment, the city had become unbearable. The constant paparazzi, the gossipy whispers, the never-ending spotlight—I had to get away from it all. And so, with my sun-kissed, chestnut hair acting as my shield, I had driven cross-country, seeking anonymity and peace in a place where nobody knew Paisley, the heiress and infamous "Runaway Bride of New York."

The town square was lively with locals enjoying the evening. Children played around a majestic fountain, while their parents sipped on freshly brewed coffee at nearby patios. A soft folk tune wafted from one of the cafés, and I couldn't resist the pull. Parking my car, I decided to explore the town on foot.

As I strolled, I noticed a local art gallery displaying vibrant paintings. Being an art-lover, I couldn't resist a peek. The artistic essence of Valle di Sole enveloped me, soothing my nerves. It was clear that the people here had a deep appreciation for the arts, and that was something I could resonate with.

"My, my, you seem lost," an elderly voice remarked, pulling me from my reverie.

Turning, I met the twinkling eyes of an old woman, her silver hair pulled into a neat bun. She had a mischievous glint in her gaze that made me think she'd seen and lived a lot.

"In more ways than one," I chuckled, tucking a loose strand of hair behind my ear.

She smiled. "Valle di Sole has a way of attracting souls looking for a fresh start."

I raised an eyebrow. "That obvious, huh?"

Her laughter was musical. "To an old soul like me, yes. Come, let me introduce you to the heart of our town."

Taking me by the arm, she led me deeper into the gallery.

Each painting told a story and, with her by my side, I felt a connection to the essence of Valle di Sole. The community, the art, the serenity—it all felt like a balm to my bruised spirit.

By evening, I'd found a cozy apartment above a local bookstore, with a view of the sunflower fields. The landlady, a kind woman named Anna, seemed to sense my need for solitude and offered the place without asking too many questions.

That night, as I lay in bed, the whispers of the ocean lulled me to sleep. For the first time in a long while, I felt at peace, away from the shackles of my past, ready to paint a new chapter of my life in this sun-kissed haven.

"You really have outdone yourself this time, Paisley," I whispered to myself as I wandered through the maze of quaint streets in the town. The previous chapter of my life felt like a foggy dream, distant and almost unreal. Here, surrounded by cobblestone pathways and inviting cafés, the weight on my shoulders felt considerably lighter.

Every corner of the place seemed to hum with a serene vibrancy. It was as if the buildings, the streets, and even the blooming flowers whispered tales of love, life, and second chances. The cafés beckoned with promises of aromatic coffees and delectable pastries, and as I walked by one with open French windows, the strains of a soulful melody reached my ears. I couldn't resist looking inside.

Sitting at the window was a man strumming his guitar, lost in his own world, music flowing seamlessly from his fingers. Locals sipped their drinks, nodding along to the tune, their conversations a gentle hum in the background. The scene before me was something straight out of a painting, and a wave of nostalgia washed over me. How long had it been since I had last picked up a brush and let my feelings pour out onto a canvas?

Lost in thought, I almost missed the art studio nestled between two cafés. The sign outside read "Claire's Creations." Inside, vibrant canvases graced the walls, each capturing the essence of Valle di Sole in a unique way. The paintings spoke of passion, dedication, and a love for the town that resonated deeply with me.

As I gazed at a particular painting showcasing the town square bathed in the golden glow of sunset, a voice behind me remarked, "That's one of my favorites too."

Turning around, I met the smiling eyes of a woman, probably in her mid-thirties, with raven-black hair cascading down her shoulders. "You must be Claire," I ventured.

She laughed, a sound like wind chimes. "Guilty as charged. And you are?"

"Paisley."

"Paisley. A beautiful name for a beautiful lady. What brings you to my little corner of the world?" she asked, her eyes searching mine, perhaps trying to piece together my story.

"Seeking a fresh start," I admitted with a soft smile. "And rediscovering old passions," I added, glancing at the array of brushes and paints on a nearby table.

Claire seemed to catch my drift. "An artist, are we?"

I shrugged modestly. "Used to be. Life got in the way."

She walked over to the table, picking up a sketchbook and a pencil. Handing them to me, she said, "Why not start now? Valle di Sole is the perfect muse."

Feeling the weight of the sketchbook in my hands, memories of my art school days came flooding back. Without a second thought, I began to sketch. The town square, the man with the guitar, the children playing by the fountain—every detail came alive on the pages. Time seemed to stand still as Claire and I lost ourselves in our respective arts, occasionally exchanging words, stories, and laughter.

When I finally looked up, the sun was dipping below the horizon, casting the studio in a soft, amber hue. Claire, her face illuminated by the dying sunlight, looked at my sketches with appreciation. "You, my dear, have a gift. Promise me you won't let it go to waste again."

The weight of those words made my cheeks warm. "Thank you, Claire. Truly," I whispered, my voice full of gratitude.

She winked, her lips curling into a knowing smile. "You're welcome. Just remember that every blank canvas has infinite possibilities."

The night had blanketed Valle di Sole and, as I looked up, the stars twinkled down, each one seemingly brighter than the one next to it. The beauty of the evening was so captivating that, for a moment, I forgot the rumble of hunger in my stomach.

Following the delicious aroma of baked dough and melted cheese, I found myself standing in front of "Stella's Pizzeria." The rustic sign swayed gently in the night breeze and the chatter from within promised a bustling atmosphere. Pushing the door open, I was immediately greeted by the intoxicating smell of freshly baked pizza. The lively voices, the clinking of glasses, and a soft Italian tune playing in the background created an inviting ambiance.

"Table for one?" a friendly voice pulled me from my thoughts. A cheerful, middle-aged man with a bushy mustache and warm, brown eyes stood by the entrance, a menu in hand.

"Yes, please," I replied, offering him a smile.

He led me to a cozy corner table by the window where I could see the streets outside and the starry sky above. Once seated, I quickly scanned the menu and placed an order for a classic Margherita pizza and a glass of red wine.

While waiting for my dinner, I pulled out my sketchbook, the memories of the day urging me to capture them. Flipping through the pages, I revisited each scene, from the sunlit art studio to the soulful musician in the café. Each stroke, each line was a testament to my rediscovered passion.

The waiter soon arrived with my pizza and wine. Setting them down in front of me, he remarked, "That's some impressive work there."

Blushing slightly, I closed the sketchbook and smiled. "Thank you. Valle di Sole has been quite the muse."

He grinned. "It tends to have that effect on people. Enjoy your meal."

Taking a sip of the smooth wine, I allowed the rich flavors to envelop my senses. The pizza, with its thin crust and perfectly melted cheese, was simply divine. Each bite was a reminder of why I had chosen this town for a fresh start.

As I dined, the soft Italian tune transitioned to a more upbeat rhythm. The ambiance of the pizzeria was infectious, and soon I found myself tapping my foot and humming along. By the time I finished my meal, I felt rejuvenated, the worries and scars of my past seemingly fading away.

"Is this your first time in Valle di Sole?" a voice interrupted my musings.

Looking up, I was met with the curious eyes of a young woman, probably in her late twenties. She had olive skin, dark curly hair, and a smile that was genuinely friendly.

"Yes, just arrived yesterday," I replied, intrigued.

She extended her hand. "I'm Isabella. I couldn't help but notice your sketches earlier. You're quite talented."

Blushing again, I shook her hand, "Thank you, Isabella. I'm Paisley."

We chatted for a while, sharing stories and laughs. It turned out that Isabella was a local journalist, always on the lookout for interesting tales. She expressed interest in writing about my art, an offer I promised to consider.

By the time I left Stella's Pizzeria, the streets of Valle di Sole were quiet, the stars shining even brighter. The events of the day, from my encounter with Claire to my delightful meal and newfound friendship with Isabella, filled me with a sense of contentment and purpose.

As I walked back to my apartment, the town's serene beauty and its welcoming residents reaffirmed my decision to start anew. With my sketchbook in hand and a heart full of hope, I was ready to paint my future in this enchanting town.

Access Billionaire's Secrets by clicking here

Printed in Great Britain
by Amazon

38071765R00139